THE EMPRESS
AND
THE MOON

Book 4 of the Nightcraft Quartet

Shannon Page

Published by Outland Entertainment LLC
3119 Gillham Road
Kansas City, MO 64109

Founder/Creative Director: Jeremy D. Mohler
Chief Operating Officer: Anton Kromoff
Editor-in-Chief: Alana Joli Abbott
Senior Editor: Scott Colby

ISBN: 978-1-954255-84-5 (paperback), 978-1-954255-85-2 (ebook)
Worldwide Rights
Created in the United States of America

Editor: Alana Joli Abbott
Copy editor: Bessie Mazur
Proofreader: Ariel Kromoff
Cover Illustration: Matthew Warlick
Cover Design: Jeremy D. Mohler
Interior Layout: Jeremy D. Mohler

Printed and bound in the United States of America.

Visit **outlandentertainment.com** to see more, or follow us on our Facebook Page **facebook.com/outlandentertainment/**

ALSO BY SHANNON PAGE

NOVELS

Eel River
Our Lady of the Islands (with Jay Lake)
The Fate of Alizar (Forthcoming)

The Nightcraft Quartet:
The Queen and The Tower
A Sword in The Sun
The Lovers Three
The Empress and The Moon

The Chameleon Chronicles (with Karen G. Berry,
writing as Laura Gayle)
Orcas Intrigue
Orcas Intruder
Orcas Investigation
Orcas Illusion
Orcas Intermission
Orcas Afterlife (Forthcoming)

COLLECTIONS

Eastlick and Other Stories
I Was a Trophy Wife and Other Essays

EDITED BOOKS

Witches, Bitches & Stitches (anthology)
The Usual Path to Publication (collection)

PRAISE FOR SHANNON PAGE'S
THE NIGHTCRAFT QUARTET

"Page's enchanting worldbuilding and charming heroine will draw readers in, and an exciting cliffhanger ending sets things up nicely for the next in the series. This fascinating blend of science and fantasy is a treat."

-Publishers Weekly

"Page fashions an intriguing and hugely gifted heroine who, nevertheless, struggles with problems that have bearing on our own. The first book in the planned quartet kept me up all night until I had finished the last page."

-Antoinette L. Botsford, *Amazon review*

"The magic system is powerful but subtly intwined. The characters use it so nonchalantly, I sometimes forget I'm not also a magical person walking around San Francisco."

-C. G. Volars, author of
Static over Space: Gravity and Lies

"The history, the folklore and the world-building in this novel are written together beautifully. The characters are well developed and the information that is given about the world is intertwined with the story in a way that does not feel like an info dump. Some characters I fell for instantly, others I am wondering if they are who they say they are. In a world where warlocks and witches can live for centuries, who knows what hiding in their back closets; but I am looking forward to finding out."

-Richelle Reed, *She Reeds by the Sea*

"Witches and warlocks and covens... Oh, my. An absolute pageturner filled with mystery, spells, and romance. Not to be missed!"

-Barb Hendee, *New York Times* best-selling
co-author of the Noble Dead Saga

For Emily

─── CHAPTER ONE ───

The closet looked very different this time.

I had investigated this under-stair closet in my house many times since I'd moved in. From day one, Elnor, my familiar, had paid way too much attention to it—insisting on being let in, sniffing around inside. Typical cat stuff.

Then the scryers had placed several of their scanning stones in it after my dear friend Logan departed this plane without showing up in the next one.

Months later, my young student Gracie had visited me, telling me she had come through the "cat portal."

Which, in turn, was months *before* actual cats started popping in and out of the place.

I stepped into it now, holding Elnor, not knowing what to expect. I was following a pair of white cats who had previously appeared to me only in a dream. A very unpleasant dream, in which a rather scary human woman had insisted I adopt the cats...whereupon the cats had turned frightening as well, biting me and trapping me in the dream. *You must listen to the cats*, they had somehow conveyed to me.

Now they had shown up for real. I knew I must follow them.

After my first step, the closet was no more. I was in non-physical space, though not ley space—the energetic lines of the earth, which we witches use to facilitate travel.

I still had full awareness of my body, my physicality, but it was clear that I was not in regular earthly space. The twin white cats were still before me, still moving their legs as though they too were walking, though I could see no floor or ground beneath their feet. Nor was there any under mine, I realized. I looked down at Elnor in my arms; she looked back up at me, utterly unafraid.

Oh, how I wished our cats could communicate with us. With words.

I walked, following the white cats, though I could perceive no sense of the space around me, or even whether we were making progress or just…moving our legs. There was no color, no light, no walls or ceiling or trees or sky.

No scent. No sound.

We were moving forward, I decided, though I couldn't say whether I perceived that or just needed it to be true.

Elnor gazed ahead, perfectly content to be carried. Unusual, for her.

I told myself that was a good sign and kept walking.

And then there were others around us, other presences. I could still see nothing, but I knew that we were no longer alone.

"What is this place?" I tried speaking aloud. My voice, shocking in the unearthly stillness around me, sounded almost normal, but not quite. Thinner than usual.

Elnor looked up at me again when I spoke. So, the sound was real. Probably.

The sense of others around me grew sharper. Somebody I knew was near—but I felt a tip-of-the-tongue elusiveness; I *knew* who this was, but just couldn't quite grasp their name.

"Are we…in the Beyond?"

"No," said a voice. An achingly familiar voice. I strained to see, then closed my eyes and used my witch-sight, but nobody appeared.

"Where are we?" I tried. "Who are you?"

"Callie, it's me," she said, and I opened my eyes and saw Logan.

I gasped and tried to reach for her, to pull her into my arms and never let her go again—but my arms were already full of Elnor, and I somehow knew I could not put her down, couldn't set her on the not-ground; that if I did I risked losing her forever. Or losing *myself* forever, in this cat-space. And anyway, Logan wasn't really there, or else *I* wasn't really there. The whole experience began to take on more of the feeling of a dream; I had an almost-rational thought that maybe all this was an unusual kind of lucid dream—

But then Logan did something, shrugged, and flicked her fingers, and the edges solidified. Now we were standing in a real room, in a real place. It still felt somewhat hollow, but my feet were on solid floor, and Logan, my dear friend Logandina Fleur who'd had her soul stolen from her body nearly a year ago, stood before me, intact and alive.

"Is that better?" she asked.

"Logan!" I breathed, my heart flooding with joy at the sight of her. I set Elnor down—our connection safe, now, I somehow knew it—and reached for my friend, and now I actually could draw her to me. She came easily into my arms, and I hugged her tight, so tight. "Logan!"

"Callie," she said again, drawing back after one final squeeze. She looked so completely herself, yet also...not.

And she looked very sad. She gazed at me. "I am so sorry."

"Sorry for what?" I asked.

She shook her head. "I didn't imagine that he would catch you too. I thought..." She trailed off. "You're so strong. But I suppose he was always stronger."

"He who? Gregorio?"

She nodded, looking even sadder.

"But—no, he didn't catch me!" *Did he?* I wondered with a terrible sinking feeling. I shook it off. He didn't; he couldn't have. I would not let that be true. "I journeyed here myself—where *are* we?"

"Here." She motioned behind her, but I could still see nothing. "We've been trapped for—well, so long, but I don't know how long. Just...long. I never imagined he could catch you."

Now I saw shadowy figures behind her. Lots of people...moving closer, but still barely visible. "Is this everyone who Gregorio stole souls from?"

Logan nodded. "He's trapped us here, betwixt and between. No one can reach us from either direction." She shook her head, as if I had said something. "I know no one can; you and I tried so hard to find my parents, but we couldn't, because we couldn't get here." She blinked at me. "And I know *you* would have tried to find me."

Elnor had been prowling around the space. It still looked like a real room, though its boundaries were murky as though lost in shadows. Now my familiar returned and looked up at me, then turned again and began walking forward.

"I think she means for me to follow her," I told Logan. "Walk with me."

Logan looked sad again, and apologetic. "But there is nowhere to go." Even so, she took my hand and fell in beside me. We walked, following Elnor. I could no longer see the white cats, and the shadowy figures kept just a bit ahead of us, or off to the side.

But I could feel Logan's hand in mine, and that was so good. Even if I couldn't really see the walls. "I've missed you," I told my friend. Such an understatement. "I did try to find you, desperately."

She squeezed my hand. "I know. I've missed you too. I've missed...everything."

I squeezed back, and her hand felt solid and real—warm, smooth, soft yet strong—but that couldn't be, could it? If this was her spirit, here with me, then this could not be her body. In fact I knew where her body was—

As I had this thought, Logan stopped and dropped my hand. "Callie, don't," she said urgently. "Doubt is what makes it all worse. You have to believe, to trust, and then we can do anything."

"Except go anywhere?" I asked.

She gave a soft laugh. "Oh, we can go everywhere, except that it's nowhere."

I searched her face, but it told me nothing. "If this is not the Beyond and it's not the earthly plane," I said, "then...where are we?"

"I...um, well, betwixt and between." She gave a frustrated sigh and then waved her hands again, indicating the barely-seen others around us in the mists. "Daddy, you tell her. You explain it better."

Now her parents stood before us. Though I had not seen them since I was a teenage witchlet, Augustus and Lorenna looked just as I remembered them. But of course they would; they must have been frozen in time then, stolen away from our world but never allowed to move to the Beyond.

Augustus smiled gently at me. "Calendula Isadora, it is good to see you." He reached out his hand.

I took it, and we shook warmly. I hadn't known him well. He'd been my best friend's dad: a boring old warlock, just as her mom had been a boring old witch. Just like all grown-ups.

His smile fell away as he let go of my hand and gestured to Logan and Lorenna, standing beside him. "You are not truly here, as we are." He glanced down at Elnor, at my feet. "Nor your familiar."

"But Daddy, they are here, can't you see?" Logan protested. "They're *more* here than we are; their bodies are here too!"

"That's just it," Lorenna put in. Her voice was thin and hollow, even more like the space around us than the voices of her consort and her daughter. "Because she and the cat are with their bodies, they cannot be as we are."

"But...maybe she's come to rescue us!" Logan suddenly looked fourteen again: plumper in the face and thinner in the arms. Her blond hair was more unruly, yet her long thick bangs threatened to tumble into her blue eyes just the same as ever.

I glanced down at myself, but I was still forty-six, and a post-baby forty-six at that.

"Have you?" Logan said to me, and now she was her true age again. "Can your body take us out of here? How did it get in here?" She was so excited. It broke my heart.

"I don't know—" I started, but Lorenna patted her daughter gently on the shoulder.

"Darling, you know it is not as simple as that. If it were, we'd have escaped long ago."

Augustus nodded sadly. "There are many layers of bonds that hold us here. And also—" He cut himself off and gave a small yet hopeful smile. "However, this is something we have not seen before: someone other than Gregorio Andromedus able to move through these realms. Perhaps his grip is loosening." He peered at me searchingly. "You do not know how you came to be here?"

"I...there's a portal in my house. That cats use." Elnor nudged my calf, leaning against me. "I don't understand how it works, but tonight, it suddenly opened for me, and some strange cats—not Elnor—wanted me to walk through. Of course they vanished as soon as we were in here…" And then the rest of why I was here flooded back to me—I could not believe I had forgotten it, even for an instant. "My mother—he's taken her—he's going to do this to her too—"

Lorenna shook her head, looking sympathetic. "We have not seen Belladonna Isis among us."

"He said he took her to his 'special clinic,'" I said, nearly seething. "If he hasn't stolen her soul yet, he's about to."

"We will watch for her," Augustus said.

"Oh, Callie," Logan said. "I'm so sorry. Somebody needs to stop him."

I turned to her, realizing that I was squandering a priceless opportunity to learn crucial information. In my defense, there was quite a lot happening all at once, and I'd been asleep when it started, not all that long ago. "What's the last thing you remember? Before coming here, I mean?" I asked her.

She looked puzzled for a moment. "Your dinner party?"

I nodded. "Yes. What do you remember from that night? Specifically?"

"I felt ill, after your boyfriend Raymond showed up drunk. Then…" She closed her eyes and looked pale. "I didn't know then what he was doing to me, but I had the weirdest sense that Dr. Andromedus was…reaching into me." She looked at her parents. "He still does that," she said, much more softly.

Lorenna closed her eyes and turned away briefly. Augustus patted her arm and said to me, "It is why he has left our bodies living. One cannot harvest essence from a corpse."

Horror spread through me. It wasn't that I hadn't had a pretty good idea of what Gregorio had been doing, but to hear it put so starkly, and by one of his victims…. I shuddered, then forced myself to focus. "He took your essence?" I asked Logan. "In my *house*? At my dinner party?"

"I…I think so, yes. I was talking about what happened to you guys," she said to her parents. "To a, um, warlock." Now she blushed, and I felt even worse, though that hardly seemed possible. She'd had a crush on Jeremy; in fact, they'd been tentatively moving toward dating.

She could have no idea I'd gotten involved with him after she was gone. That I had been on the verge of signing a contract with him.

Oh, so many things she didn't know...

"But then I just couldn't move or think, hardly," she went on. "Someone carried me upstairs to a bed. I know everyone was worried. Did the healers come?"

"They did," I told her, "and Dr. Sebastian Fallon was also there. Everyone tried to figure out what had happened, but you slipped away before we could save you. Then—oh, there's too much to try to explain—but more witches got sick, and warlocks too."

"Yes, we know that part," Logan said. "More folk keep joining us here."

"Gregorio eventually told us all it was a terrible crime committed by one of the junior doctors, stealing essence for his own gain, in cahoots with Old Country criminals.... Of course it was a lie, and we punished an innocent warlock. But—does anyone know how Gregorio did it? How he does it?" I asked Logan and her parents. "If I could narrow that down—"

Lorenna was shaking her head, but Augustus said, "He is working with a cadre of Old Country folk. They build his machines. But he didn't need a machine for what he did to us."

"We were just an experiment, I think, Augustus and I," Lorenna said, very sadly. "It is as Logandina said: he initially reached into our bodies, just with his hand and his magic, and took something vital. Not just essence, though that as well. Once he had that other piece, we could not hold body and spirit together. And then we were trapped, and he takes from us as he pleases."

"What was it, that he took at first?" I asked. "Something physical?"

But they all shrugged. "Probably not," Lorenna said, "or it would have been detected by all the healers and researchers who have been trying to understand."

"I am still encouraged that you have managed to come here, and with your body and essence both," Augustus said.

Logan looked suddenly frightened. "Oh, you must make sure he doesn't know you were able to do this. He would be very angry."

I laughed, but without any humor. "I'm afraid that ship has sailed."

"Are you in danger?" my best friend asked.

"I have been for some time," I told her. "But he hasn't gotten me yet. Or—" I had been about to say *my daughter*—yet another thing she did not know about. "So let's see what we can do, okay? Maybe I *can* rescue you. Can you all try following us back out of here?"

Logan's eyes widened; her parents looked both dubious and hopeful. "There are so many others..." Lorenna said.

"If I can get you guys out, I'll come back for more," I promised. "But let's just start with you three." I reached out for Logan's hand; she took it, and I turned and started walking back the way I'd come. Or at least, what I *thought* was the way I'd come...Elnor brushed against my ankles before I'd taken two steps. I reached down and scooped her up with my other hand, not letting go of Logan's hand.

"Oh, wait," Logan said, and flicked her fingers. The space around us lost its shape, its solidity (such as it had); the mists surrounded us again. "If it's going to work at all, I think it has to be this way."

"I agree," said Lorenna, behind us.

We began walking. "How do you tell if you're making any progress?" I asked, after a while. "It all feels like floating through space to me."

"I had hoped you would be able to tell, being in your body," Augustus said sadly.

"Let's keep trying," Logan said.

"All right."

We walked, and walked...and walked some more. "How long were you here before I found you?" Logan asked.

"Um...it's kind of hard to tell, but not this long, I don't think," I said. "Not very long at all."

Behind me, I could hear Lorenna sigh softly. "It was never going to be this easy."

"Walk ahead of us a bit," Logan said. "See if you get anywhere if we're not with you."

"I don't want to lose you!" I said.

Logan put her hand on my arm. "You found us once; you'll find us again."

I hesitated, thinking about it. Could it hurt to try? I hoped not. "All right," I said, nodding. Still carrying Elnor, I started forward, and in under a minute, I began to sense the difference. I couldn't quite see it, but I knew my house—my under-stair closet—was just ahead. In my arms, Elnor perked up. "Hey!" I called back behind me. "Can you hear me? I found it!" Maybe we just hadn't walked long enough...

They didn't answer. I called again, and then headed back for them.

Logan and her parents were waiting for me. "It's there—just a bit farther. Come on!"

I couldn't really see them; I could just feel their reluctance, their dejection.

"Hey," I went on, to Logan. "Didn't you tell me that doubt makes it all worse? You have to believe! Just a little ways forward, and we'll be in my house in San Francisco."

She smiled bravely, and they walked with me, through the fog, the gloom, the nothing. We got nowhere.

At last even I had to admit defeat. I stopped with a sigh. "I'm sorry."

"We had to try," Augustus said.

I turned to them, though they were nearly impossible to see. "Even if I could lead you out," I said, "what would happen then? You wouldn't have your bodies. I'd just be bringing your spirits into my home."

"It would be better than being here," Logan said. "It would be a start." She waved her fingers again, and not only did everyone become visible, but another actual room appeared around us, this one with chairs and a small table. A window on the far wall looked out on an impossible view of San Francisco—as if the ocean were just beside downtown, and a wide strip of greenery ran down the middle of each street. Sidewalk cafés crowded against high rises; flowers bloomed everywhere. It was lovely, if weird. Elnor squirmed in my arms; I set her down, and she began exploring the space. Logan sank into a chair, frowning.

Her parents looked at her fondly. "She does like to paint her pictures," Lorenna said to me. "We long since gave up trying to change things around here."

"Everything I spend doing this is that much he cannot take from me," Logan muttered.

My eyes widened as an idea sprouted in my brain. No, it was impossible...but what if it wasn't? "So—how does he draw essence from you?" I asked.

Logan shrugged, but Augustus and Lorenna looked at each other thoughtfully. "Part of it does have to do with our bodies," Augustus said, "but they are tethered to our spirits here." He tapped his chest. I stared where he pointed; he smiled and shook his head. "I didn't mean literally there. But..." He sat down and nodded at the chair beside him. "Come, sit. I will try and show you."

When we were seated, he turned and took both of my hands in his. Unlike when he'd shaken my hand earlier, now his hands felt as substantial as Logan's had; this illusion was quite thorough.

"Close your eyes, I think," Augustus said. "Listen to my senses. Listen to my feelings. Listen to my thoughts."

I don't know how to do that, I thought, but did not say it. I didn't know how to do any of the things I was doing here, but I was doing them, wasn't I? So I tried. *Think positive. Don't doubt. Trust.* I opened every sense I had and thought about...receiving.

Elnor brushed against me. I leaned my leg into her a little, accepting her help, opening to her feline energy as well as the spirit-energy around me.

And then I saw it. It had the same odd feeling as the cat portal in my closet...except it resided in Augustus. Not in his heart, or his belly, or anywhere physical like that; not exactly, anyway. But there was an opening. "Oh," I breathed, and sent the tiniest bit of intention toward it. Just the gentlest nudge.

Elnor began to purr, and Augustus sighed. "You found it."

"Is that...where our magic lives?" I asked, unsure even of my question. "I mean, I know our whole bodies and souls are imbued with magic, but is that...the core of it?"

"We do not know," Lorenna said. She stood beside Augustus,

her hand on his shoulder. Even with my eyes closed, I felt her, knew where she was. "But that is where Gregorio taps our essence from."

I took a deep breath. I had no idea if this would work, but what did any of them have to lose? If worse came to worse and I untethered them from their bodies, then they could move Beyond, and embark upon the next phase of their journeys. I would release them from this limbo-prison. "May I try something?" I asked.

"I think we are all hoping that you will," Augustus said quietly.

"All right." I took another breath and focused my intention. I honed and sharpened it, but with thoughts of love and protection and healing…unlike when I had done something like this before. When Jeremy and I had performed the cautery, we'd honed our intentions into a stiletto to burn every trace of magic out of Flavius Winterheart.

And then I reached into Augustus and didn't quite know what to do.

If it's a valve, then I should close it. The metaphor helped. I imagined turning the valve down, lessening the flow that would be available to pour through it.

But how much? If I closed it all the way, would that harm him? Would Gregorio be able to detect that I had done so—or even that someone had done something?

Too many questions. I couldn't know any of the answers, so I settled for reducing the potential for flow by about half. (If I understood what I was feeling, anyway…) I sent my senses through Augustus's "body" before I withdrew, ensuring that everything still seemed to be functioning as it should.

I mean, besides the fact that this isn't his body, and he's been trapped in a mysterious in-between space for decades, being preyed upon by an evil ancient warlock.

I opened my eyes and leaned back in my chair. "I turned down the channel—closed it but only partially. How do you feel?"

Logan's father smiled kindly at me. "All right, I think; it's difficult to say. I won't really know until…"

"Until he comes to tap us again," Lorenna finished for him.

"Does he do that often? And—to everyone, or just some of you?" I felt suddenly fearful; what if he showed up and found me here?

"It varies," Lorenna said. "He takes more now, but there are more to take from."

"We try not to be grateful for their presence," Augustus said, looking abashed. "But you are wondering whether what you have done will be discovered?"

"Well, yeah. I don't want to..." *Get you guys in trouble* sounded ridiculous, and as I'd already reasoned, even if the worst happened, they would get to move Beyond. "Should I have closed it all the way?"

They glanced at one another, seeming to confer silently. Then Logan said, "No, partway is probably best. Can you do me and Mom now?"

I left them soon after that, having—I hoped—protected them as best I could from Gregorio's predations. Maybe, if they proved too hard to harvest essence from, he'd turn his attention to his newer victims.

I hadn't wanted to leave them, but both Logan and her parents insisted. "The longer you stay here, the greater the chances of him catching you," Augustus said.

"You can't help us further from within this place—not right now. I feel quite certain of that," Lorenna added.

Logan nodded. "And if you got here once, you can do it again."

I wasn't sure I agreed, but who knew? I had to take the chance, though it was a terrible calculus to make. I promised myself I would defeat Gregorio, and that I would free everyone. That this was part of the process.

That I *would* be back.

So I walked with Elnor into the fog. As before, I was back in sight of my home very quickly. I stooped, looking for the opening—

—and was back in my under-stair closet.

Elnor jumped out of my arms and strolled out into the hallway.

"I think she's back," I heard Christine say. Rosemary made happy noises as I followed my cat out, and into the front parlor.

I'd handed Christine the baby before I'd left; now I stopped, surprised, as I saw that Rosemary was in Raymond's arms, on the sofa.

He glanced up at me, his face echoing my surprise, and gave me a hesitant grin. Rosemary, for her part, looked pleased but not at all desperate to see me.

My heart gave a little thunk. Raymond, holding our child… Rosemary, happy in her father's arms…it was kind of all too much to process in the moment.

"What happened?" Raymond asked, jiggling the baby on his lap. "Did something go wrong?"

"No—I mean, I don't know, but I don't think so. Why?"

"Did you find your mom?" Christine asked.

My heart panged. "No, but a lot of other interesting stuff happened." I walked over to the sofa and sat down. Raymond leaned over and handed me the baby; as I took her from him, I could feel that his grip was gentle but assured. Well, it would stand to reason he would know how to handle a baby—his sister was a midwife, after all.

Astonishingly, Rose didn't immediately start grabbing at my shirt, but just sort of gazed up at me, looking content. This, and how nonplussed Raymond and Christine seemed about my return… "How long was I gone?"

"Maybe five minutes?" Christine said. "Ten at the most."

"Wow. It felt longer." It had felt like hours and hours—the walking, the conversations, the magical work I'd done in Logan and her parents. I rolled my shoulders, working the tension out of them. "Where's Flavius?"

"He went back to bed right after you left," Christine said. "But he said to wake him if we needed anything. We were kind of trying to figure out what to do now ourselves—we didn't expect you back this fast."

Only then did I notice an unusual energy in the air—and not from the mysterious portal. "What's going on? Is something wrong here?" I asked, turning to look for Petrana.

"Uh," Raymond said, looking uncomfortable.

"The, um, warlock has been at the door," Christine said. "We didn't let him in—we couldn't, even if we'd wanted to. I think the house hurts him."

"The warlock?" I gasped, my arms tightening around my daughter. "Gregorio?"

"No, the other one," Raymond said, with a frown. "Jeremy."

———— CHAPTER TWO ————

What in the name of the Blessed Mother…? I got up and went to the front windows, looking out. Jeremy stood on the sidewalk, arms folded across his chest, staring darkly at the front door. Of course he'd know I had returned, despite my wards.

What do you want? I asked him, ætherically.

He turned and looked at me through the windows, a desperate, stricken expression on his face. *Callie! Can you please let me in?*

I snorted softly, bouncing a little to soothe the baby, though she had made no complaint. *I don't think so,* I told him. *Why should I?*

You were right. I was wrong. And…I fear I'm in danger. Please, Callie, for the memory of…whatever we once had…please trust me.

What kind of danger are you in? I asked, telling myself not to believe a thing this warlock said. Given the harsh words he'd flung at me just hours ago… *I'm supposed to believe your own father would do you harm?*

I do not know what he might do. He looked at me in growing desperation, taking a step closer to the house, then flinching as he brushed the edges of my wards. *He does not like to be crossed. And I…have news of your mother. Straight from your father.*

Fear, nearly panic, clutched my heart. *Oh Blessed Mother…* I breathed, trying to consider what it meant that he'd heard from my father—who had been cloistered away in the Elders' meeting and out of contact with me—before I had. I told myself that Jeremy was manipulating me, saying the one thing he knew would get me to do what he wanted...but what if it were true?

Had Jeremy ever knowingly lied to me? I couldn't be sure, but I didn't think so. Yes, he had sided with his father against me, even when I'd told him the truth about what was going on, but that had been my word against Gregorio's.

Jeremy had lived his whole life admiring his father—largely from afar—aspiring to become closer to him. To emulate him. To have his father regard him as worthy.

To gain his father's love.

Tell me, I sent. *Tell me about my mother: is she safe?*

I have every reason to believe so, he sent back at once. *At least for the time being. But it's complicated.*

I rolled my eyes. Of course it was complicated, everything was complicated. When were things ever *not* complicated? *I need more than that.*

Please, I must get off the street. My father does not know I'm here, but he will figure it out before too long.

How does he not know you're here?

Jeremy looked at me imploringly. *He rushed off suddenly, without telling me why. I believe something happened, perhaps in Berkeley, perhaps... farther afield. But I fear he won't be gone long.*

I looked out at him. He looked...he looked like the Jeremy I had fallen in love with. Back before the world was different.

All right, I finally told him. *But I'm getting backup here, just in case you try to do something unwelcome. So you're going to have to wait out there for a few minutes more. Hide behind a tree or something.*

His eyes widened; the streetlight reflected a flash of green at me. *Backup?*

I smiled grimly. *Just sit tight. Even your father can't get back and forth from Berkeley in an instant.* If that was even where he went.

If any of this was true.

I stepped away from the window and turned to Raymond and Christine, who had been watching our silent exchange with uneasy expressions. "That's just so weird," Raymond said.

Christine nodded. "It's like, we could see that you were talking, but you weren't speaking; I mean, just from your face, we could see you in conversation."

I shrugged. "Well, sit tight, I'm about to do it again." I turned away from them, still gently bouncing the baby, and opened a channel to the coven house. *Niad? Can I get your help with something over here? Kind of urgently?*

But of course, dear sister, she replied almost immediately. *You need only ask, and I shall appear.*

I rolled my eyes and sent a civil reply. *Thank you.*

A minute later, I felt her approach on the ley line; I opened the wards at the back of the house and let her in. She materialized in the kitchen, then walked down the long hallway and into the front parlor.

The siblings were clearly surprised. Christine covered it better than Raymond did. Niad, enjoying the effect, took her sweet time strolling in. "What can I help you with?"

"Jeremy's outside and he wants in."

She looked at me, bemused. "And?"

"And I don't know whether to trust him or not, and he's more powerful than I am. But he's not more powerful than you and me together."

"Ah." She smiled, pleased, and looked around the room. "Your human friends cannot help, and neither can your infant. Or…" I could see her casting her vision through the house. Then she tsk'd. "Or a former warlock with no magic, or even a golem or a cat. Oh, Callie. It's almost as if there were a *reason* that witches decided to live together, in households of greater numbers than one…"

"If you're not going to help me, just say so," I ground out. "I'll get somebody else."

She tossed her head and laughed. "Of course I will help you. I was just…seeking to understand the situation."

I looked at my friends, wishing I could silently send them the apology they deserved. Raymond looked as if he wanted to punch Niad in the face. Christine held her emotions closer to her vest, but she certainly looked wary.

"I'm going to let him in now," I told everyone.

Niad shrugged.

I loosened the wards and sent to Jeremy, *Okay, come in*, as I stepped to the front door to open it.

He was inside in an instant. I locked the door and reset the wards. He shivered as he felt their effect, but wisely did not say anything about it. "Thank you," he said instead.

I nodded and turned to usher him into the front parlor when I felt a nudge against my ankle. I glanced down, expecting Elnor, but it was Willson—Logan's familiar. He sniffed at my leg very thoroughly. As if he recognized a scent on me… I didn't say anything aloud, still not at all sure whether to trust Jeremy.

Instead, I just balanced the baby on one hip as I leaned down and petted the tom, then said, "In here."

Jeremy again clearly held his tongue as he walked in and was surprised to find humans there. He glanced at me; I waved him toward his usual chair and took my own.

Rosemary had been so placid during all this activity. She was watching with interest, not seeming hungry or tired or impatient.

My sweet, strange baby.

"What does a witch have to do to get a drink around here?" Niad asked. She had taken a seat in one of the overstuffed chairs, crossing her slender legs at the knee, showing off a clearly precisely calculated amount of thigh in both Raymond's and Jeremy's direct line of vision. I mean, I almost had to admire her thoroughness, her dedication to her art. It was truly impressive.

"What would you like?" I asked her.

She gave me an amused smile. As if she'd followed my thoughts and was considering a naughty answer. But she only said, "I heard your golem can make Smoldering Dragonflies."

"She can indeed." I glanced around at the humans, and at Jeremy. "Beers, and brandy?"

"It's three in the morn—" Christine started, but Raymond interrupted her: "Beers, absolutely."

"I would have a brandy," Jeremy said quietly. "The, ah, usual kind."

Petrana, clearly overhearing, appeared in the doorway. "And a Smoldering Dragonfly for you as well, Mistress Callie?"

Sure. Why not? "Yes, please."

Jeremy clutched his brandy snifter, looking quite uncomfortable. He'd downed more than half of it in the minute since Petrana had served us, and now he held his hands protectively around the glass.

"All right, I'm listening," I said to him.

He glanced around the room, then back at me. "Are you sure you want to have this conversation in front of...everyone?"

"Entirely sure," I said. "It's the secrets that are killing us all—quite literally, in fact. I'm done with secrets. I've told everyone in my coven," I glanced at Niad, who nodded, "along with as many other witches as I could, everything about what your father has been up to—as much as I've been able to learn, that is, which is plenty. Flavius Winterheart is upstairs, and he knows he was framed and then punished for crimes he did not commit. And by the way, these humans know about magic now, so you can stop freaking out when I say things like 'coven' and 'witches' in front of them, and stop being cagey about your Bulgarian frog brandy too."

Jeremy blanched and looked nervously at them. Christine gave him a cold nod; Raymond managed a smile, but it wasn't a friendly one. Niad just smirked, still amused.

I mean, what did he think they thought when Petrana walked into the room?

"So, go ahead and tell me why you're here," I went on.

The green-eyed warlock took another bracing sip of his brandy. Then, with a visible effort, he set the glass on the table beside him. The lamplight picked up the drink's color and glinted prettily. He cleared his throat. "I. Um. It's like I said when I was outside: You're right, Callie. I was wrong, and I am sorry. My father..." He swallowed, looking anguished. "My father has been harming all of us, and he needs to be stopped."

Niad leaned forward, an expression of polite interest on her face.

"Tell me about my mother," I said, before she could say something snarky. "What is he doing to her?"

"I don't know for certain, but your father is worried—it was he who came to me with this, straight from the Elders' meeting. He pulled me aside…he has been working with my father for centuries, of course, but he has grown increasingly worried of late. My father has become much more secretive, Lucas told me, while intimating that he is on the verge of some astonishing new breakthrough. And, while his power has been as strong as ever, if sometimes erratic, his mental acuity has been…challenged."

"He's losing his mind," Niad put in, helpfully.

Jeremy nodded sadly, but looked puzzled. "I fear he might be. And yet his strength—"

"I told you he's stealing essence from others," I blurted, tired of dancing around the issue. "That's what he's doing with it: He's using it on himself, to make up for his failing powers. This isn't just some *research* project." I felt a sudden fury. "He started decades ago, with Logan's parents. At least, those are the first people I know about; there could be more, there probably are. But his need for stolen essence just keeps growing, so now he's got a whole roomful of bodies, and souls held hostage in an in-between, limbo space." I got to my feet and started pacing, unable to stay seated. In my arms, Rosemary seemed to be listening with intense attention. She didn't even appear to mind my emotion.

"I know," Jeremy said, looking stricken. "You told me, and…I didn't want to believe it. Not being a biological researcher, I didn't understand. What he told me made sense."

I had more I could tell him, now that I had traveled to the in-between space and seen the trapped souls for myself. But not until I was positive I could trust him. "Don't feel bad," I said to him, more gently. "I *am* a biologist, as is my father, and Gregorio fooled us both."

Jeremy shook his head, looking grim. "Did he tell me the truth about anything?" he asked quietly.

"That is the question, isn't it." Rose was finally getting a little heavy in my arms. I headed back to my chair, and, not incidentally, my drink. I settled us back down and took a sip.

Niad leaned forward, looking intrigued; the humans were both listening intently, though I could see the exhaustion on their faces.

Not even rock-musician Raymond was accustomed to completely sleepless nights.

"What you told me about my mother," Jeremy whispered. "She died when I was so young…"

"Yes," I said, almost as quietly. I hadn't told anyone else, certainly not Niad—though I had told her of her own supposedly-impossible hybrid parentage. I shot her a helpless look, without quite meaning to; she knew there was one other, but she didn't know it was Jeremy.

Except now she did, because she wasn't stupid. She raised an eyebrow and sent me a silent, *Oh, interesting.*

Thankfully, Jeremy didn't seem to notice. "I just don't know what to believe."

"I understand that," I said.

Petrana appeared in the doorway. "Does anyone need another drink?"

I glanced around the room, catching Christine in a huge yawn. And Raymond—was he actually asleep? He'd finished his beer; his sister had made it halfway through hers. "I think some of us need to get to bed," I said.

Raymond gave a soft snore, sinking a little further into the corner of the couch.

Niad rose elegantly to her feet. "I'm satisfied, thank you," she said to my golem. When had she started being so polite to Petrana? It was kind of weirding me out. She turned to me. "Would you like me to stay here tonight, Callie? For continued backup?"

"I would, actually," I said. "If that's all right with you."

"I would be happy to."

Jeremy cleared his throat. "Actually…I was hoping I could stay here too. If he hasn't already, Father will certainly discover my absence soon. And I fear he won't be confused about where I've gone and what I've found out. Your wards feel…quite strong. I would be safe behind them."

"They are, and you will be," I said, feeling proud of myself even as I tried to figure out where I was going to stash everyone. He didn't imagine he was going to sleep with me, did he? Letting him into my house was one thing; welcoming him back into my bed was quite another.

And I hadn't forgotten that he still owed me an answer about my mom.

"I can make up a pallet in my office," he said quickly, reading my expression.

That made perfect sense, and yet…I suddenly found I didn't even want him on the same floor with Rosemary and me. And I certainly didn't want him in space he still considered "his." Way too much of a slippery slope. "Hold that thought for now," I told him, adding silently, *I'll find you something.*

"Ah. Well. All right."

"Let's get these folks to their rooms." I got up and walked over to the couch, where Christine and Raymond sat. "Can you climb the stairs under your own power?" I asked her.

She yawned massively again. "I think so, but you might have to bewitch my brother."

Niad chuckled. "Not a problem." She raised her arms, fingers crooked menacingly—like the TV sitcom version of an evil witch. I swear even her eyes flashed red and her nose grew a fraction of an inch.

"Stop it!" I said, more sharply than I'd intended. Rosemary shifted in my arms, and Petrana was by my side; I handed her the baby and leaned down to nudge Raymond. "Hey," I said to him. "Time to get up and go to bed."

"Mmmmph," he groaned. "Sleep here…"

Christine got up, and Raymond slid down into the space she'd vacated. Now he was almost entirely horizontal.

"Fine with me," I said, trying not to think about the last time he'd passed out on my couch…the night Gregorio stole Logan from me.

——— CHAPTER THREE ———

I gave Niad the room I'd made for Raymond and asked Petrana to take Rosemary to my bed, then led Jeremy up to the attic.

Part of me hated to let him into my private research space, but this was better than having him too close. And honestly, it was the best place to contain him should he turn out to be untrustworthy after all.

Besides: no more secrets and all that. This would be a good test of my resolve.

I pulled a small but comfy fully made bed from the showroom of a furniture store out in the avenues—I'd return it in a few days, or drop money into the store's bank account if I turned out to need it longer—then brushed the dust off it before sitting down. "Make yourself comfortable," I said, patting the space beside me—close, but not too close. "And then tell me everything you know about where my mom is and how we can get her back."

Jeremy sat where I'd indicated and let out a quiet sigh. "Well, I don't know the precise physical location, but I am quite certain we can figure it out. I have an idea."

My heart sank, even though I wasn't all that surprised. Of course Jeremy had pretended to know more—he'd been desperate for me to let him in. I told myself not to get furious with him. He could help me, and he would likely be more willing to if I was civil with him.

"He said he took her to his 'special clinic,'" I told him, "but he was clearly mocking me, trying to get a rise out of me. But you're saying she's not in Berkeley?"

"No, nor the regular San Francisco clinic either," Jeremy said. "I would know."

I didn't ask how he would know that. "So, what other safe holdings does he have?"

Jeremy looked down at the floor between his feet. "He told me that he recently brought property up the coast, a little cabin north of Mendocino. He even said that we should go there together, for a… vacation." He looked up at me, looking very pained. "But I haven't seen it—he kept postponing our trip."

"What aren't you telling me?" I asked.

Now he looked away again. "Our vacation…it was to be a celebration, just father-and-son, of my signing my first contract. A celebration of our growing family."

Oh Blessed Mother… "You know how weird that is, right?" I asked him. "Like—you were supposed to go on your honeymoon with your *dad*? And without me?"

"I know, it seems absurd now…" He sighed. "A lot of things seem absurd now, as I look at them from a different perspective. I just…I trusted him. I didn't understand that he was not telling me the truth about things."

Tell me about it, I thought.

"Like my mother being human," he said, very quietly. "That is true, isn't it?"

"I'm afraid so."

He stared at the floor for a long moment. "He…he cannot have not known?" he finally asked, but shook his head even as he said it. Witchkind can tell with a pointed glance who has magic and who does not. "Why?"

"Why did he form a union with a human? Why did he have a child with her? Why did he keep this from everyone?"

"All of that," Jeremy said, helplessly.

"I wish I knew." I gave him a rueful smile. "But I'm not about to pop over to his house and ask him."

"No, of course not." He shivered, and then looked even grimmer. "I wonder how she died, really. Because it was clearly not the magical wasting disease he pretends it was."

And there we were: I had wondered the same thing myself. I reached over and squeezed his hand. "I am sorry."

He squeezed back, then let go, sighed heavily, and dropped his face into his hands.

I got up and walked across the attic room to gaze out the back window, giving him space.

A long moment later, I heard him clear his throat. I turned around; he was looking sorrowfully at me. "We have to stop him."

"Yes, we do." I walked back over to the bed and sat down beside him again. "But first we need to get my mother away from him." I remembered another thing. "Wait, you said you talked to my father: Where is he?"

"As far as I know, he is still at my father's house. He agreed to cover my absence, to make an excuse if my father returned and looked for me." He must have read something in my eyes, for he added, "Don't call to him, Callie. He's walking a dangerous line as it is. It will be hard for him to cover up communication with you, should my father be looking for such a thing."

I shook my head. "I hate this."

Now Jeremy tentatively reached out for my hand again; I took his and sighed. "I hate it too," he said. "I feel very…" He paused, laughing sadly. "Words like 'confused' and 'lost' feel rather inadequate right now."

"I find it helps to concentrate on tangible stuff when I feel that way," I said. "Like, how are we going to find your father's Mendocino property and get my mother out of there?"

"I don't know anyone on the north coast…" he started, but I interrupted.

"Hang on: I'm being stupid," I said, and then called through the æther to Leonora—hoping desperately that she and the coven mothers were finished meeting.

To my great relief, Leonora responded at once to my ping, and within minutes, she was putting the word out through the coven mother network. *Get some rest*, she told me. *We should know more by daylight.*

I didn't feel tired, but I saw the wisdom in her words. Besides, Rosemary would surely be wanting a snack by now.

"Sleep well," I told Jeremy. He gave me a brave smile as I did not kiss him and did not invite him to come downstairs with me.

Perhaps someday we would work out where we stood, but this was not that day.

At least I didn't ensorcell him in there, I thought, wondering if I should have. But if he wanted out, well, he could just leave, couldn't he? I wasn't the one who needed him here.

Back in my bedroom, Petrana was standing watching Rosemary, asleep in her crib. "She's not hungry?" I whispered.

"She went down as soon as I laid her in there," my golem whispered back.

I nodded as I crawled into bed, nudging a sleeping Elnor with my feet.

"Rest well," Petrana said, and left my room, closing the door softly behind her.

I lay in bed, wishing I could look through physical space all the way to Mendocino. Sadly, peering across town was about the extent of my powers, and even that went more easily if I was familiar with the space I was looking to.

I would just have to wait and see what the north coast coven mothers came up with.

I closed my eyes, wondering if sleep would find me, or if my mind would just noodle over everything until the sun rose...and then suddenly Nementhe was speaking to me. Nementhe, our departed coven sister, returned to Circle every week to give us advice and counsel—and now she had come to me.

"Calendula Isadora," she said. She stood before me, her long hair and white dress billowing around her in an unseen wind. "Luna will help you. Heed my words..."

"What?" I asked. "Luna?"

And then, just as suddenly, Nementhe was gone and the two white cats were back. They walked into my room and jumped up onto the bed.

Elnor woke abruptly and leapt to her feet in one smooth motion. She stood bristling at my feet, her fur raising, her back arched, her tail high. I reached down for her; she jumped away as both white cats turned to me, each biting me on a hand—as they had done in my dream.

I yanked my hands back in shock and pain, but they had no wounds on them.

"You must listen to the cats…" Had someone said that? Nementhe, or someone else? Or was it just a memory? Oh—it was a dream; the scary human woman had told me this in a dream…

Wait, I knew this. But why was it so vague? Was I dreaming, still, again?

I must have been, for I was now standing, and fully dressed. Elnor was beside me; she nudged my leg. Her fur was still raised, but now she stared at the white cats. They stared back at her, then up at me, then turned and marched forward.

Only then did I realize we were no longer in my bedroom but were back in the misty white fog of the in-between space where Logan and her parents had spoken to me.

Elnor gazed up at me, then turned and followed the white cats.

Were the cats called Luna? They were ghostly-white, like the moon. Was this what Nementhe had meant?

Not knowing what else to do, and not wanting to lose Elnor to this strange vagueness, I followed as well.

I walked, once again without any sensation of my feet on the ground (or floor). There was barely even any feeling of movement. All I could see was my black and white cat, and two strange white cats before her.

The not-scenery did not change; it was as though we swam through fog.

After an uncountable span of time, the edges darkened. Was there something there? "Logan?" I called, but my friend did not answer. "Logan? Lorenna?" My voice no longer held the hollowness of that in-between place, and the space around me began to feel familiar. "Augustus?"

The white cats marched on ahead of us. We followed. My senses continued to insist that we were approaching something, but nothing materialized.

Was this a trap, set by Gregorio? He must know by now what I had done to Logan and her parents. Had I been an idiot, setting off after some strange cats?

But warlocks never worked with cats.

Don't underestimate him, I reminded myself. I stopped and glanced behind me, but it was all blankness. Too late to turn back now. I took a moment to wrap myself in a protection spell, at least.

The white cats stopped as well, then came back toward me and nipped at my heels aggressively. "Hey!" I said, trying to step away from them, but one of them...grew blurry? The cat's edges wavered, and then it abruptly resolved into the healer Manka, nearly buried in her pale swirling robes. She reached out to me, but my protection spell prevented her hand from landing on my upper arm.

"Callie! Come with us," she hissed. "Now!" As I turned, bewildered, I saw the other cat was now the second healer, Nora, and both healers were gesturing me forward.

I hurried along behind them, Elnor at my heels. Manka suddenly gave a flick of her wrist, and now we were on a ley line, traveling somewhere. I had no control; Manka pulled me with her own magic.

Before I could react, we emerged. I gasped in a breath and blinked, taking in my surroundings. We were now in the house on Potrero Hill where Nora and Manka lived, and where they had seen patients before Gregorio had built his fancy new clinic—but this was not a room I'd ever seen before. The magic and energy in here felt...different. Not quite normal. I had a momentary sensation of light-headedness and put a hand to my forehead, trying to ground myself. I was clearly no longer asleep, or dreaming—if I ever had been.

Elnor began sneezing, as she always did after traveling on ley lines.

Manka stalked through the small room, checking something at every corner, though I could not detect any wards or spells. Apparently satisfied, she sighed and turned to me. "My apologies, Calendula, but there was no time for explanation."

"It's all right," I said. "What's going on?"

Nora smoothed back her short auburn hair with both hands. "We must speak." She and Manka exchanged a glance. I felt reassured just being in their presence, though part of me wondered if I had any reason to be. Recent events had shown me so powerfully that I could no longer just blindly trust everything I'd been told by my elders.

Yet the healers were in a class of their own. On no one's side. On everyone's. And they had so capably and lovingly tended me through my pregnancy and Rosemary's birth. If I could not trust them…I didn't even finish the thought.

"Please, have a seat," Manka said. Her own long salt-and-pepper hair was held firmly in a braid down her back, woven with a white ribbon.

I sank into a plush chair as I let my protection spell fall away. Elnor jumped into my lap, though she still had one small sneeze in her. I managed to keep most of her cat-spit off me.

Manka took another chair beside mine, watching as we got settled. I could feel that she was also scanning me magically, as she had done many times during my pregnancy and periodically afterwards. She nodded after a minute and looked up into my eyes. "You are well."

"And you did well to follow us," Nora added, sitting on a small couch across from us. "We apologize for the haste, but we could not have Dr. Andromedus finding us in the not-quite-here."

Then the full force of what I'd just seen struck me: "Wait, can you guys change into *cats*?"

"Of course not," Nora said with a surprised chuckle. "Why do you ask?"

"What *were* those cats?"

Manka's brow furrowed. "Did you see cats?"

"Uh, yeah," I told them. "Two white cats." They both stared back at me blankly. "They've been in my *dreams*," I went on. "But they were also real, because they bit me." Though, had they? I held up my hands, looking at them. Still unwounded.

"We had to do a bit of archaic magic to reach you where you were," Nora said. "That might have caused some confusion."

"Maybe. Do you know what *Luna* means?"

They glanced at each other and shrugged. "The moon?" Manka said.

"Nothing more specific than that?"

"No," Nora said. "We're sorry, and we do apologize for alarming you."

I shook my head. "I'm okay. But, you guys, there's so much you need to know. Gregorio kidnapped my mom and has taken her some-where up north. And, in that in-between space, I saw Logan and her parents! I talked to them, and I helped them, just a little, I hope…" I trailed off, yet again hoping I hadn't actually doomed them. Both healers looked at me quizzically. "He's been draining the essence of his captive souls for his own use," I said. "I…figured out a way to block some of his access to their essence. But just with those three."

Manka said, "We are aware of Dr. Andromedus's laboratories in Berkeley. We did not know precisely what he was doing there; we knew the coven mothers were looking into it, and we have been expecting to hear from them. For now, I will want to hear more about what precisely you did for Augustus and Lorenna and their daughter."

I described what I knew, what I had learned. As I spoke, they nodded, exchanging occasional glances and looking grave. When I was finished, Nora said, "It is worse than we feared—and we did indeed fear. That warlock has much to answer for."

"Nora and I have retreated from his so-called clinic," Manka said. "We once again see patients here only."

"I rue the day we ever entered the cursed place," Nora said. "Our healing vows are some of the most sacred oaths a witch can possibly take." Her voice was pained, bitter. "It seems he very nearly caused us to rupture those vows entirely. We will be long atoning for our deeds."

"It wasn't your fault—" I started, but Nora went on.

"We should have seen it, long before now."

Manka looked at her partner. "The warlock's deceptions run deep," she said quietly. "He has harmed so many, for so long, so subtly."

Nora frowned.

"It's true," I said. "It's all tumbling out now, though. He can't cover his tracks anymore—too many people know too much. The coven mothers are telling all their covens, and even the Elders are talking about what to do. Leonora is contacting north coast covens about finding my mom. Everyone's sharing information." Gregorio had worked so long in the shadows, trading in secrets and lies and threats; pretending to have everyone's best interests at heart even while he was preying on us.... I shook my head again. "I'm glad you guys are up to speed."

"We aren't, not entirely," Nora said. "We don't know—"

She was interrupted by a soft knock on the door. I jumped, startled, but neither healer looked alarmed. Nora got up and opened it a crack. A young witch dressed in traditional acolyte's robes stood there, holding a tray.

"Ah, thank you, Peridot," Nora said, and opened the door widely, motioning her in. The young witch nodded at us, set the tray on the low table in front of the couch, and retreated, pulling the door shut behind her.

The tray held tea, cookies, and a tall, thin bottle of a sweet, strong liqueur. Nora poured and passed the plate of cookies to me. I hadn't thought I was hungry. Showed what I knew.

After a minute, Nora set her empty cup down and said, "I was about to say that we have been unable to locate Sebastian Fallon."

In my lap, Elnor shifted. She'd already eaten most of one cookie, even though cookies aren't for cats. "I am told he is safe and does not want to be found at the moment," I told the healers. "For everyone's protection."

Nora and Manka both frowned. "Flavius Winterheart told you that," Nora said. It was not a question.

"Right." If they knew that, they also knew Flavius was still at my house—along with the rest of my little slumber party.

Manka said, "I mislike this, taking the word of one who has deep cause for distrusting and disliking our kind."

"I know," I assured her and Nora both. "I was very wary when he showed up. He does seem—well, sad and broken." My heart ached to think of his pride, his diffidence, barely masking the terrible wounding. Not only had we rendered him incapable of working magic, we'd cast him out of our community altogether, without equipping him for the human world we'd dumped him into. "But I believe him. He has no reason to lie to us, about this."

"Revenge?" Nora asked, pointedly. "It seems to me he has abundant reason to lie to us—to you in particular. To hurt us in any way that he can."

"Well, maybe," I conceded, "but I honestly don't think so. He was found by Willson and all the other familiar-cats whose witches Gregorio is holding, and he's been taking care of them. It was the cats who brought him to me—they obviously like him. Logan's cat would never trust someone wicked."

"That is indeed strong evidence," Manka said thoughtfully. Then she leaned forward and put her hands on her knees as she peered at me. "We would like to speak with Dr. Winterheart, but first we would like to understand how you came to walk between the worlds."

"I...don't really know how it happened," I said, and told them about the under-stair closet. "The white cats led me there."

Nora patted the cushion beside her on the small couch. "Come, sit close, and I shall scry. Your body may well know things your conscious mind does not."

I got up and sat beside her. Nora put a hand on my arm, beginning her work. I leaned back and relaxed, feeling warmth from the healer, more than just her body heat. It grew, filling my body, like settling into a lush, fragrant bath. I sighed and closed my eyes.

"You may speak if you like," Nora said softly. "It won't disturb my work."

"All right." I thought a minute. "I don't really understand the white cats."

Manka looked over at me. "You said you dreamed them—tell us this dream. When did you have it?"

"Recently—maybe a week or two ago." Time seemed to have sped up; I wasn't really sure how long it had been. But I related the uncomfortable dream to them: the human woman's insistence that I listen to "the cats," the creatures' aggression and forcefulness, the painful bites, and how I'd been stuck in the dream until Sebastian had come from across town to rescue me from it. It was the night all my memories had been restored. "That's part of why I wasn't reluctant to follow them into the so-called cat portal."

Manka continued to gaze at me. "Calendula," she finally said. "I am struck by this new openness to intuition in you."

"What?" Of course I was open to intuition. That wasn't new.

"As you know," she said with a small smile, "magic is all about balance—because magic is intrinsic to nature, which is also always seeking balance. It is just as much of an error to lean too hard into your scientific training, to seek to measure and quantify everything without listening to the quiet voice inside yourself, as it is to let a dream or a tarot spread—"

"Or a cat," Nora said softly, shifting her hand.

"Or a cat," Manka agreed, "govern your actions. We all, whatever our natures, must use both approaches, listen to both messages. Only when we have achieved a true balance between the rational and the intuitive can we know our path."

I nodded. "That is all true, but it leaves me no less mystified about the white cats," I said, smiling. "They don't seem much like any of the others. I'm still not entirely sure they're real. And...I could have sworn that they changed into you two."

Nora just gave a wordless hum; she had both hands on me by now, one on my upper arm and the other at the back of my neck. It was soothing and comfortable.

Manka said, "Traditionally, of course, the color white symbolizes purity and cleansing, or a fresh start."

"I like the idea of a fresh start," I said. "I'd like to freshly start by finding my mom, and then maybe freshly punching Gregorio in the face."

"It would be good if we could talk to Sebastian Fallon," Manka said quietly, frowning at my joke. Which wasn't really a joke.

"I'm worried about him," I admitted. Yes, Flavius had said he was safe, but... "He's been messing with magic that nobody understands. Magic that's clearly powerful and dangerous."

"Oh?" Nora asked, moving her hand to the base of my neck,

sending radiating heat down my spine. It felt marvelous and relaxed me another notch.

"Yes." I told them about the golden ring, the one that Gregorio had leashed and monitored me with. Of course they had known it was there during my pregnancy, and they knew that I had tried to take it off and suffered a powerful blowback in the process.

Manka nodded slowly as I spoke. "And the ring released itself after you gave birth, and Dr. Andromedus never returned for it? Never asked about it?"

"Yes, it did; and no, he didn't," I said, feeling my discomfort grow again.

"That is interesting." Manka fell silent. Nora continued scrying on my body, moving her hand down my arm, her slender fingers encircling my wrist.

Finally, after a minute, Manka spoke again. "Dr. Andromedus knows that you have been working with Dr. Fallon?"

"Probably," I said. "I mean, we should assume so."

"He also contacted you specifically to tell you that he had taken your mother—that sounds very much like gloating to me," she went on.

I nodded. "That's how it sounded to me too."

"Would he not then have done the same if he had Dr. Fallon in his clutches? Either physically, or tethered in some way by the ring?"

I thought about it. "Maybe? Honestly, I don't know. Like I said, I don't think any of us really understands what that ring can do." I gave a rueful chuckle. "Correct me if I'm wrong."

Manka looked at me, her eyes hard and serious. "You're not wrong, Calendula. I now regret that we did not follow up about the ring sooner." She shook her head. "So many things are clearer in retrospect than they were at the time. No matter: we can only move forward. We would speak with Flavius Winterheart, and go from there."

"And what should I do?" I asked.

The healers glanced at each other again, this time long enough to consult silently, if that's what they were doing. At last, Nora said, "I observe something." She removed her hands from me; the heat they had generated slowly dissipated. I missed it, but I was glad to have my body back under its own direction again. I shifted on the sofa and stretched.

"In my body?" I asked.

"Yes." Nora stood up and began slowly pacing the small room as she spoke. "Your channels are unusually oriented."

I frowned up at her. "What does that mean?"

"I am not certain." She shook her head. "And it is quite subtle, but I am now sure of it." She came back to the couch and sat beside me again, looking into my eyes. "As you know, Calendula, because of your pregnancy, both Manka and I have had occasion to look very deeply into your entire system for over a year now. There is probably nobody we know as well as we know you, inside." She gave a ghost of a smile. "We noticed early on in your gestation that there was a different...feel, for lack of a better word...to your magic."

"Again, very subtle," Manka put in.

Nora nodded. "Much more recently, when Leonora told us the truth about Rosemary's sire, we imagined that was the cause of what we were seeing: her human parentage. A half-human being, sharing your most intimate bodily functions: that would explain any discrepancy."

"But I gave birth three months ago," I said slowly.

"You did. So any trace of your shared blood, your shared systems and essences, should have only lessened since then. Except this... anomaly has grown stronger."

"You mean I'm stronger?" I asked, still not quite understanding what she was trying to tell me.

Nora exhaled through her nose. "Yes. No. Not like that, anyway." She gazed helplessly at Manka, who shrugged. "Let us just say that you were an unusual witch to begin with, and you are only growing more unusual as time goes by."

"And we do not know why," Manka said.

"But it seems likely that it is this new aspect within you that has given you access to the in-between space," Nora said. "Which is interesting, and potentially useful."

"Useful?"

"Oh indeed," Nora said with a smile. "You have already, as you put it, turned down the spigot on three of Dr. Andromedus's captive souls, rendering them more difficult for him to drain."

"As you point out, the old warlock is clearly using this stolen essence to bolster his increasingly failing faculties," Manka said. "If you were to return, visit more of the victims, cut off even more of his supply…"

I was already nodding, until it occurred to me: "Wait," I said. "You guys can come with me, you can help me—you came into the in-between to bring me here, right?"

They glanced at each other. "In a manner of speaking," Nora said. "Though we do not walk those passages as you clearly did."

"We, rather, reached in for you. As it were," Manka said.

My heart sank. "So I will have to do it alone."

"That seems probable," Manka agreed.

"And dangerous," Nora added. "As healers, we do not like to send anyone into danger—particularly not a new mother."

I snorted. "I can't say I like the idea a whole lot myself." Power of suggestion: my breasts suddenly ached, just at the reminder of Rosemary. I sent my vision back to my house, checking on her. She was still sleeping peacefully, a tiny fist in her tiny mouth. Petrana, bless her stone heart, had realized I was gone; she was standing in my bedroom, watching over the child.

"But nobody is safe while Gregorio Andromedus preys upon us all," Manka said, bringing my attention back to the room where we sat.

"If I can cut off enough of his supply," I said, "we ought to be able to…defeat him." Even now, even knowing what he'd done to us all, I couldn't bring myself to speak of killing the warlock. My old mentor. My father's best friend. Jeremy's father.

"He belongs in the Beyond," Nora said firmly. "It is long past time he took the next step of his journey."

"I'll do it," I said. "Whatever I can. And…" I bit my lip. "If it doesn't…go well…you guys will make sure Rosemary gets taken care of?"

Both healers smiled gently at me. "I fear we would have to stand in line to even babysit the witchlet," Nora said. "Does she not have an entire coven of doting aunties wrapped around her little finger?"

I shrugged but smiled back at them. "I guess she does."

Manka cleared her throat and turned to Nora. "I respect your caution, but I actually disagree with your assessment. I do not believe the danger is as great as we may imagine."

"Oh?" Nora looked interested, if skeptical.

"For all his threats, Dr. Andromedus does appear to not want Calendula dead, or even permanently harmed."

"Taking my memories seemed pretty permanent," I said, my smile falling away. "And he threatened me pretty fiercely when I was supposed to cover up the fact that Raymond was Rose's father."

"But that is not how things have ended up, is it?" Manka said. "You have your memories, and your daughter is safe at home."

"My mother isn't," I said, pointedly.

"All the more reason to press now, since you have found a vulnerability," Manka went on. "Deprive him of access to his ill-gotten essence. Weaken him further. Send him away from our midst." Her voice strengthened as she spoke.

Nora nodded slowly. "You have a point, my friend. He has done such great harm to so many, while leaving Calendula largely unharmed. We do not even know if Belladonna Isis is in any discomfort or danger."

"That's the problem," I argued. "We *don't* know. I want to go find her, get her back home!"

"We understand," Manka said. "And others are working on that. For now, the thing you can do—perhaps you and *only* you—is cut off Dr. Andromedus's source of power."

I felt a shiver—of fear, of pride. And an increasing discomfort, as both healers looked at me expectantly. "Um…you think I should do that now?"

"I see no reason to wait. Do you?" Manka asked.

I stifled my nerves, with an effort. I saw all sorts of reasons to put this off—I needed to get home and nurse my daughter; all my houseguests were going to need breakfast pretty soon; didn't we want to think this through a little more carefully?—but I shook my head. "Well. Um. Okay." I got to my feet, hopelessly wishing that they would somehow stop me, but both healers rose as well. Nora put her gentle hand on my back, lending me her strength.

"We will be right here," she said.

I nodded. In my arms, Elnor looked up at me, clearly wondering what was next. "How do I start?" I asked the healers. "My first time in, I walked through the cat portal in my house; my second time, it felt like you guys pulled me from a dream."

"Just step forward," Manka said.

——— CHAPTER FOUR ———

*J*ust step forward, Manka said, so I did, feeling foolish, until—

—I took a second step and I was in the fog once more.

I stopped and looked behind me, imagining I would look back into the healers' room, but it was not there. Just fog, in every direction.

Elnor fidgeted, clearly wanting to be set down. "Are you sure, kitten?" I asked her.

Still, she'd "walked" through this space before, and I hadn't lost her. I should be able to trust her to know what she was doing. So I let her down.

We both walked forward, for a span of time. "Logan?" I called out, periodically. "Lorenna? Anyone?" There was no reply. Was it not going to work? How long should I keep trying? How would I get home again if it failed? "Logan?"

Suddenly my friend was beside me.

"Logan!" I cried, delighted to see her again, relieved that I wasn't lost forever in an endless mist between realms. "Oh, thank goodness I found you. The healers want me to try—" I cut off, seeing her face. "What's the matter?"

She sniffled, shrugged, and glanced around us. We were now in a dark, empty room, bereft of all warmth and color and hope. "He knows," she said quietly.

"He...Gregorio found out what I did?" I asked. My heart pounded with fear once more. But of course he would find out, we'd expected he would...all the more reason to push our advantage...

"He took my father away." She sounded miserable. "We didn't tell him what had happened, that it was you, anything—but he knew something was wrong. He took Daddy." She sniffled again. "Callie, I'm so frightened that he will..." She looked at me, her eyes wide. "You can't do this to any more people."

"But that's just it," I argued, shaking my head. "It clearly worked, or he wouldn't have reacted this way. If I can do a *lot* more people, right away—"

"I don't mean you shouldn't," she interrupted me. "I mean you *can't*. He's cut Mother and me off from everybody else as well; I wouldn't even know how to help you find them." She shivered. "Oh, I knew it was too good to be true. I hope he isn't torturing Daddy..."

I pulled her into a hug. It felt like a hug, even though her form here was only half-substantial right now. My heart ached. "Oh Logan, I'm so sorry," I said. Why oh why hadn't I insisted on staying and turning the "valves" on more people when I was here before? I should have known Gregorio would make a countermove, would outflank me. When would I ever learn?

I couldn't even reassure her that her father was probably fine. Clearly, he wasn't.

"I'll get Gregorio," I promised instead. "I will stop him, if it's the last thing I do." *And it probably will be*, I added silently.

"Could you...undo what you did to me?" she asked in a tiny voice.

I looked at her. "Really? I mean, maybe, but why?"

"I don't...want him to take Mother too. If we cooperate..." She bit her lip. "If we behave..."

My heart, already fracturing, broke the rest of the way. Logan wanted me to make it easier for Gregorio to harvest more of her essence, to spare her mother. And could I blame her? I would do the same for my own mother. The only reason I wasn't punching Gregorio in the face right now and snatching my mom back was because I didn't know where they were.

"Are you sure? It'll just make you more helpless."

"I'm already helpless."

I stared at her, thinking. "What if I undo it most of the way? Maybe even leave you a latch to, I don't know, undo my undoing if things change?"

"You can do that?"

"I have really no idea," I admitted. "All of this is new to me. I don't understand it. But I don't like leaving you with no options."

"I suppose we could try that," she said. "But you'll have to teach me what you did."

"If I can."

She nodded, and tried a brave smile, suddenly looking achingly young again. "I know you can, Callie. I know you can do this, and that you can fix everything. Right?"

"Oh, Logan. I wish I had your faith." I took a deep breath and put my hand out. "When you're ready."

She took my hand, and together we placed both our hands on her chest. "So the first thing I did was just feel, energetically, for the source..." I said, guiding her through it.

Logan vanished back into the mists after I'd reopened her channels most of the way, and I'd coached her as she manipulated them. "And it might not even come to any of that," she'd said. "Mom and me, we can't hide from him, but we can sort of...make ourselves scarce, at times. Especially now that he's cut us off from the others."

After she left, I walked forward again, setting my intention toward my home, the cat portal there. It was the most familiar anchor I had, though I did not understand how this place worked. Did I have any control here? It was so hard to know.

But all I could do was try, Elnor by my side.

After another unmeasurable span of time, I felt the edges harden around me, and then—I was in my under-stair closet.

I exhaled a huge sigh of relief. Elnor sniffed the corners of the closet, then walked toward the door, which was ajar, as it should be. She paused in the doorway, then stepped out into the hall.

I followed her, blinking in the strong sunlight pouring through the window in the front door. It was morning.

"Hey," said Christine, stepping in from the front parlor. I could hear other voices in there; the household was clearly awake. "We were wondering where you'd gone!"

"I told everyone not to worry," Niad said from behind her, "that you would not abandon this precious child...but I confess, it was a bit of a puzzle." She held Rosemary in her arms.

"Maaaa!" my daughter sang out, joy and delight in her piercing voice. I reached out and took her. For a wonder, she didn't immediately begin pawing at my blouse. She waited nearly a whole minute before doing that—time enough for me to sit down, at least, and glance around the room. Everyone except Flavius was here; I could hear Petrana rattling around in the kitchen.

"Want some coffee?" Christine asked me.

Raymond and Jeremy both started to speak, then stopped. A dark look passed between them.

"What?" I asked.

Raymond shook his head and muttered something under his breath.

"She drinks tea," Jeremy said.

"Yes, I know that," Raymond barely whispered.

Hmm.

"*Any*way," Niad said, "once we determined that you weren't here, despite us all having agreed that we were to stay indoors behind these industrial-strength wards for our own safety, we began discussing how long we should wait to order up some breakfast."

"I'm sorry," I said, "but I didn't have any control over it. I was asleep, I think, and then suddenly I was pulled into the in-between space again—and then pulled right back out of it, by Nora and Manka."

Niad raised an eyebrow and leaned forward. "Indeed? Do tell."

I told them everything I'd done and learned (and hadn't done, and hadn't learned). "And now I should let the healers know the same," I told them. Rosemary had finished nursing; I buttoned up and shifted her to face forward into the room.

"I can check on breakfast," Christine said, getting to her feet.

"I'll help," Raymond said at once, and followed her to the kitchen.

I looked over at Niad, and then at Jeremy. "What's going on here?" I asked. "What happened?"

"Nothing," Jeremy said, too quickly.

Niad just shrugged. "Oh, everything's fine. Make your report to the healers, and then we can call to Leonora and see if she's heard anything from the north coast covens."

"Right." I looked at Jeremy. He looked back at me for a moment, then down at the floor.

I sighed. "Look: I know this is awkward—"

His eyebrows shot up. "That's putting it mildly."

"—but I invited *him* here. *You* just showed up, later, begging to be let in."

"I understand. My apologies."

I watched his face. His expression had closed down; he looked quite convincingly blank, if not exactly innocent. "You don't have to like him, but I need you to be courteous."

"I shall be courteous."

I told myself that was probably as good as I was going to get—at least for now. After watching him another long moment, I turned away and closed my eyes, so I could concentrate on my ætheral conversation, and called to Nora and Manka.

They were of course disappointed, but neither of them seemed terribly surprised. *So the next step will be to find his north coast stronghold*, Manka said.

Stronghold? I asked. Jeremy had described it as a little vacation cabin...

What else would you call it? she said, sounding surprised. *A fortified remote place where he is most likely holding your mother captive—and perhaps others. For all we know, that is where he has taken the spirit of Augustus as well.*

We have to stop him, I sent.

Indeed.

By the time I finished that call, breakfast was served.

Flavius Winterheart did come down and join us in the dining room, though he was nearly silent. I watched him as we ate. He looked a little less drawn and ragged, but he clearly had no emotional connection with either the humans or the witchkind in the room. Or appeared to want one.

I noticed that Jeremy avoided interacting with the former warlock. Not in a rude or overt way, just...stepped around him, conversationally.

Well, at least he was being courteous. As promised.

Oh, it would be good when this awkward little household could disperse, and everyone could get back to where they belonged. And then I had a sudden stab of guilt at the thought. Where did Flavius belong? Nowhere, of course. He had once belonged among our kind, but we had destroyed that.

I was reaching for the platter of toast when Leonora called to me through the æther. *Calendula Isadora? May I enter?*

Enter? I cast my glance to the doorway, and indeed, my coven mother was standing on the front porch. "Of course!" I said aloud, as I leapt up to go ease the wards and open the door. "Leonora!" I said, stepping aside. "Please, come in. We're just finishing breakfast; can I get you anything?"

"I have broken my fast," she answered, stepping into the front hallway with a swish of fabrics. She was clad in long dark green skirts, heavy and full, with a short grey jacket above, trimmed with jade beads and large occluded emeralds. Restrained, for her. The jacket buttoned up to her neck; the buttons were mismatched, but all of a type: big, squarish, dark. "But I would take a cup of tea."

At the far end of the long hallway, Petrana stepped out of the kitchen, already holding a teapot in one hand and a cup and saucer in the other.

"You, ah, know who-all is here right now?" I asked Leonora, very quietly.

She gave barely a glance toward the dining room. "In addition to you, I see Niadine Laurette of my coven; Jeremiah Andromedus, the son of the warlock who is trying to destroy us all; two humans, the sire of your daughter and his sister; your daughter, asleep in a bassinet; and Dr. Flavius Winterheart, the former warlock to whom you are apparently giving asylum."

"Uh…yeah," I said.

"And of course your golem, and some assorted cats."

"Right." Actually I wasn't at all sure how many cats were here right now; I'd only seen Elnor, but in a three-story house, and given the way they came and went, there could be any number, anywhere. "And you're okay talking in front of…everyone?"

"If you are hosting them here, I can only presume that you have taken them into your confidence. Should they hear something that confuses or frightens them, that is not my concern." She fixed me with her steely gaze, though I felt a brush of warmth in it. "Was it not you who informed us that the time for secrets was over? I am merely honoring your wishes."

I stifled a smile. "Well, all right then." But I shook my head in wonder as I followed my coven mother to the dining room.

She strode in, took an empty chair, nodded to everyone at the table, and accepted the cup of tea from my golem. "I have come in person rather than calling," Leonora began, "because of the sensitivity of the matter. And because there *is* one from whom we must keep secrets."

"Oh?" I asked, settling back into my own chair.

She sipped her tea and set the cup in its saucer with a gentle clink. "Yes. As we know—or at least, as I *assume* we know—the warlock Gregorio Andromedus has stepped outside of the bounds of reasonable and decent behavior, and it is the duty of witchkind to stop him."

Everyone nodded, even Flavius, who seemed a little overawed by Leonora. Well, she was a formidable presence.

"His latest misdeed is the kidnapping of Belladonna Isis, under the guise of treating her for a mysterious ailment." She snorted softly. "As if we are meant to be deceived by *that* ruse over and over again. He appears to have taken her to a relatively new property acquisition of his, in a tiny village between the towns of Mendocino and Fort Bragg, on the northern coast." She glanced at me. "I did receive word from Magenta in the Mendocino coven that a house on substantial grounds, formerly owned by a member of their warlock community, has been purchased by a shell company, disguising its eventual occupant's identity, but that powerful magic continues to be worked there. It would be a rather astonishing coincidence if that were *not* Dr. Andromedus."

"Right," I agreed.

Jeremy was also nodding. "My father did tell me it was north of Mendocino proper."

"Magenta and her coven are going to look into the situation further, but I see no reason why we should wait here for word from them, particularly given the challenges that we face in traveling to Caspar."

Now it was my turn to snort. "*Casper? Really?*"

Leonora gave me a quizzical look.

"Like, the friendly ghost?" I said, now starting to feel foolish, as both Jeremy and Flavius were also looking at me like I was nuts. "That's where our crazy warlock is building his new fortress?"

Raymond, however, was laughing with me. "Obviously no one in witch-land knows about ole Casper. Why should they? Ghosts aren't real."

He really was coming along nicely, after having had his whole world turned upside down just a couple of days ago. I wondered if I could have told him the truth sooner…and then I pushed that thought away. The important thing was, I hadn't, and now wasn't the time for what-ifs…even if I did wonder what this might mean for the future.

"Cas-*par*," Leonora said, with a slight emphasis, "as I was saying, will pose some challenges for us. Specifically, to travel there."

"Why?" I asked. "Are the ley lines awkward or something?" Places near the coast could be oddly organized, with channels often ending abruptly. We were lucky to have such good thick lines in San Francisco.

Leonora shook her head. "For the same reason that I came here in person, in a taxicab, Calendula: please attend."

I could almost hear Niad's quiet snicker. *Oh, that's right, dear sister, little Callie's in trouble again,* I thought, but kept my eyes off her.

"Every use of magic exposes us further," Leonora went on, "sending information to Dr. Andromedus, opening our channels to possible encroachment. We do not know the extent of how he has misused his ill-gotten essence. He could have planted traps on the ley lines; he could intercept ætheric communications; we simply do not know what means he has prepared to thwart anyone challenging his dominance." She took another sip of her tea, frowning. "Now that he is no longer able to hide his actions, he will likely switch tactics altogether—in fact, he almost certainly already has, going on the offensive rather than skulking about in the shadows."

Niad leaned forward, looking concerned, and quite sincere. "We should travel carefully on the lines, then; perhaps always taking at least one other practitioner with us at all times."

"No," Leonora said, "we should stay off the lines altogether. He will be looking for us there. Sadly, we may need to rent a vehicle, and somebody will need to drive it." She shook her head. "I have not driven a car in some years, I do not know if I would recall the precise mechanics of it…"

Raymond caught my eye. "I got my truck here. I'll drive you to Caspar. It's a tiny little town—if you can even call it a town. Houses are all spread out. Only about three hundred people live there." He shrugged. "I've been up there before."

Everyone at the table stared at him. Even Leonora's eyes widened. Then she nodded slowly. "That is a most excellent idea," she said.

"Wait, what?" Niad said, looking affronted. "That's silly; it'll take forever. How far away is this Caspar place—hundreds of miles? It'll take days!"

I could see that Raymond was stifling a smile, having clearly already perceived what a bad idea it would be to laugh in Niad's face. "Three, four hours, tops," he said. Beside him, Christine nodded agreement.

"And that's no way to keep Gregorio from spotting us!" Niad went on. "He knows we've got humans here; if we thought of this, he certainly will."

"We didn't think of it," I pointed out. "Raymond did."

"I don't like it either," Jeremy said. "How big is this truck? How many people will it carry?"

Raymond leaned forward. "My offer was to take *Callie*. Not anybody else. If you-all want to rent a car or go on the whatever-lines as a distraction or something, go for it." He glanced at Jeremy. "My truck carries two people comfortably, three in a pinch. Three hours crammed in a cab on winding roads is a long time."

"The human man will take Calendula," Leonora said, with a note of finality. I kind of wanted to remind her that Raymond had a name, which I was pretty sure I had just uttered a moment ago, but this didn't seem like the time. Niad had opened her mouth to say something more; it snapped shut, and she picked up her teacup. Jeremy looked disgruntled but also kept silent. "I shall remain in San Francisco," Leonora continued, "and begin working with alternate means of communication."

"Alternate?" I asked.

"Yes," she said. "All these cats are clearly trying to tell us something. I will work with Sapphire and her coven to see if we can assist in their efforts."

I nodded, even though I didn't think they'd find out much of anything. Cats were wonderful creatures, and our familiars were bonded to us in complex and beneficial ways; but cats never did run around carrying messages between witches.

Unless... I turned to Flavius. "The cats who brought you here: how did they tell you how to do that?"

He shrugged. "Pretty much like you'd expect. Nipping at my heels, meowing at closed doors, not letting up till I did what they seemed to want."

I sighed. "That sounds familiar," I muttered.

Leonora got to her feet. "You should leave as soon as possible," she told me. "Go to Magenta's coven in Mendocino first." She reached into a hidden pocket in her bodice and handed me a folded slip of paper. "They will take you to the warlock's house and should be able to provide protection and guidance as well." She glanced around the table, looking firm and resolute. "Together, we will prevail. The days of one warlock, however powerful, harming all of witchkind are about to draw to a close."

Then she turned and swept out of the room, queen of dramatic exits that she was. The humans watched her wide-eyed; Niad gazed after her with nothing but respect showing on her face, though I knew her well enough to know she was rolling her eyes inside. I hurried to my feet and followed my coven mother so I could open the door for her, like a good hostess.

"Be careful," she said to me in a whisper, then stepped down the front stairs and into a taxi, which appeared at a flick of her fingers. A moment later, she was gone.

I shook my head and returned to the dining room. In her little bassinet, Rosemary awoke, stretching and yawning. Then she turned her gaze to me.

"You hungry, little one?" I asked, stepping over and reaching for her.

She came into my arms happily enough, but she sent me a silent word: *Journey*.

I gave a start.

"What is it?" Niad asked, ever alert.

"She said *journey* to me," I told her, as I sat down and situated my daughter on my lap. Rose didn't start reaching for my boobs, which was nice. Well, she'd just eaten less than an hour ago.

"That's a complicated word for one so young," Niad observed.

"I thought the same."

Raymond shifted in his chair. "I, uh, I mean if you wanna…the truck is big enough for a little bitty thing like her, but I don't have a baby seat or anything…"

Christine's eyes widened. "You are *not* taking an infant in that awful truck of yours. Car seat or no."

I glanced down at Rosemary, who was watching the conversation attentively. "It will likely be dangerous there," I said.

"The child should stay here," Jeremy said, definitively, but with a remarkably restrained expression. *The child*. The child he'd thought was his…as had we all, at least for a while. The child he'd begun to bond with.

But of course he would still care about her. If he cared about me, how could he not?

"Petrana is very practiced at taking care of her," I said, giving Jeremy a warm and grateful look, "as of course is Niad—in fact all of my coven sisters are. I'll express some milk before we go, just in case we…"

I trailed off as I felt the telltale soft nudge of a voice in my head—just a momentary flicker. I thought it was my daughter saying something further. Was she going to agree, or object? But it wasn't her, it was a male voice, and older than her… *Callie?*

I gasped his name aloud. "Sebastian?"

Everyone at the table became intensely alert. "What did you say?" Niad nearly snapped, as both Raymond and Christine gasped, and Jeremy started to ask something as well.

I closed my eyes and covered my ears. *Sebastian?* I sent. *Where are you, what's happening?*

Did Flavius Winterheart find you?

Yes, he did. He's here now.

Sebastian sent a sigh of relief. *Don't let him out of your house. He cannot defend himself.*

He is safe here, I told him. *But what is happening? Are you safe?*

A slight pause. *I have had to…make an adjustment. I am no longer where Flavius knows, but I should say no more than that. If he thinks it through, he may be able to* catch *a hint.*

He gave the word "catch" the slightest emphasis, though such things were so hard to tell in ætheric communication. It was possible I'd imagined it, or that the lines were uneven, or…

And I'm going to go now—I will be in touch when I can—be careful, Callie!

With that, he was gone.

Sebastian! I sent, though I knew it was futile. I dropped my hands from my ears and opened my eyes. Fortunately, everyone knew enough not to keep talking at me when it was clear I was listening to a voice in my head, but they were staring at me now.

"Sebastian is in danger, and he called to you and can't tell you where he is," Flavius guessed.

Niad shot him an annoyed look; clearly, she'd been about to make the same observation.

"He said if you thought about it, you could *catch* a hint," I told

Flavius. "And maybe 'catch' is part of the clue; he sort of leaned into that word."

Flavius frowned. "Catch? I'm not sure what that refers to."

"Well, think about it perhaps," Niad said, snippily. "Don't just shrug your shoulders and give up."

"All right," I started to say, as Christine leaned forward.

"Let me help," she said, "with anything—with everything. I've already called in to work, told them I'm taking another personal day. I can take care of the baby; I can help figure out clues; I can help look for your friend, probably better than most of the rest of you. Right?"

Now we were all looking at her. "What do you mean?" Jeremy asked.

She pushed her long red hair back; her blue eyes shone with sudden purpose. "It makes sense—after what your coven mother said about staying off the ley lines, and not talking magically, and about going to Caspar in Raymond's truck. My car's here too. Human stuff flies under the magical radar—humans ourselves do. Don't we?"

"Well, not exactly like—" I said.

"But yes, exactly like that!" she cried. "Witchkind can't pay attention to us—there's too many of us, you'd be watching us all day long. You basically ignore us, even though you live among us. If *you*, Callie, went to hunt for your friend, there would be all sorts of sensors, or triggers, or however it works that would alert Gregorio that you were there. But me? Would he have any way to guard against me?"

I looked at both Jeremy and Niad, who had fallen thoughtfully silent. "Likely not," Jeremy said after a minute. "Oh, certainly a warlock could set wards or spells targeted for general or even specific humans, and he will use mundane door locks just as anyone else would, but knowing my father..." He shook his head. "I believe you are correct, Christine. He does not take humans seriously, and he does not see any individual human as a threat."

I didn't like how Christine's eyes were shining, how her cheeks were flushed with excitement. "Guys," I said to both her and Raymond, "this isn't a video game or an action movie. This is *real*. You know so little about the magical world, about how powerful Gregorio is, how he operates. He could kill you, and you wouldn't even know what to expect. You'd never see it coming."

"Then I shall go with her," Flavius announced.

We all stared at him.

He shrugged. "I'm not witchkind anymore, but I do have an understanding of the world, even still," he said dryly. With a pointed look at Niad, he continued, "Together, we can even *think through* Sebastian's little riddle."

"Wow," I said, leaning back in my chair, jiggling Rosemary on my lap. She had continued to watch the conversation quietly but attentively. Now, she sent me *journey* again, then repeated it twice. I looked down at her. "You think it's time we all got started on our journeys?" I asked her, aloud.

"Ready when you are," Raymond said, pushing back from the table.

Petrana came in and began clearing the dishes. "I understand you are leaving Rosemary Leonora in my care," my golem said.

"I'll be here too," Niad said, a bit stiffly. As though I'd forgotten her.

"Do you want me to call a few more sisters over?" I asked her, my gaze surreptitiously—I hoped—flitting to Jeremy.

Niad shook her head. "No need. I can call to them as easily as you can—in fact," she added thoughtfully, "it might be a good idea to start a lengthy, chatty conversation between here and the coven house. If the lines are compromised, rather than staying off them, it seems to me that sending a lot of irrelevant or even misleading information back and forth is a wise move." She smiled, wickedly. "I will be sure and mention how you are absolutely, certainly here in your house—napping, playing with the cats, bathing—"

"Pumping milk," I added, getting up to go get my supplies. "Gregorio will *not* want to spy on that, I'm quite sure."

Even Jeremy laughed then. But he looked a little uncomfortable a moment later.

"What will you do while we travel?" I asked him, pausing in the dining room doorway.

He shrugged elegantly. "May I stay here? I still feel safest behind these...walls."

"You may." I resisted the urge to glance at Niad, to see if she was okay with continuing to supervise him. He'd proved trustworthy so far, even helpful.

"Thank you."

In the kitchen, I got the breast pumps out of its drawer and then considered where to set up. So many people in my house...but, well, it was *my* house, right? I sat down at the kitchen table and strapped on.

When I had filled two bottles, I handed them to Petrana. "I hope I'll be back before you need to use all this, but in case I'm not..."

"I am sure you won't be gone this long," she said, placing the bottles carefully in the freezer. "And perhaps it's time we started the girl on real food? Something besides milk?"

"Don't you dare," I said, though I was smiling. "My daughter is not going to take her first bite of porridge from anyone's hand but my own."

"Yes, Mistress Callie," Petrana said, in a fair approximation of her initial monotone.

I shook my head and went out to the front parlor, where Raymond was waiting. On my way, I saw Niad and Jeremy in the second parlor, talking softly about something. Niad held Rosemary, who relaxed comfortably in her arms, not even reaching for anyone's hair. My coven sister glanced up at me as I walked by, then returned her attention to the warlock.

I wondered what they were talking about. They had plenty in common...more than they knew, or at least than Jeremy knew; Niad had figured out their shared secret.

"Hey," Raymond said when I joined him in the front room. "Ready?"

"Yeah." I looked around. "Where are Christine and Flavius?"

"They already left."

"What?"

Raymond gave a diffident shrug. "Christine thought—and Flavius agreed—that not only should they get going right away, but they shouldn't tell you, or any of us, where they were going. Just in case…you know. In case the bad guys can reach into our brains and find what they wanna know."

As much as I wanted to say *That's not how it works*, I—sadly—was living proof that that was, in fact, very much how it worked. Evil Old Country warlocks had reached into my brain and harvested a vast quantity of my memories. I was lucky to have them back.

"Okay," I said. "They're right."

"So." He gave me a weak smile. "Ready?"

"I am." I reached down and picked up Elnor.

Raymond's face fell. "Uh…"

"What?"

"Cats, uh, don't usually like to go for car rides."

I blinked at him. "Elnor is different." And there was no way I wasn't taking my familiar with me.

"Okay…do you have a box for her, maybe?"

"What? No, she doesn't need a box. She'll let me know if she needs to go to the bathroom."

He frowned. "No, not a litter box—just, a box to hold her in? So she doesn't freak out?"

"I told you, she's different. She'll be fine, won't you, kitten?"

Elnor wriggled a little in my arms, as if to say, *I don't know why you picked me up but whatever it is, let's do it.*

"See?" I said to Raymond. "Perfectly fine."

He just shook his head.

——— CHAPTER FIVE ———

Raymond's truck was faded red, a dozen or more years old, and smelled like a combination of Doritos and motor oil, plus something swampier underneath. The suspension was so tight, I had to cross my arms firmly under my boobs so I didn't put an eye out every time we hit a bump in the road. (Hmm, maybe there *was* something to this idea of getting the baby on solid foods... it would sure be nice to go back down a cup size or two.)

Raymond made quick work of navigating San Francisco's crowded streets to the Golden Gate Bridge. I kept mostly quiet, not wanting to distract him...and not really knowing what to talk about.

Elnor sat on the seat between us, gazing out the front window. Every now and then Raymond looked at her, clearly waiting for her to freak out. She would just glance back at him, blink slowly, and then resume watching our progress out the window.

Once we were on Highway 101 and through Marin County, the traffic opened up and the scenery settled into something less stunning. Raymond finally seemed convinced that my cat wasn't going to panic and scratch his eyes out; now, however, he glanced over at me a time or two, as if he wanted to say something.

"Thanks for doing this for me," I said, figuring I'd give him an opening.

"Oh sure," he said quickly. "It's no big deal, really."

"No big deal to uproot your life and drive me several hundred miles north, to maybe confront an evil warlock who kidnapped my mom?"

He snorted. "Okay, maybe a little bit of a big deal." Then he grew serious. "But Callie, I just...I know we hit some rough patches, but I never hated you. And nobody should be kidnapping anyone's *mother*. That's just *wrong*."

"I agree," I said with a small smile. "Anyway, I appreciate it."

"Sure."

We fell silent again for a while. But it wasn't an uncomfortable silence, exactly. Yes, there were the huge unresolved issues between us—he was human, I was not; he was Rosemary's father, but hadn't known it until very recently; I had been about to effectively marry another man without being honest with Raymond or even really cleanly breaking things off with him—but for now, all that stuff seemed...like we could tackle it later. After we did this bigger, much more important thing.

It felt good to be doing such a thing with Raymond, I realized. He had always been so honest, so solid, so reliable. Simple? Not exactly, no. And certainly not stupid. But...he was a straightforward man. What you saw was what you got.

Basically the opposite of everything I lived with among witchkind.

We drove past a field of cows, grazing among the occasional majestic live oak tree. I had to admit this was still pretty picturesque. By the time we left Marin County and entered Sonoma County, Elnor had given up watching out the window and had curled up for a nap.

"Making good time," Raymond ventured.

"Yeah." And then finally I just decided to ask it: "What happened between you and Jeremy when I was gone?"

Raymond darted an alarmed glance over to me, then whipped his eyes back to the road. "Nothin', really," he said. Before I could protest, he went on. "He just told me that, well, his 'intentions toward you have not changed,' and I oughta stay out of his way. Though he said it a lot softer and prettier than that. But I knew what he meant."

I leaned back against the saggy seat back and blew out a breath. "Seriously? I was afraid it was something like that."

He nodded, still staring straight ahead. "I wasn't gonna tell you—why do his work for him?—but you asked."

"I did ask, and thank you." I also gazed out the windshield, thinking. "I don't know what to do about him," I finally admitted.

"Do you love him?"

I looked over at Raymond, surprised. "I...well, to be perfectly honest, I don't really know. I don't know how many of the lies he's told me were his lies and how many came from his dad, and Jeremy just believed him because he didn't know any better. Or because he wanted to believe him."

"Hm."

"Hm?"

"Well." Raymond paused, thinking. "Jer's magical, and he's, what, a hundred years old or something?"

"Late sixties," I said, though that probably seemed much the same thing to late-twenties Raymond.

"Right. So. Shouldn't he be, you know, smarter or something about that kinda stuff? Do you really think he would fall for what his dad told him?"

"Gregorio is over eight hundred years old, and pretty crafty. And Jeremy...he really admires his dad. Or at least he did."

Raymond thought further. "So do you trust him? Jer, I mean?"

"I don't know if I can," I said. "Or if I *should*. I mean, I trust him enough to shelter him in my house, obviously." *With backup,* I added silently. "I want to give him a chance to at least not be my enemy, but...I can't just let him back into my life in the way we used to be. And I certainly don't want to sign a contract with him."

"Contract?"

I described witchkind contracts to Raymond, how because of these very lengthy lives of ours, we did not marry "forever" as humans did, but bound ourselves using agreements with stipulated end dates.

"So you don't divorce either?" he asked, after I'd laid it out as simply as I could.

"Oh, sure, contracts can be broken or dissolved," I said. "It isn't super common, because frankly, domestic contracts aren't all that common either. Most witches live in covens, and there are far more witches than warlocks anyway."

"Really? How come?"

Traffic was growing thicker; we were passing through Santa Rosa. "Because most witches decide to have daughters, not sons."

He turned and stared at me, then quickly whipped his attention back to the highway in time to not rear-end the sedan in front of us. "Seriously?"

"Seriously."

"You can do that?"

"So I hear," I said, wryly.

"That's not what you did?"

"Raymond, I explained this to you already—I didn't decide to get pregnant in the first place. I didn't think it was possible, with... with you."

"I guess I'm pretty potent," he said with a teasing grin, though I still detected a wary air in him. As if he were wondering if it was okay to joke with me like this. To talk about any of this.

I reached over the sleeping Elnor and patted his arm. "I guess you must be," I teased back. Then, more seriously, I added, "I honestly don't know what happened there, but of course, obviously, it *is* possible for us to conceive with humans. Rare, but possible. I didn't choose Rosemary's sex, though. That was something she did herself, I suppose."

"Huh."

We both fell silent for a while, as he navigated the traffic. Eventually, it eased up once more and we were back in suburbs, then countryside—this time filled with vineyards. Elnor had sat up again through Santa Rosa, and spent some time grooming, but was now sleeping again.

"She's pretty cute, though," Raymond said.

Enough time had gone by, I was a little confused. "Who?" Was he talking about Elnor?

"Rose. Rosemary."

"Ah. Yeah, she is." I paused, studying him. He seemed...at some kind of peace, or ease. "We should be proud of ourselves," I ventured.

Was that a small smile I detected? "I'm glad I..." He cleared his throat. "However it all turns out, I'm glad you let me know—well, everything."

"Me too." I resisted the urge to touch him again, even a pat on the arm. "Me too."

We left Highway 101 north of Cloverdale for narrow, winding 128. Until then, I'd been thinking it couldn't possibly take us all of three hours to get to Mendocino; now, I wondered if that estimate had been low. "Ugh, is it like this the rest of the way?" I asked, hanging onto the door handle as Raymond navigated another sharp turn.

"Mostly. We can stop in Boonville for a breather if you like."

"Nah, I'm okay," I semi-lied. "Well, maybe a bathroom break. Elnor might need one too."

Boonville was a cute funky town in a big, wide valley, which provided a respite from the curves. Short-lived, sadly; I was reluctant to leave the combination gift shop-restaurant-visitor's center, and I was really curious to know more about the town's very own invented language, but knew we had to get back on the road. Soon enough, we left the valley and were driving into dark, spooky woods, and the temperature dropped noticeably. Huge trees filled the sky all around us, rising higher than I could see out the truck's windows. Really interesting trees.

"Are these redwoods?" I finally asked.

Raymond glanced over at me. "Have you never been up here before?"

"I...uh, I don't think so," I admitted.

"You grew up in San Francisco and you've never been to the redwoods?"

"Um. No."

He shook his head. "Wow. Something I've done that you haven't."

"Raymond!" I said, astonished. "You've done a whole bunch of things that I haven't done."

He snorted. "Like what?"

"You're a rock star, or at least a rock-star-to-be. You've traveled all over the country! And beyond that, you know how to build a deck, and repair plumbing, and probably change a tire. Heck, you know how to drive this big truck."

"You can do freakin' *magic*," he countered.

"That's not an accomplishment. It's just who I am." Well, that wasn't entirely true, I allowed, but only in my own mind. The main point held. "You're an amazing, remarkable man, and don't you ever let any fussy, over-bred warlock make you think otherwise."

His eyes widened. "How did you..."

"It's pretty easy to see," I said, gently. "Jeremy with all his Old Country sophistication and breeding...that's actually what I like least about him, if you want to know the truth. The Jeremy I grew closer to was the genuine, honest, vulnerable man underneath the veneer." I added, more quietly, "If I ever do decide I can trust him again, that will be why. Not because he's somehow better than humans...than *you*."

"Oh." He shrugged. "Um, thank you, I guess."

"You're welcome, I guess." And then, a moment later, "And thank you for bringing me to the redwoods. They're amazing."

"If we had more time, we could stop and walk through them. You wouldn't believe how that feels. How it smells in there. It's awesome."

"I'd like that. Maybe..." But I trailed off. Maybe when? We were kind of booked up here, what with having to find Gregorio Andromedus's secret stronghold and rescue my mother and, oh yeah, defeat the evil warlock, probably all by ourselves, and send him off to the Beyond where he should have gone a century or two ago...

My breasts ached at the thought. What? Creepy! Or, no, wait, it was just getting to be time to pump-and-dump, which I hated the thought of doing, but I didn't want to dry up either—and I didn't want to have to magically spell my lactation any more than strictly necessary.

"Yeah," Raymond said, thankfully not privy to my thoughts. "Maybe some other time."

"Let's," I said, definitively.

The last part of the drive was just as narrow and curvy as the previous hour, but on gorgeously terrifying (or terrifyingly gorgeous) cliffs overlooking the Pacific Ocean far below. We passed through a couple of tiny towns, then more astonishing scenery, over a bridge or two, and then—

"It looks like a little New England village," I said wonderingly, seeing Mendocino across a stretch of river-into-ocean. "I mean, I've seen photographs," I quickly added, "but I didn't realize it looks just like this."

Elnor had sat up by now, attending to our journey with interest again.

"I still can't believe you've never been up here at all," Raymond said. "All your life you've lived in San Francisco."

I shrugged. "It does seem kind of crazy, now that I think about it. I guess it just...never came up."

Perhaps other witchkind communities got around more—certainly many of the witches I'd met in the Old Country last fall had seemed more worldly—but I was realizing more and more all the time that San Francisco witches were a pretty insular bunch.

Another thing it was high time to change.

"So, where do we go?" Raymond asked, as we crossed one last long bridge and approached the town.

"Hang on." I pulled the note Leonora had given me out of my purse and unfolded it. "Um, 777 Ukiah Street. She says it's the first exit into town—so pull off here."

Raymond did, and we drove down into the adorable little town, past cute shops, and a water tower, and lovely little well-tended gardens. Eventually, I thought to pull out my cell phone and open the map app. "Oh, we overshot; turn right here," I told him.

We found Ukiah Street two blocks up, and turned right again. Raymond squinted at the addresses on the business and houses. "Uh, are you sure about that number?" he asked, after we'd gone most of the rest of the way back to the highway. "It doesn't look like—"

"There it is," I said, pointing to a large Victorian-style house.

"Huh," Raymond said, but he pulled over.

Elnor stood up on the truck seat and stretched, arching her back. She gave a tremendous tuna-scented yawn and looked at me expectantly. "Yes, I imagine there will be new familiars to meet," I told her. "Shall we?"

"Do you…should I come in too?" Raymond asked. "Or is this a just-you kinda thing?"

"Hmm." I thought a moment. A little more guidance from Leonora might have been nice—what had she told this coven? "Maybe stay here for the moment," I said. "But I'll tell them what's going on and that we're working together. If they have a problem with it, well, we'll figure it out from there."

"Okay." He gave a small smile. "I *am* gonna get out and stretch my legs, at least. That was a long time sitting on my ass."

"Understood."

We all got out; Elnor disdained to be carried, jumping down from the truck cab herself, and followed me up the coven's front walk.

I felt the gentle brush of wards as soon as I stepped through the low front gate: inquisitive, not repellant. The deeper wards, assuming they had them, would be further in; this looked like a house that received mail and packages, and maybe even gave out candy on Halloween. It was integrated nicely into its block, though it was the grandest dwelling, painted a lovely shade of coral, trimmed in cream and lilac. The colors complimented the proliferation of roses, Shasta daisies, sweet peas, and other flowers that filled the yard.

At the front door, Elnor stepped before me and gave it a sniff, then raised her tail happily. So I knocked.

A witch of perhaps two or three hundred years—middle-aged, in other words—opened the door and smiled at me. "You must be Calendula Isadora." She had long, snow-white hair worn in two simple braids, twitching gently at the ends. The rest of her garb was equally simple: well-worn blue jeans, a clean but rugged plaid flannel shirt, and bare feet.

"I am," I said.

She nodded. "I am Magenta. Welcome to my coven."

I thought I'd felt *coven mother* energy coming off her. How gracious of her to answer the door herself. I tried to imagine Leonora doing the same.

"Thank you."

"Come in, please. And your familiar as well...?"

"Elnor," I said, and only then noticed Magenta's cat standing behind her.

"This is Primrose," Magenta said, indicating the calico.

Elnor marched straight up to Primrose, tail up, nose forward. Magenta's familiar, clearly a bit shy but definitely interested, sniffed warily at my cat but didn't hiss or flee.

Magenta laughed. "We can leave them to that. Come along to—" She paused, glancing behind me. "But who is your companion? You may bring him in as well. We have no rules against his kind here."

"He's human," I said, just in case she hadn't perceived that from this distance, in case "his kind" had just meant "male."

"I can see that," she said kindly. "If he would rather wait outside, we would understand. But he is welcome."

Gosh, they sure did things differently up here on the north coast. "All right, let me check."

Of course, since I couldn't call to him mentally, I had to walk back out to the truck to convey the message.

"Really?" Raymond asked.

"She says it's up to you," I told him. "Your call."

He shrugged. "I'll come in. I've never seen your witch head-quarters in the city. This might be my only chance to see one of these *boardinghouses*." He gave me a wink.

"Oh, hush, you," I said, but I silently thanked him yet again for being so mellow about all this.

A few moments later, we were seated in what was apparently the coven house's only major gathering room—it looked like the original small front and second parlors had been combined, the pocket doors removed, and the walls replastered. Mismatched but comfortable chairs and sofas were scattered about, making several seating areas.

"May I get you anything? Tea? Wine?" Magenta asked.

"I would take some tea, thank you," I said.

Raymond looked at me in surprise. "I thought we..."

"We are in a hurry," I said, "but I'm also thirsty and tired, and we need to talk. I might as well refresh myself while we do." *Not to mention I now really need to pump-and-dump,* I added to myself.

Magenta nodded at both of us. "And for you?" she asked Raymond.

"Uh..."

"Do you have any beer?" I asked her.

"We have anything and everything, as you know," she said to me with a smile, and a slight question in her eyes.

I had to stop myself from sending her a silent message: we were trying not to do that. "Raymond knows what we are and what we can do," I told Magenta. "He's only learned it recently, but he's coming to terms with the whole reality remarkably well." I smiled at both of them. "Bringing him a beer from a bar down the street was the first overt magic I showed him."

"Wait, overt?" he asked.

I patted his knee. "I'll tell you later."

"Uh. Right."

Magenta rose to her feet.

"May I use your restroom?" I asked her.

"Of course, it's just this way." She led me into a hallway. As soon as we were out of Raymond's earshot, I told her what I really needed. "Oh, then you'll want the meditation room," she said, and showed me to a small room at the back of the house, furnished with low, comfortable couches and large floor pillows.

"Thanks. I'll only be a few minutes."

She studied me a moment, then said, "You needn't destroy the milk. If you are willing, we would use it here, in our spells. And we would use it respectfully."

I hesitated only briefly. "That would be lovely, actually. I hate to throw it away, but I just wasn't sure..."

She smiled. "I understand. Well, take your time; I will keep your companion entertained until you return."

As I sat and expressed the milk, I thought again about what a different feel this coven had from any I knew in San Francisco. It was a little more like the group I'd met in Canada, on my way to the Old Country; but even they had a formality that this house didn't seem to have. And I hadn't even met any of the sisters here. Just the coven mother—and the house itself, its colors, furnishing, even the feel of its magic—told such a different story than the one I'd grown up in.

What would it have been like to be raised in a place like this?

When I returned to the parlor, a steaming cup of pennyroyal tea was sitting beside my chair. Raymond was holding a half-empty glass of amber-colored beer, and Magenta was sipping something fragrant and red in a thick, obviously handmade pottery cup.

"So," she said once I was settled, "Leonora tells me that the warlock who purchased the old Grandison place is up to no good."

"That's putting it mildly." I told her a little bit of what had been going on, what Gregorio had been doing. "We believe, at the very least, that he has my birth mother there, and perhaps others he is preying upon. Beyond that, he might be planning to increase his field of victims, spread it around a bit—he's cut a pretty deep swath through the San Francisco community."

Magenta frowned. "Does he not imagine that we will communicate with one another?"

"I think he's—well, not exactly rational these days. I'd love to think he's panicking and that we've backed him into a corner, though that's probably going too far. But he is running short on options." I sipped my tea. It was delicious: potent and nourishing, deeply satisfying. "So we are hoping that your house can help us—can get us to his house at least, perhaps cover our tracks a bit?"

"Of course. That and more." She took a measure of her own drink. "I would like to send one of my junior daughters with you, if you don't mind. Her magic is powerfully intuitive, and rather out of the ordinary."

"That sounds good—that's the kind of help I was hoping for." Before I could begin to wonder why this coven sister wasn't meeting with us now—indeed, why none of the house members were here save their coven mother—Magenta went on.

"She is at one of our businesses in town. I would have sent you there first, but I wanted to meet you myself and understand the situation better." She smiled down at Elnor and Primrose on the floor, now playing happily together. "And get my familiar's nod of approval, of course."

"Of course."

CHAPTER SIX

Ten minutes later, we were back in the truck following another set of handwritten directions; three minutes after that, we were parked in front of a long string of shops and businesses on Main Street, facing the bluffs that overlooked the Pacific Ocean far below.

We walked down the wooden sidewalk to the address I'd been given. "The Empress and The Moon," I read on the sign over the shop's door.

"Sounds witchy," Raymond noted.

I pushed open the door and stepped inside under a cheerfully ringing bell. Elnor trotted in after me.

"Can she—" Raymond started, looking worried. "It's okay for her in here?"

"In this shop? I expect so," I said, looking around.

We seemed to be the only customers, at least at the moment. (Had the witch kept everyone but us away?) The shop had the look of a typical hippie-flavored "spiritual seeker" store, with shelves of books about herbs and divination cards and dream journeys and self-empowerment and a jillion other things; the entire right-hand side of the shop was filled with various crystals, from giant lumps of rose quartz all the way down to exquisite (and probably very spendy) jewelry. In the middle was a small fountain burbling with water over colorful stones; soft sitar music played; and the smell of patchouli incense touched the air. At the very back of the shop, I saw the telltale sign of a tarot nook, complete with a lush purple privacy curtain.

"May I help you?" A young witch with exuberant red curls, cleverly held mostly motionless with an assortment of beaded strings but not otherwise confined, stepped toward us.

Her eyes held the same question Magenta's had, so I gave her essentially the same answer: "I am Callie and this is Raymond, and we've just been to your house to speak with your coven mother." Another quick glance around the store—adding my witch-sight this time—confirmed that we were alone here. "She sent us to talk to you—assuming you are Geneva?"

"I am, yes," she said, still looking puzzled about Raymond but clearly trusting her coven mother. "She mentioned you would be coming by; I didn't know you were here already."

"Our coven mother deemed it wisest to stay off the ley lines and the ætheric communication, at least for the time being," I told her. "Except to send false and distracting messages."

"Ah." She nodded. "Shall we sit down?"

I ignored Raymond's impatient squirm beside me. At least he didn't say anything this time; I knew he was eager to get moving. But we were making a pretty big ask here, of witches we'd never met before. We had to respect the process. "I would love to, yes."

She led us to the back of the store, behind the tarot nook. There was a second, much smaller room back here, before the stock room; it might have been an office in an ordinary store, but here it was a typical witch's cozy, with soft furniture, bowls and cups and plates on a small shelf above a sink, and of course a hot plate with a teakettle. A stack of well-thumbed paperback novels sat beside a loveseat covered in the same purple fabric as the tarot curtain.

"The Empress and The Moon," I said as we made ourselves comfortable. Elnor finished exploring every corner of the room and came to settle on my lap. "That refers to the tarot cards, I assume?"

Geneva smiled, though she looked a little apologetic, perhaps even defensive. "Yes, it does. I know that tarot isn't a traditional witch's tool, but I find it to be very revealing."

"My best friend read tarot cards, and my mom works with them too," I assured her. "My friend made her living that way, but she also really believed in it. She was always trying to read my cards. I did not always share her belief in the tool at the time, though I have come to a deeper understanding and appreciation over time."

"You speak of your friend in the past tense," Geneva observed.

I nodded. "She was one of the first witches whose soul was captured by the warlock we're trying to stop, up in Caspar," I told her. "She is not dead, but she is no longer among us on this plane either."

"Ah, I am sorry to hear that. Tell me more."

I gave her the same run-down I gave Magenta. I was getting good at summarizing a whole pile of confusing—and heartbreaking, and terrifying—information by now. "No one is quite certain how powerful he is right now, and how mad—and in what proportions," I finished. "I did temporarily reduce his access to the essence he was stealing from his captives, but he struck back, so we have to assume he's replenished himself."

"It is never good to underestimate one's enemies," Geneva said.

I looked at her in some surprise. How many enemies would a north coast witch who ran a crystal shop have?

She noted my expression and smiled. "You would be surprised at what goes on in small towns. But mostly—" She glanced down at the stack of paperbacks. "—I read a lot of mysteries and thrillers."

Raymond chuckled beside me; Geneva's smile grew even warmer. She was intentionally making him feel more comfortable, more welcome. Including him. I'd already liked her; now my feelings for her warmed further.

I scritched Elnor's ears. "So, can you take us to the Caspar property?"

Her smile faded. "Of course I can, and we shall go there; but I would like to do a little exploration first, to prepare, and find out what I can. If you don't mind?"

"Not at all," I said, "but—safely, yes?"

"Absolutely. I had a divination in mind. Nothing using the aetheric or ley lines."

"Good." I gave her an apologetic look. "I don't mean to tell you your business…"

"You aren't," she said, her voice kind, "and I wouldn't mind if you did. But I do need a private space for this. There's a nice ice cream parlor just a few doors down, if you're hungry."

Raymond perked up, but I said, "I think I'd rather stay off the streets, at least for the moment."

Geneva nodded. "Why don't you both go wait out in the shop, then? Make yourselves at home, look around, do whatever you like. I will probably be ten minutes, not much longer than that."

"Sounds good."

We left her in her cozy, the door shut. If she had a familiar on hand to help with her divination, I didn't see the cat. Elnor sniffed around in the main room just as she had done when we'd walked in, as if things would be different now than they'd been a few minutes ago.

Raymond picked up a crystal, examined it, and set it back on its shelf with a musical clink. "What if a customer comes in?" he asked, glancing at the front windows, the floods of tourists constantly walking by.

I opened my witch-sight again and looked at the windows too, and then the door. "They won't," I said. "She's got some mild wards set, basically just a 'go-away-nothing-to-see-here' message."

"That can't be good for business."

I chuckled. "I don't imagine they're always active. And in any event, the business probably isn't really for making money."

"What is it for, then?"

"Well, any number of things. A community meeting space—a safe place to bring together witches and humans, if that is needed. Obviously, storage." I thought about my own reasons for moving out of my crowded coven house. "Geneva clearly performs important work here; this is likely her 'office' away from home. And doing tarot regularly will keep her in practice, if she uses that magic for her witchly work."

Raymond still looked confused. He stepped over to the tarot nook and peered inside. "Someday I should get you to do my cards," he said.

"I don't really do tarot," I told him. "My mom's been trying to teach me, but it was really more Logan's thing than mine."

"What do these cards mean—hey, aren't they the ones the shop is named after?"

I walked up to the nook and saw that Geneva had laid those two cards out on her lace-covered table, next to the rest of her deck, stacked in a neat pile. "Well," I said, remembering back to my mom's lessons, "The Empress is obviously about women—female power and other feminine attributes."

The golden-haired Empress sat on a cushy chair—not unlike the furnishings in Geneva's cozy room, now that I looked at it—in a field of ripe wheat. An orange pillow was propped against a red bolster with a tassel; she leaned against this plush softness, holding a golden orb and wearing a crown of stars. She was draped in a lovely gown with a design of roses, and beneath her was the traditional "female" symbol.

"She does seem witch-ish," Raymond said. "I mean like Glinda the good witch."

"Yeah." I smiled. "There are other female-centric or female-focused cards, of course—all the Queens of the various suits—but the Empress is kind of at the top of all of them."

"The boss lady?"

I shook my head. "Not exactly. The thing about tarot is that these are all symbols, not literal characters. The Empress is the pinnacle of all that it means to be female. Fertility, giving birth, being a mother—"

Raymond gave me a pointed look.

"—but also creativity and, like I said, female power."

"Not to sound like a dumb construction worker, but what's the difference between girl power and boy power?"

"You're not dumb, and you're not even a construction worker anymore, Mr. *Rock Star*," I said.

He snorted.

"And if you thought about it for even a minute, you'd know the answer to your own question. Stereotypically, males just brute-force things. Right? If something doesn't go where it's supposed to, just hit it with a hammer? Just push harder? Just, oh, kidnap people and syphon their essence out of them for your own personal use?

"Whereas female power," I went on, "is—I don't want to say

gentler, but it's more, hmm, rounded. Less direct. Women persuade, where men push. Like I said, this is a total stereotype—I know plenty of women who push on things—"

"Your bossy blond sister, maybe?"

I chuckled again. "Niad? Actually, yes and no. Again, if you think about it, she's pointed and snotty and kind of abrasive, but she's also totally indirect. Right? She hints, she deflects, she sits across from you and crosses her legs *just so,* so you can look up her skirt."

Raymond swallowed uncomfortably and glanced away. "I. Uh."

"You didn't think I noticed," I said, "but I've been living with that witch all my adult life. There's nothing about her that surprises me now." Though even as I said it, I wondered if it were true. She was being unusually helpful and sympathetic to me these days—though, to be sure, in her own special, snarky way.

"So The Empress," Raymond said, obviously desperate to change the subject. "Woman power and mama power and all that. What about The Moon?"

I frowned as I looked at the second card. This was a much darker illustration: two scrawny dogs or wolves snarled at the frowning moon overhead, by the side of a pond or stream. Inexplicably, a lobster was posed emerging from the water, waving its claws to the moon as well. Forbidding towers stood in the near distance; dark mountains lay beyond them.

"This card is about fear and anxiety," I told him. "And sometimes about trusting your intuition—your dreams." My thoughts flashed to the white cats, to Nementhe in my dream, to the strange permeability between waking and dreaming I'd experienced several times lately. "It's usually more of a warning than The Empress is—a sign that things aren't what they seem, that you need to watch out, to be more careful and attentive. Or even to change direction altogether."

"Huh." He stared down at it too. "I'd have thought it would also mean female stuff—you know, water, the monthly, uh, cycle, and like that."

I glanced up at him.

"Christine tells me stuff," he said quickly.

"I'm not surprised you know any of this," I said. "I told you:

you're not stupid." *Even if I treated you like you knew nothing, and could never be trusted to know anything, the whole time we were dating,* I thought ruefully. "It's true: the moon governs the tides, and it does affect women's menstrual cycles, but, uh, mostly human women, rather than witches."

"Really?"

"Really." I glanced back at the closed door at the back of the shop. Surely Geneva was going to be done with her divination soon? Surely I didn't have to stand out here explaining witches' periods to my ex-boyfriend? Alas, no such luck. "We don't follow the twenty-eight-day cycle that human women do—well, that the *average* human woman does; there's plenty of variation among humans as well."

"What cycle do you follow?" I could almost see the gears in his head turning.

"A healthy witch of child-bearing age might have two or three periods a year," I told him.

He nodded, grinning. "I always wondered about that! When we, uh, you know, it just seemed you were never, uh, indisposed."

Not the time to tell him I wouldn't be indisposed even if I were in my cycle, I thought. If it would *ever* be that time. "But the moon, and hence The Moon card, is about a lot more than just female stuff," I said. "It lights our nights—except during the dark part of its cycle. It brings us strength and energy, and sometimes madness—like the word lunatic, you know?"

"Oh yeah. Right."

"The moon is captive in the gravitational hold of the earth, but did you know that it is ever so slowly moving away?"

He shook his head. "It is?"

"Yes, though we won't be around to see it escape."

"Not even you? With your long life?"

I laughed. "Nope. I'm talking, like, billions of years. The sun'll become a red dwarf long before that. And all of witchkind will have moved Beyond."

"Wow." He shook his head in wonderment. "I read a science fiction novel a few years ago about the moon exploding."

"Oh?"

"Yeah. All kinds of terrible things happened to the planet. Almost everyone died."

"That seems about right," I said.

We both stared down at the odd card for another moment, and then finally, the cozy-room door opened, and Geneva walked out. She held a fluffy white cat in her arms; for the briefest moment, I thought, *The white cats!*, but her familiar was much smaller than my mysterious visitors.

"I'm ready to go to Caspar now," Geneva said. "This is Chelan."

"Great," I said, much relieved, though now I was suddenly nervous about what we would find there. I'd successfully pushed my nerves aside for a while, but now… "My cat is Elnor, by the way."

Hearing her name, Elnor stepped forward. Geneva set Chelan down, and the familiars greeted each other warmly.

"We'll stop at the coven house for two more of my sisters," Geneva added. "We will want to approach the Caspar house from several directions at once, and quietly."

She locked up the shop and, I was interested to see, lifted the "nothing to see here" wards. Then she added a handwritten note to the door: "Short-staffed; closing early today. See you tomorrow at 10 a.m.!"

"Enough locals do remember there's a shop here," she explained, to my questioning look. "I don't like to put the deflection wards on unless I really need to be left alone."

"Makes sense."

Since we were only a few blocks away, we all walked back to the coven house, to not only pick up more witches, but also a car large enough to carry us all. All too soon, we were driving north on Highway 1 in the coven's large, rambling station wagon, vintage 1973 or so. Geneva was behind the wheel; I rode shotgun; Raymond sat in the back seat, between Rosalinda, a witch about Niad's age but pleasant and dark-haired, and Phoebe, closer to my age. Whatever color Phoebe's hair had once been, it was now a striking shade of lilac, and cut so close to her scalp as to render it quite incapable of twining around under its own accord and interfering with things. *Well, that's one approach*, I thought, wondering what it must be like to have such short hair.

My hair was often a hassle, but I couldn't imagine living without it. How much of our magic resided there?

Or was that just superstition?

"Mother Magenta should already be starting the distraction," Geneva said as she drove. "We'll be in Caspar in about five minutes; hopefully Dr. Andromedus has already noticed the chatter and will be paying attention to it."

The idea was, after a period of unusual ætheric quiet among both San Francisco and Mendocino County witchkind, furious communications would start up—between my coven and Magenta's, between Magenta's and other nearby covens, between Leonora and other San Francisco covens—whatever they could do to flood the channels with noise, while we snuck onto his property and had a look around. It wasn't much, but it was what we had.

Geneva pulled off the highway at a narrow, unmarked road and headed toward the ocean. We could no longer see the water, but its scent hung in the air. Cypress and other coastal trees surrounded us. Geneva drove slowly, looking for something; in her lap, her familiar watched intently through the front window.

Finally, at some sign or signal I couldn't see, she pulled over onto a wide shoulder and turned off the car. "All right, this is as far as we dare go," she said quietly.

We all got out, making as little noise as possible. Which was silly, on one level—if Gregorio Andromedus had ears out here, whispering wouldn't make any difference after the noise of a car engine—but emotionally, it felt right.

"I kinda wish I had a cat too," Raymond said softly, just by my ear, as Phoebe's Siamese and Rosalinda's calico (a virtual twin to Magenta's, probably a litter mate) led Elnor and Chelan in our vanguard.

I patted his arm. "Even if you did, no one would mistake you for a witch."

His chuckle was just a quiet exhale.

A narrow path led off the road, hardly wider than a deer trail, I thought—nothing like the normal approach to a house. We followed our cats, single file, through thick trees.

After a minute, the path widened, then opened into a small

clearing. As Geneva put her hand up to stop us, the cats spread out immediately, disappearing into tall grass; only the occasional movement of plant life over their heads provided any hint they were still there.

"All right," Geneva whispered. "It's just ahead."

I couldn't see anything, but I followed her forward. She kept near the tree line on the left. Raymond, behind me, reached forward and brushed his hand against my back; I reached back and took his hand, giving it a quick squeeze.

Two more steps and I did see the house. I stopped in my tracks.

"Uh. Wow," Raymond whispered.

"That's…really ugly," I whispered back.

Phoebe came up from behind Raymond. "It's kinda famous for that," she said softly. "Humans built it originally, if you can believe it." She cast a glance at Raymond. "No offense."

"None taken," he said. "That place is a horror show."

It was a huge, sprawling house, entirely out of scale for the landscape and any other houses we'd seen so far; but the size was only the beginning. It perched at the edge of a high bluff, so perhaps it had large windows on the ocean-facing side; but from what we could see, it resembled nothing so much as a maximum-security prison. With peculiar decorative flourishes, like marble columns and a tall tower.

And gargoyles. *Lots* of gargoyles.

Don't get me wrong: gargoyles are great. I'm a huge fan of gargoyles. It's just…they don't belong on modern architecture, or whatever this was supposed to be.

"I guess if you're looking for privacy…" I mused.

Geneva stepped back to us, drawing us all together with a gesture. "The main entrance is around the right-hand side, which is why I brought us this way. Of course he's going to be watching all doors and gates, at least passively, I imagine; so I think we should wait here at least a few minutes, let the cats do their thing, and see if it seems like anything got tripped. Then we'll separate."

We all nodded. Rosalinda screwed up her face in frustration. "I wish we could look inside."

"Yeah, well," Geneva said. "Any use of magic around here is bound to raise alarms."

I saw the telltale sign of cats moving through the tall grass, toward the house, away from the house, exploring the few outbuildings, circling around and periodically checking in with each other. I couldn't see which cat was which, but they were clearly all working together. I was glad Elnor was pulling her weight.

And even as I had that thought, I saw her black tail sticking up out of the grass as she bounded back toward me.

I bent down; she leapt into my arms. "What is it, kitty?" I asked her. She seemed—not frightened, but very excited. Pleased with herself?

"What's in her mouth?" Geneva gasped.

I drew back and looked. Something glinted between Elnor's teeth. "Kitty?" I asked and put out my hand.

But she pulled her head back, then dropped the item on the ground.

I reached down for it, only to have Elnor nip at my arm. "Ow!"

"It's a ring," Geneva said, which is when I understood why Elnor bit me. "A gold ring."

"Nobody touch it," I said. "Not with your hands, anyway; use something to pick it up, like a stick."

"I have these," Rosalinda said, pulling out a pair of substantial-looking black leather gloves and drawing them on.

I hesitated. "That might work," I finally allowed. "But drop it at once if you feel anything."

Because this wasn't just any ring. This was *the* ring, and the fact that it was here meant...

"Sebastian," I whispered, my heart sinking. "What has he done to you?"

— CHAPTER SEVEN —

Rosalinda carefully picked up the ring, brushed a bit of dirt off it, and held it up for us all to see. "What is this thing?" she asked in a hushed voice. "I can't feel it through the gloves," she quickly assured me, "but I see…I'm not sure what I see, actually. But it's not normal."

"It isn't," I told her, and the others. "This ring belongs to Gregorio. I don't know if he created it or just, well, adopted it or something, but it's not okay. He required me to wear it for months and months, though he kept most of its nature disguised from me. But it…controlled me, and I believe it communicated with him. I tried to take it off once, and nearly destroyed my golem in the process."

"Your *golem*?" Phoebe asked, incredulously.

I shrugged. "Long story. Anyway, it came off by itself when I had my daughter, and I gave it to my friend Sebastian for safekeeping."

Everyone looked at me, knowing what I was about to say.

"It is not good, finding it here," I finished.

"We were told the warlock Sebastian had gone into hiding," Geneva said.

I nodded. "He did, not telling even me where he was going, to protect me—and himself. We got a message that he was safe, and then, later, that he wasn't." I looked over at the terrible, forbidding house. "I guess we know where he is now."

"We will find him," Geneva said softly.

I sighed. "Yeah." I looked at the ring again, looking so innocent, so pure. Just a circle of gold. "I wonder if I will ever learn to stop underestimating Gregorio Andromedus?"

Elnor nudged at my leg, then looked up at the house after she got my attention.

"What is it, kitten?" I asked her, though of course she could not answer.

The other familiars had all returned to us by now. They looked up at us as if they were waiting for something. Waiting for us to follow?

"Can you lead me to Sebastian?" I asked Elnor. "Is it safe?"

Raymond looked puzzled, but the witches understood what I was doing. No, cats didn't understand our language…but a witch's cat could understand more than a regular cat. And even regular cats picked up more than most realized.

"Take us to where you found the ring," I told Elnor.

She stared up at me another moment, then turned and headed back through the grass. The other familiars were close on her heels.

"All right," Geneva said. "New plan: we're no longer separating. I want everyone to stay very close—in fact, I think we should all be in physical contact, holding hands. And anyone can call a halt, at any time, for any reason. Understood?"

There were murmurs of assent all around.

I went first, since it was my familiar leading the way. Raymond took my hand, and Geneva took his; then came Rosalinda and Phoebe at the end. We stepped silently through the field, or as silently as we could through the dry rustling grass and dense undergrowth.

Elnor headed straight for the house at first. My heart pounded, and my mouth went dry. *I'm not ready!* Then, to my great relief, she made a turn when we were still twenty or thirty yards away and led us toward a small outbuilding, nestled among a stand of trees—some kind of shed or garage, perhaps, though no driveway led to it.

Was Sebastian captive in there?

Elnor stopped before she'd reached the shed's door, looking up at me once more, then down at the ground. I stopped too and bent over, looking at the dirt in front of her paws. Was this where she'd found the ring? I didn't dare even whisper; if anyone was in the shed, we were close enough to be heard.

I saw a disturbance in the dirt…was it the letter S, scratched into the dust? Or was it a C, and the tail part was my overactive imagination? Or was it *all* my imagination, hoping desperately for a sign, hoping to find my friend, to find my mother—to rescue all witchkind from Gregorio Andromedus?

First Raymond and then Geneva crouched down beside me. "I think it's an S," Geneva nearly subvocalized. "And I feel some heightened spark in the dirt here—this must be where your cat found the ring."

Okay, good: independent verification of that much, at least. I nodded, then looked significantly at the shed, with a question in my eyes.

Geneva nodded, biting her lip, then pantomimed walking very slowly and quietly. So that's what we did…for three or four steps, until we were well within the trees that surrounded the building—and I felt a hand on my upper arm.

I nearly yelped in surprise, wheeling around, then drew in a deep relieved breath as I saw that it was Christine. Raymond's hand clutched mine, hard, and I heard him stifle a gasp too.

"Christine!" I whisper-hissed. "Are you all right?"

She flung herself into her brother's arms, sobbing into his shoulder. He clung to her, smoothing her tangled hair, as I tried to see if she was hurt anywhere. Geneva and her sisters closed ranks around us, both protecting us and trying to see what was happening.

"Oh thank god you're here," Christine said at last, drawing a deep breath and controlling her tears. Mostly. "You've got to help—quick, come in." She pulled away from Raymond and led him toward the shed door.

He didn't even glance at me, just went with his sister. So I followed, as did the other witches.

She pulled the door open. Inside, it was dark, with only one small window letting in a little filtered light. "In here," she said, and darted inside. We followed.

Christine shut the door firmly behind us, then turned around and leaned against it. It wasn't just her hair that was a mess; her face was also smeared with dirt, and she had a cut on her cheek. "I'm fine," she said to me, before I could ask. "It's—them, you've got to help them."

I turned to see who she was talking about...and gasped.

Flavius Winterheart lay on the dirt floor of the shed, crumpled and inert. Dead? I couldn't tell. But that's not what had stunned me.

Sebastian Fallon floated in midair at the far end of the shed, halfway up the wall. He sat cross-legged on nothing, and held us all in a piercing gaze. His face..."madness" was the only way to describe it. "Give it back," he said. As with his face, his voice was not his own.

"No!" Christine cried. "You can't, it's killing you!"

"What happened?" I demanded, forcing my terror down and stepping forward. "Sebastian, what is going on?"

The closer I got to him, the worse he looked. His very skin was a strange, pale shade; his eyes glittered with manic energy. He gave me a terrible grin. "Callie," he said, in a chilling voice, made all the worse by the faux-friendly inflection. "Please tell your human friend that I need the ring back."

"I won't," I said. Geneva, Phoebe and Rosalinda stepped up to stand beside me. "I told you to be careful with that thing," I added. Then I glanced down at the limp form of Flavius before me. "Did you kill him?"

"I *saved* him," Sebastian said. He faltered in the air, dropping an inch or two, though he didn't seem to notice it. "I gave him his magic back."

I couldn't help it; though it meant taking my eyes off Sebastian, I dropped to the floor and put a hand on Flavius's arm, sending my senses through his skin, seeking—anything. To my tremendous relief, he was alive; whether he had magic or not, I could not tell.

I looked back up at Sebastian, who had slipped another few inches when I'd looked away. "Now give me the ring back and I will wake him up," Sebastian growled.

"No," snapped Phoebe, before I could answer. "This evil artifact has obviously infected you. It should be destroyed."

"Noooooo!" howled Sebastian.

"Shut up!" Christine shrieked. I whirled around. Raymond was again holding her; he pulled her tighter to him, whispering in her ear. "Stop it," Christine said to Sebastian, more quietly. "You have to stop. You cannot use that ring anymore, ever, ever." She gave another sob. Raymond patted her shoulder.

"But why?" Sebastian said, suddenly preternaturally calm. "Did I not...solve everyone's problems, hmm?"

"We have to get him out of here—we have to get everyone out of here," I said to the Mendocino witches. "Whatever is going on, we shouldn't be talking about it right here."

"Why?" Sebastian asked. "I took care of Dr. Andromedus. I locked him in his fancy basement, and he'll never never never never get out!" Then he laughed, and if I never hear such a laugh again in all my days, it'll be too soon.

"Right," Geneva said. "On my mark, everyone."

I barely had time to blink before the north coast witches stepped away from me and surrounded Sebastian. He had fallen another foot or so by now; he was only a few inches above the floor. The witches, chanting together, whipped up a spell. Almost before I could realize what it was—a collaborative containment spell—they had it completed and wrapped around an astonished Sebastian. He hollered and thrashed about, seeking the edges of the spell, trying to pull it off himself, but they had him firmly.

Geneva turned back to me, looking flushed but strong. "Can you get your friend? The one on the floor?"

"Uh, yes. Yes, I can."

I bent down and lifted Flavius, using a measure of power to assist me. It was a long walk back to the car, Raymond was busy with his sister, and Flavius was quite obviously out cold.

The cats ran ahead of us as we left the shed and headed back through the field away from the warlock's house. Sebastian protested and screamed the whole way; Geneva laid a silencing spell on top of the containment spell, muffling him to near-silence, but I could still hear his faint cries. "I need to stay and keep him captive!" he said, over and over. "It's not safe!"

"It's not safe to leave you here," I told him, though I wasn't sure he could hear me—or would understand me if he could. "Whatever you think you've done to Gregorio, I can assure you he's three steps ahead of you."

And yet we are still trying to defeat him, I thought. Because what else could we do?

Geneva drove us back to the coven house. Magenta took one look at Sebastian and hit him with a powerful knockout spell—probably the Cozy Night, though I didn't smell any sage. "Put him in the guest room," she said, giving the words just the slightest emphasis.

I was pretty sure I didn't want to see that guest room.

Geneva helped me settle Flavius in a small study behind the living room, on a sofa, under an afghan. "Later, we can see what is keeping him under, and what we need to do about it," she told me. "For now, it's probably best if he sleeps."

"Right."

"Now," Magenta said, once we'd all returned to the front room, "tell me everything."

Christine sipped at a tall glass of iced tea that another coven sister had brought her—someone I hadn't met yet. In fact, more and more sisters were finding their way in, taking chairs and cushions on the floor, listening.

"I, uh," Christine said, and put the tea down. She aimed a shaky smile at her brother, and gave me a nod; she was still unnerved, but much better than she'd been before. She pulled her hair back and tied it into a rough knot, just around itself. Oddly, it stayed there.

"Flavius and I went to look for Sebastian, after he sent a sort of cryptic message," she started. Glancing around the room, she said, "You all know who both Flavius and Sebastian are, right?"

"We do," Magenta said. "Leonora Scanza brought us up to speed before Calendula arrived today."

"Okay. Good." She took another gulp of her tea. It seemed to help calm her; probably, it wasn't just tea. "We went where Flavius thought he might be, given the clue he'd sent...long story short, he wasn't there, but there was another clue at the location. We went on a sort of wild goose chase all over the South Bay—"

"South Bay?" I interrupted, surprised. How did they get to Mendocino long enough before us for whatever had happened to happen?

Christine glanced up at me. "Yeah. Flavius's apartment is in San Francisco, and Sebastian was staying in his building, hiding in the basement; but when that felt unsafe, he headed south." She looked back at the roomful of witches. "We were following that thread when suddenly Flavius shouted and I felt this dreadful pull. We were nowhere—I can't describe it. It was like suffocating or drowning, but that part only lasted a second. Before I had time to be afraid, we were standing in a huge, weird mansion overlooking the ocean. Up there." She pointed north, in the direction of Caspar. "Two men were in the room: Sebastian, and an elegant, well-dressed older man." She shivered. "Gregorio Andromedus, of course."

"Sebastian pulled you through the ley lines?" I asked.

"I guess? I don't know; he seemed surprised to see us. Gregorio seemed surprised too, though he covered it better. The next thing I knew, Sebastian shouted at us to 'cover his back' and then he just lunged at Gregorio. Then they were—well, tussling. Fighting—though not physically, not exactly."

"Fighting with magic," Magenta said softly.

Christine nodded. "I think so. It felt…fizzy in there." She huffed in frustration. "Another thing I can't describe. Flavius looked very frightened, which scared me more than anything else up till then. And I didn't know how we were supposed to help, what in the world Sebastian wanted us to do to 'cover' him. But he looked…triumphant? Definitely manic? He was more lucid than he seems now, but…well, I'd never met him before, but Callie had told us about him, and she'd never mentioned that he had a creepy violent side. So I figured he probably wasn't quite himself.

"Mostly, though, I tried to stay out of the way of the fighting. Sebastian and Gregorio were throwing invisible things at each other. One of them brushed against me," she reached up and touched the cut on her cheek, "and I've never felt such pain in my life. I might have passed out for a minute, honestly. But the next thing I knew, Sebastian was yelling stuff in another language, and then he lifted his hand and he was kind of aiming this gold ring at Gregorio. And that's when Gregorio gave a huge shout and just vanished!"

"Vanished?" Raymond asked.

Christine nodded. "Sebastian did it; it was clearly a spell of some kind, using the ring. He thought…he thinks he defeated Gregorio, but—and I know I'm no witch, I don't have magic—but I don't believe it. I just had this sense that Gregorio was acting. Performing. But Sebastian was so delighted. He was sure he'd locked him away, that he used the power of Gregorio's own ring against him." She turned and looked at me. "But, could he? Could that be true? Are we all safe now?"

"I don't think so," I said. "I would trust your gut. If you think he was faking it, he probably was."

"I am inclined to agree," Magenta said to nods all around the room. "What happened then?"

"Flavius tried to persuade Sebastian to leave the house with us—to go somewhere safe. Sebastian didn't want to; he wanted to look around for more magical items, more stuff of Gregorio's he could steal, repurpose. 'The less he has, the easier we'll be able to defeat him,' he kept saying. But Flavius argued, saying we just needed to get out of there. Finally, Sebastian agreed to leave with us—but then he changed his mind before we'd hardly gotten out the door. Or maybe he was just humoring us—I don't know.

"We were right in front of that little shed when Sebastian suddenly turned on Flavius and hit him, knocked him down. Then he crouched over him and put his hands on his temples and…I don't know what he did but Flavius passed out. He looked dead. I thought he was dead.

"I screamed, and—I don't know what came over me, I guess I panicked. I wasn't thinking, I just turned and smacked Sebastian in the face. I surprised him; he reared back and acted like he was going to hit me, but the ring flew out of his hand or off his hand—I don't know if he was wearing it then or not, but it flew away from him, out into the field.

"He *freaked out* then. I thought he was going to kill me, too—I still thought he'd killed Flavius. So I bolted. I ran away, into the field, in the same direction that the ring had gone. Not that I was looking for it—other than to keep it away from him. I knew it was a wrong thing, a bad thing; it was so obvious.

"He chased me. I ran into the woods and hid, but he found me easily. I don't know why I thought I could hide from a warlock. He dragged me back into the shed and then he got real calm. He wove that magic bubble around himself, and offered to put one around me too—I refused, though he said it would protect me. He told me he was trying to help us all, and that I just needed to trust him. I managed to convince him to bring Flavius inside as well; he was convinced that since Flavius had his magic back, he was going to be fine and didn't need any help."

She looked at me, anguish in her eyes. "I think Flavius is hurt pretty badly. He never woke up, or moved or anything, the whole time we were in there."

"How long was that?" I asked.

"I don't know—a while. Sebastian still wanted to go back into Gregorio's house and keep hunting for stuff, and I kept insisting that we leave. We were arguing. When he sensed you guys coming nearer, he got all happy again. He sent me out to find you, to talk to you. I think he thought you would, I don't know, agree with him. That you would be on his side. You know the rest."

"Yeah," I said. "And you're right: the Sebastian I saw today is absolutely not my friend Sebastian. That ring is full of powerful bad energy...I just hope he hasn't done something permanent to himself—or to Flavius—with it."

"Where is the ring now?" Magenta asked.

Phoebe lifted it up in her still-gloved hand. "I have it. We should put it somewhere safe."

Magenta frowned, thinking. "Take it to the attic and contain it in a dragon box for now. We'll find a more permanent solution later."

"Dragon box?" I asked. "What's that?"

Magenta gave me a wary smile. "It's something we've developed here...we've run into a few unusual issues over the years and have had to find our own solutions to them. I would rather not say more at this time. I'm sure you understand."

"Uh, yeah, of course." *Unusual issues?* I wondered. That didn't sound good.

Phoebe got up and, with her familiar at her heels, left the room; three other sisters followed a moment later, following a nod from Magenta.

Then the coven mother stood up. "All right, we must resume the information flood between here and Ukiah, and open a channel to Fort Bragg as well. Now the topics should include the finding of these three; Gregorio will certainly know they are with us, so there's no point in hiding it. Begin discussing arrangements to take them to Ukiah, I think, but specify that they should *not* go to the coven house. I don't want him descending on them there." She frowned, thinking. "The lake—that should be far enough, and open enough, to keep them safe."

"Yes, Mother," said an older witch. "We'll work on that." She leaned back in her chair and closed her eyes, as did several of her sisters.

Magenta turned to me. "I would prefer you stay safe, here, and let us protect you; though I feel as though you intend to return to the house and continue your search for your birth mother."

I echoed her gentle smile. "You would be correct in that. Every minute longer she's in his clutches…"

"Yes." She regarded me and my human companions. "What is your plan, then?"

"Well," I said, totally not making it up on the fly, "if Sebastian really *did* manage to slow him down in any way, we need to take advantage of that, as soon as possible. You're right that he knows we're here, that we've pulled Sebastian and Flavius and Christine away from his place, and that we're very likely coming back for him next. There's no longer any sense in being stealthy."

Magenta frowned. "Even so, I am not at all happy about the idea of your going there to confront him. Could I persuade you to at least delay an hour, so that we can see if our diversion tactics have any effect?"

I wanted to squirm in my shoes.

Before I could answer, Magenta added, "If you were willing to wait, I could spare Geneva and another sister or two to accompany you. Hyacinth in particular—" She nodded toward the older witch across the room, still sitting closed-eyed as she sent random decoy ætheric messages around Mendocino County "—is quite powerful, and even has experience with the struggles in the Old Country, though I caution you not to speak to her of it."

This coven and its secrets! I nodded and looked at the human siblings. "What do you guys think?"

"It's your call," Raymond said.

Christine added, "We're here to help you. But…I think we could use all the additional help we can get."

She wasn't wrong—and it was pretty clear what she meant by *additional*, despite her earlier opinions about how humans could be more effective against witchkind. "All right," I said to Magenta. "An hour."

The coven mother smiled more warmly now. "If we sense that he has taken the bait sooner, then we will send you on your way sooner. But I do think this is the wisest course."

She settled into a chair and began adding her own voice to the ætheric chorus. I listened in for a minute before turning to the siblings. "Want to wait in the garden, at least?" We would be nearby, and easily findable, but wouldn't be emanating anxious impatience all over these nice witches who were only trying to help.

First, we went into the small room where Flavius still slept. I saw no change in him, though Christine said she thought maybe his color was a little better. I put a hand on his chest, sending the gentlest of probes to see what I could detect inside him. All I got, though, was "alive," which was already apparent just from looking closely at him.

I wondered if one of the witches of Magenta's house was a healer, or if they had others in the community we could call. That made me miss Nora and Manka with a surprisingly strong pang. Their assurance, their comfortable presence, not to mention their knowledge…I wished I could bring them here, now.

"The coven mother said there was something they could do for him, though, right?" Christine said, not quite reading my mind. "But that he should sleep now?"

"Yeah," I said. "I just…poor Flavius. Hasn't he been through enough?"

"Sounds like it," Raymond said.

Then we went outside and walked through the front yard. It was lovely and well-tended; I again admired the riot of colorful flowers, wondering how many of them would grow in San Francisco. A small gate led around the side of the house to the backyard, planted with many familiar witchly herbs and some unusual ones, flowers I did not recognize. A wooden bench sat under a trellis draped with fragrantly blooming clematis. I took a seat there, and Christine sat beside me; Raymond sat on a large flat stone before the bench, which was obviously used as a footstool or low table. Elnor prowled around the perimeter of the yard, sniffing everywhere, inspecting everything.

"How are you doing, really?" I asked Christine.

She thought about it. "I guess I'm all right. I mean, how would I know?" She laughed softly. "Everything about all of this is just—just completely unreal. Sometimes it still hits me. Magic! I just got sucked through time-space and deposited in the living room of an ancient evil warlock! And hit by an invisible magical beam, or whatever." She shook her head. "And right now, in that house behind us, a bunch of women are sitting around sending messages to other cities just with their minds."

"Tell me about it," Raymond said. "I keep thinking I'm gonna wake up any minute now." He gave a faint smile. "But then I remember how you pulled a beer out of thin air, and I kinda don't wanna wake up."

I laughed. "Right. You guys are both handling it really well. Honestly. I'm not sure how many other humans would be so calm about this."

"Calm!" Christine also laughed, but without much humor. "You mean when I was having a nervous breakdown earlier?"

"You were not," I told her. "You were quite understandably freaked out, and yet you still pulled it together and told us everything that had happened."

"Everything I could remember. Some of it was kind of confusing."

We sat in silence for a minute after that. It really was very pretty here. Calm and peaceful. Elnor completed one circuit of the yard and began a second, slower one. I thought about what Christine had said. "You only saw Gregorio Andromedus and Sebastian in the house, right?"

She put her hand on my arm sympathetically. "Yeah. I didn't see your mom, or anyone else. I wouldn't have forgotten that. I'm sorry."

"That's okay. That's what I thought...I just had to be sure."

"It's a big house, though," Christine said. "I was only in one room, and only for a short while."

"Right," I agreed, wishing it made me feel better.

"We'll figure something out," Raymond said, bravely. "We'll get in and get her out of there."

It was touching, how confident he was. He had no idea.

"Can you describe the layout of the house at all?" I asked Christine, thinking ahead to our next move. "Sebastian mentioned a basement, where he says he locked Gregorio. From the outside, it looks like the house has at least two stories above-ground—or is it just one with really high ceilings?"

Christine shook her head. "I only saw that one room, and then I guess the entryway when we ran out of there. But that room did have super high ceilings, and giant plate-glass windows looking out over the ocean." She sighed. "In any other circumstance, it would have been—well, not lovely, because the house was so weird, but impressive, anyway. As it was, all I could do was freak out."

"Tell me about the main room and the entryway, at least," I said.

She did, though I didn't learn much more. The front door was on the side of the house nearest to where the outbuilding was. Christine could only guess where any other entrances might be—there would at least be a back door, I figured. But we were just going to have to go there and see for ourselves.

"If we take two witches, there will be five of us," I said, thinking aloud. "You guys can try doors or windows; we can go through walls if we need to, unless the place is warded."

"Wouldn't it be?" Christine asked, surprised.

"If it had been, Sebastian—or whoever—wouldn't have been able to bring you through on a ley line," I told her. "Of course, it's possible Gregorio has put up wards since then. We'll need to determine that when we get there."

We continued planning as best we could, but there were so many unknowns, it was hard to settle on any kind of definitive plan. But we had to do something to occupy our minds. I couldn't just sit around and wait.

At last, Geneva and the older witch came out and found us in the garden. "This is Hyacinth," she said, as I stood up to shake her hand—or, tried to stand up; sometime in the last ten minutes, Elnor had finished her inspections and come to fall asleep on my feet.

"Thank you for helping us," I said to them both, once I'd disentangled myself from my cat. "Did your diversion tactics work?"

"Mother Magenta believes that she felt a force of energy leaving the compound," Geneva said. "None of the rest of us felt that, but we have all looked and do not see the warlock there."

"Of course," Hyacinth said gruffly, "we could not see him— or anyone else—even when he *was* there, so that is not saying much."

Geneva gave her an unreadable look; Hyacinth frowned back at her. "The energy feels different now. You sense it too."

Hyacinth shrugged. "I sense nothing so definitive as to be certain. Which is why we are traveling there in person, yes?"

"That is the plan." Geneva smiled at me. Apologetically? Or just matter-of-factly? Was she so used to her sister's personality that it didn't faze her?

I knew how *that* went.

Geneva went on: "Mother Magenta also said that she received a message from the Ukiah coven that indicates Gregorio followed the false trail. It was in code, of course, but she believes her interpretation to be correct."

"That sounds good," I said.

Hyacinth shrugged. "Even if true, there will be nothing stopping him from returning as quickly as he flew there."

Well, thanks a lot for all the words of encouragement, Sunshine, I thought. Old Country witch indeed; she was as dour as an Old Country warlock. "Uh, right."

Hyacinth nodded briskly. "So. Why are we all still standing here with our thumbs in our ears?"

CHAPTER EIGHT

Geneva drove us back to Caspar in the coven's rattletrap old station wagon. The trip seemed to go faster this time. Maybe it was because we worked out the details of our plan along the way. Or maybe it was because Geneva went ahead and parked in Gregorio's driveway, rather than halfway up the road and us covering the rest of the way sneaking through the woods.

We all got out of the car. I looked around, with both regular sight and my witch senses. I certainly didn't detect any signs of life here—beyond deer and squirrels and birds in the woods, and some interesting marine life in the ocean far below. I looked back at my companions; Geneva seemed to be doing the same, while Hyacinth remained inscrutable. Our familiars, including Hyacinth's black tom, Melyx, prowled around a bit, but kept close by.

Raymond pulled a well-worn baseball cap out of his back jeans pocket, smoothed it out, and donned it. "Ready?" he asked.

"Just a sec," Christine said, pulling her hair into a bun and securing it with a scrunchie. "Okay."

The two witches and I nodded at each other, then at the humans. "Okay," I echoed Christine.

We spread out. Raymond approached the front door, where he would knock, just like he was a regular dude from the neighborhood, coming to ask about coordinating on some repairs in the fence between this estate and the next one over. We were of course counting on the door *not* being answered; nobody had any idea if Gregorio had ever met his neighbors, or if he would recognize Raymond in his brilliant ballcap disguise.

Christine headed around to the back door. By the time she got there, we would know if Gregorio had answered Raymond's knock. If he hadn't, she was to try knocking herself, then see if she could get the door open.

Geneva and Hyacinth and I were spread evenly around the house's lower windows. We planned to see how much of the inside we could spot through them. If all looked clear, and there were no wards preventing it, we would head in.

Simple.

Terrifying.

Elnor and I had just gotten to my window when I heard Raymond's knock. He rapped loudly and rang the doorbell for good measure. Then he waited twenty or thirty seconds before knocking again. "Hello?" he called out, in an innocent, friendly voice. "Anybody home?"

I stood, holding my breath. Nothing happened. Through my window, I could see the large living room Christine had described. Ugh, had Gregorio chosen this furniture? On purpose? It was ostentatious, too large and too white, sharp-edged and uncomfortable looking. It was Statement Furniture. People were actually supposed to sit on that stuff?

It had to have come with the house, I decided; Gregorio's taste had always been good. I'd admired the lovely things in his San Francisco home.

I stifled a sigh, thinking of the simpler, more innocent times when Dr. Gregorio Andromedus had been my father's good friend, and my mentor, and our avuncular community elder...not a madman preying on us all.

Or so we'd thought.

Shoving the memories away, I peered inside again, then sent my witch senses in once more, seeking any signs of life. But it not only seemed unoccupied; it gave the impression that it hadn't been occupied in some time. Months, years even.

Which of course was not true. So he had laid disguising spells over the whole place.

But not wards.

I glanced down at Elnor, who looked back at me. Waiting for my direction.

Christine's knock came next, followed by another one of Raymond's.

I so badly wanted to send a message to the other witches, asking them if they'd seen anything, but we'd agreed we still couldn't send true information ætherically. So, after sixty seconds with no detection of life and no response, I reached for my magic, let my body become one with the glass, and stepped through the window. I was in the house.

Even though we had detected no wards on the place, it felt beyond strange to just be able to enter like this. It felt like a trap...and, well, it obviously could be. I paused just inside the window, Elnor beside me, both of us listening, sensing, waiting.

Nothing.

As I stood there, I heard the other two witches doing the same: stepping inside, holding their breaths, exhaling softly. Hyacinth murmured something to Melyx. "Callie?" Geneva said, from the next room. Her voice was low, but not quite a whisper.

"I'm in," I said.

"Me, too," said Hyacinth. "Let's go get the humans and get busy."

I opened the front door for Raymond while Geneva let Christine in the back. "It feels strange in here," Christine said, when we'd reconvened in the main central room.

"Different from how it was when you were here before?" I asked.

"I don't know. I was...kind of head-spinny then. Maybe that's it. It feels, I don't know, almost more normal now."

"That might have something to do with the fact that you entered normally and not through ley lines," Hyacinth said. "Have you ever traveled that way before today?"

"Never."

"It feels strange to me as well, sister," Geneva said. "I think she's picking up on something."

I told them about my sense that the house was giving off a "long abandoned" feeling.

"It could be that spell," Hyacinth allowed.

"It could," Geneva said, frowning. After a few seconds she added, "I feel that too, now that I seek it."

Hyacinth looked at her. "Is that all you detect?"

"So far."

"Well, let's search, then," I said, looking around. Two hallways branched off the main room, probably heading for separate bedroom/bathroom suites as the kitchen and dining room were clearly behind us. I headed for the right-hand one.

Raymond was immediately by my side. "Not alone, you're not," he said.

I smiled at him, touched, and not pointing out that I wasn't alone: I had a black-and-white familiar at my heels. "Thanks."

"Sure." He shrugged. "I didn't drive you all the way up here just to let you do this part by yourself."

"He is correct," Hyacinth said. "We should search together. Geneva and Christine, come with me; we shall take this side."

Generous of her, I thought; or maybe she was just trying to keep the witch-human ratio in something closer to balance. Either way, I appreciated it.

Raymond and I stepped into the hallway. At the first door, he reached out to open it. "Hang on," I said softly, and hovered my hand just above the doorknob, then touched it. No booby traps, no spells or wards. I glanced at him and dropped my hand. "I just had to check."

"Got it." He opened the door, revealing a small bedroom with all the personality of a convention center hotel—a budget one. At least the bed looked like it might be comfortable. And there was no one there.

The next three rooms—a study, a bathroom, and a second small bedroom—were much the same: bland, empty.

The hall ended in a big set of double doors, where I guessed one of the suites would be. Again, I put my hand near and then on the knob; again, I felt nothing. I looked through the door with my witch-sight and saw a bland, empty room.

"Ready?" Raymond asked.

I nodded, and he opened the door.

Everything happened at once. Raymond sucked in a sharp breath; Elnor hissed; somewhere far behind us, Geneva screamed; I had no time to do anything, because Gregorio Andromedus, standing in the center of the room, reached up and slapped a spell on me that immobilized me completely. I fell to the floor like a cut tree, only escaping hitting my head because Raymond caught me.

Gregorio let Raymond ease me to the floor, then flicked his fingers at him, freezing him as well; he crumpled beside me. Gregorio lifted his hands and flung another spell in the direction of the others, across the house. I heard soft thuds as the three of them also fell.

I had no idea if he'd gotten Elnor as well; she wasn't in my line of sight.

Gregorio lowered his arms and stepped over, looking down at me. "Calendula Isadora," he said. "Always where you do not belong. Always prying into things you do not understand."

I couldn't move my mouth, couldn't access my voice. I supposed I was lucky he let me keep breathing. But now there was no reason to not communicate ætherically, I realized. *Help, he's caught us all, he's here!* I sent to Magenta. And then, a moment later, to Gregorio, *You wanted me to come after you. That's why you told me you had my mother— you knew I wouldn't stay home and wait for you to drain her essence. You wanted me to be here.*

"I did not imagine you would come to *this* place," Gregorio said. "I will not ask you how you learned of it; I imagine my faithless son told you what you needed to know." He glanced disdainfully at Raymond. "Despite the fact that you are apparently still keeping company with this human."

That didn't merit a response. *Where did you think I would go— Berkeley?* I asked. *Where all your captive bodies are? Was I supposed to believe that was your "special clinic?"*

"Clearly you did at least stop by there," he said. A flicker of anger passed over his face, there and gone in an instant. "It took me some effort to undo the mischief you unleashed upon my...experiments. But I did."

I was confused. I hadn't gone to Berkeley...I'd gone to the

in-between space, where I… Then I was very glad that every muscle in my body was frozen, because the relief that flooded through me would have shown all over my face. If he did not know that I'd been to the in-between space…what else did he not know? *Sorry to put you to all that trouble,* I sent, as snottily as I could manage. *I suppose you've got your pipelines all running smoothly again now, filling you up with essence that doesn't belong to you.*

"I have told you, and everyone else, any number of times, that I am doing this research to benefit *all* witchkind. It is so disappointing to be doubted, although I suppose I should expect such things by now. Nobody has ever understood my insights. Not even you, talented and intelligent as you are."

Uh, thanks, I sent. *For the compliments, I mean. Now can you let us all go, please?*

He chuckled. "So you can run off and imagine you have defeated me? As poor Dr. Fallon clearly thinks?" Gregorio *tsk*ed. "He showed promise as well; it is sad, really. So much wasted potential."

I stifled my fear for Sebastian as best I could. *He's going to be fine,* I told Gregorio, defiantly. *He is in good hands now and he will recover from whatever your poisonous filthy ring has done to him.*

"Ah, Calendula." He shook his head. "Ever the optimist."

What are you trying to do, even? I asked in desperation. *To "benefit all witchkind," I mean? Explain it to me.* If I could keep him talking… it could buy time for Magenta to respond. And maybe I would even learn something.

He seemed to puff up a bit. "As you would know if you had remained working with me, rather than maneuvering behind my back at every opportunity, I have made astonishing breakthroughs in understanding the nexus between body and essence, breakthroughs that would never have been possible with direct experiments upon living volunteers. My next efforts will involve replacing the essence into the vessels from whence they came. Provided, of course, that I am given the chance to conduct those experiments, rather than being forced to dance all over the state of California to avoid being harangued by former research assistants."

I wondered if he actually believed this—any of it. *I don't remember*

Logan volunteering for any experiment, I sent. *Or her parents. Or my parents, for that matter. Are they here? Or do you have them in some other secret villain lair?*

Magenta still hadn't answered me. Should I be worried? Or maybe that was wise of her: yes, Gregorio had us in his clutches, but if she did not tell me what her intentions were—or even confirm that she had gotten my message—he wouldn't be able to overhear her.

If he could do that.

"There are volunteers, and then there are *volunteers*," Gregorio said.

What does that even mean?

He stood a little taller. "Not every witch, not even every warlock, is capable of fully understanding their duties to our race. In older times, the common folk respected and trusted their elders; they did not question them. They did as they were told, and their betters looked after all witchkind in return."

Ick, could he *be* more odious? *Where are my parents?* I demanded.

He stood, staring down at me for another long moment. "I sometimes wonder why I waste my breath. Did I not just finish noting the inappropriateness of questioning one's elders? It appears that if I am to persuade you to listen at all, I shall have to do this, at least." With a heavy sigh, he stepped around Raymond and me on his way out of the room.

I lay, frozen, immobile; I couldn't even follow him with my eyes. Couldn't even look at Raymond, though I knew he was still beside me, where he'd fallen, as his arm rested against my side. And I could feel him breathing, thank the Blessed Mother.

I listened to Gregorio's footsteps, following his progress as he clearly headed toward the others; my witch-sight was blocked by the spell, so I couldn't look that way either.

And where was Elnor? Frozen at my feet, or prowling around somewhere, still mobile? She would be smart enough to keep out of sight, if she could.

Long minutes passed. I heard not a sound. If Gregorio was talking to Christine or the witches, the sound of his voice did not carry this far. If they were talking to him silently, it did not come through to me.

Then his footsteps returned, and he was standing over us once more. "Do please join us in the front parlor, if you would be so kind." He pointed his long index fingers at Raymond and me.

The power that flowed out of his hands raised us to our feet. I still had no control over a single muscle; my eyes, frozen in my head, passed over parts of the room as he moved me. I did not see my familiar, mobile or otherwise.

Gregorio puppet-mastered Raymond and me forward, out of the bedroom suite and back down the hall into the central living room, where he sat us on a square white sofa. I'd been right: it was as uncomfortable as it looked. And I couldn't even shift or fidget.

"That is an improvement," Gregorio said. "Wait here, and I will fetch the others." He smiled at his own un-funny joke: of course we were going to wait here, what else could we do?

Christine was puppet-marched in, followed by Geneva; Gregorio sat them next to each other on a matching awful couch. Then he raised his hands once more, bringing in not Hyacinth but—

I wanted to gasp. *Mom!* I sent her, before I could even wonder if that was a bad idea.

Hello, darling, she sent back. She was just as frozen as the rest of us.

Gregorio marched her to a chair of her own, directly across from me. He looked between us and smiled. "There," he said to me, with apparent satisfaction. "Alive and well. Happy now?"

I looked at my mother. Okay, she was alive, I'd give him that. Was she well? How well could anyone be when they were locked in a spell of freezing and had no control over one's body? *Are you all right?* I asked her.

I have been better, she sent me. *I have been worse.*

Is Dad here?

He is. He and Dr. Andromedus have quarreled, however, she sent. *They are taking some time apart, in hopes that they will cool down, and remember themselves.* A pause. *Themselves and everything they have gone through together, over their long lives.*

She was trying to tell me something. This was not how she usually talked. But with likely no privacy (even in our ætheric conversation) and no control over our bodies, not even to flick a glance in a particular direction, to widen our eyes, to shift our heads, I was going to have to just figure out what it was.

He's okay, though? I asked, trying to buy time. Trying to think. "… everything they've gone through together, over their long lives…" They grew up together in the Old Country—no, that wasn't quite true, was it. Gregorio was already several centuries old when my father was born, but when Dad began his biological research studies (called something else at the time, of course, humour studies or natural philosophy or some such) with Gregorio, they quickly became close. Their mentor-student relationship matured into a warm collegiality…though with Gregorio the master and my father the pupil, ever and always.

Had my father minded? I used to wonder, but Dad always seemed content with their relationship, with his position in it. He liked and admired Gregorio, as I was taught to do.

Now Gregorio was watching us, my mother and me; amused, perhaps, though his expression remained muted. He knew we were communicating. How much could he "hear?" I wished I knew.

Normal witches and warlocks could not spy on one another's ætheric talk. An eight-hundred-year-old warlock—at least this one—already possessed a great deal more power than a younger witch or warlock; one who was suffused with essence stolen from dozens of our kind…there was no telling what he could do.

I have been assured that he is, Mother answered, after a rather lengthy pause.

Assured by Gregorio, of course. *I am so very, very relieved,* I sent. *I've been worried about you both—you especially, Mom.*

Her response was quick this time. *Oh, as you can see, I am quite intact.*

Apparently growing bored with this latest game, Gregorio cleared his throat. "I asked you a question, Calendula. Are you happy now?"

I am thrilled beyond measure, I sent him. *I would be delighted to show you just how thrilled I am if you would let me out of this chokehold.*

He chuckled. "Yes, I am quite sure you would. But I prefer rather more calmness and decorum in my home. There is no need for all this unpleasant struggling." His smile grew, ever so slightly. "Particularly when you are all so thoroughly overmatched."

Following a sudden inspiration, I told Mom, *Sebastian attacked Gregorio—right here in this room, that's probably what he's complaining about. Sebastian's been using the ring that Gregorio thought was lost. It's given him so much power! It's incredible that we managed to hang onto it.*

There, Gregorio, chew on that.

Mother of course did not budge, so any eyebrow-raising I imagined was, well, only my imagination. *Well now, that is fascinating,* she said. *What a good student of the master Dr. Fallon has turned out to be.*

As good as Dad?

No one can replace your father.

So Dad *was* in danger, had perhaps already been harmed. Well of course; we were all in danger. I just needed to know where he was…oh and get all of us out of here…without being able to move a muscle, much less use my magic…

What have you done with Hyacinth? I asked Gregorio.

"My, what a busy little mind you have," he remarked. "Unable to focus on any one thing for more than a moment at a time. First your mother, then a sour, shriveled-up old hag you only met earlier today. Shall I tell you all the secrets of the universe, then?"

Did they have history, he and Hyacinth? The Old Country wasn't a small town like Caspar, but someone like Gregorio Andromedus would have made an outsized impact there. Without knowing more, there wasn't much I could do with my speculations. *Yes, please tell me all the secrets of the universe, Gregorio. After you let us all free.*

He sighed. "That was what is known as a rhetorical question, Calendula. I see that you are going to require rather more time to think things over, and I have numerous errands I must attend to elsewhere. But you and your little party of troublemakers will be secure here. It is a good thing I purchased such a large domicile, with plenty of space for—"

There was a shriek and a sudden trembling everywhere around us; I thought I might fall off the couch, unable as I was to move and catch myself. Gregorio froze, clearly quite startled.

But I only had a moment to notice that, because a black-and-white blur, still wailing and hissing, flew through the room and leapt at Gregorio, claws and teeth out—

And the air in the room tore in two and—

"Rosemary?" I gasped, almost not registering that I could suddenly speak and move again, because in the next moment Petrana was there, too—

And my golem reached out her massive hand, the one not holding the baby, and grabbed my hand—

And then the three of us were in my kitchen in San Francisco.

"The others!" I cried, but I needn't have; in a blur too fast to see, my infant daughter and my golem were there and back and there and back and there and back—

Until Christine and Raymond and Geneva, along with Elnor and the other two familiars, Chelan and Melyx, had all been tumbled through ley lines to join us. What a relief! We'd all been freed—

Except—

"Mom!" I yelled, looking desperately around the room. She was not here, not with the others. I turned to Petrana. "My mom—Gregorio had her, you need to get her, too!"

"I am sorry, she is no longer there," my golem said, handing me the baby. "We tried for her just after you, but the warlock had already removed her. He is gone as well."

"Blessed Mother!" I swore.

"Where is Hyacinth?" Geneva cried, sounding near panic.

Petrana turned her big head in the witch's direction. "I saw the warlock take Belladonna Isis. I retrieved everyone else I found."

"My father was there too!" I said. "Are you sure? Did you look everywhere?"

"Everywhere in the house and on the grounds," my golem said. "That was everyone." At our expressions, she added, "I am sorry."

CHAPTER NINE

Tears filled my eyes, but Rose was pulling at my blouse; I sank into a wooden chair and started unbuttoning on autopilot. My milk responded—or maybe I'd needed to express again and had just been a little distracted. Or frozen out of all bodily sensations. Or something.

Geneva blinked, looking around my kitchen. "Are we...we're in San Francisco!" she said. "What happened?" Her cat and Hyacinth's wended around her legs, meowing. "We have to save Hyacinth! She is strong, but she's no match for a warlock wielding *that* amount of power." She fell into a chair and took both familiars into her lap, soothing them.

Christine was absently rubbing the wound on her face; Raymond looked unsettled but at least not confused. My human friends were getting more accustomed all the time to what they had always understood to be impossible.

"Somehow my golem rescued us," I started, answering Geneva, who looked up in surprise at Petrana. *You really do have a golem,* I could almost hear her thinking.

Petrana spoke up. "It was not me," she said. "Rosemary led the action; I merely opened myself to her magic and lent a hand."

"*Rosemary?*" I looked down; she was already nursing greedily. "What did she do?"

My daughter looked up at me, big eyes gazing into my face while her mouth remained latched onto the nipple. It was freakin' adorable. A look of pure innocence exuded from her. I mean, of course she was innocent, she was a baby.

Except...how had she done what Petrana said she had just done?

Yummy, she sent me, and then *Luna moon ah. Moon-ah. Luna.*

"What do you mean?" I whispered, smoothing down her soft red hair. "What about the moon?"

"The moon?" asked Geneva. "Is she talking to you about the moon?"

Moon ah. Luna.

"Yes, I guess, but...I don't know why, or what she's trying to tell me," I said.

Petrana had busied herself making tea; now she poured cups for everyone, without even asking who wanted one. Smart golem.

Very smart golem.

I felt about ten steps behind—well, everything.

"I cannot tell where Dr. Andromedus has taken them," Petrana said from the kitchen counter. "If indeed he took this Hyacinth, Belladonna Isis, and Lucas all to the same place. I am sorry I was unable to gather everyone. Everything happened very fast."

"You did good," I said, though the stricken look on Geneva's face matched what I felt. *Mom...* And then I remembered who else had been left here at the house when Raymond and I had headed north. "Where are Niad and Jeremy?" I asked Petrana.

She set my cup on the table before me. Fragrant steam rose into the air, along with a heavy, inviting scent of honey. "Leonora called for them; they have gone to the coven house."

"*Both* of them?" Of course warlocks weren't barred from the coven house—we had plenty of them there for our annual Samhain party, among other occasions—but it was not the usual way of things.

Of course, these were not usual times.

"Yes. Actually, your coven mother first only called for Niadine, but Niad asked if Jeremy could come along as well. They had been talking together for some time, and she felt his input would be helpful. Leonora agreed."

"Fascinating..." My left-side milk began to run down; I eased Rosemary off the nipple and switched her to the right side, remembering only belatedly to keep this whole business covered when I saw Raymond blush and turn away. Oh for crying out loud, I thought. It wasn't as though...

And then I felt bad for feeling irked at him. What must it feel like, watching your ex-girlfriend nurse your daughter, knowing that you might never again be close to your former lover, that you might not get to share your life with your daughter?

"Would you like to let Leonora know you are returned, or shall I?" asked Petrana.

Blessed Mother, I was still seventeen steps behind myself. I reached out with my free hand and took a sip of my tea. Sweet, and restorative. "I'll call to her." Instead, however, I reached out to Niad: *I don't know exactly what happened or how, but we're back in San Francisco, with a north coast witch who was helping us. Sebastian and Flavius are still in Mendocino; something's badly wrong with Sebastian, and possibly with Flavius too, but they're safe for the moment, I think. Gregorio has my parents, both of them, plus another witch; he fled somewhere with them, but we don't know where. What's going on there?*

My goodness, came her reply a minute later. *Certainly not so much as all that; mostly talking, although this house is beginning to fill up with cats almost as much as your house has.*

Really? I felt a tentative excitement as the next step became clearer. *That's great—let's see if they all want to come to Berkeley with us.*

Excuse me? Niad asked. *We're going to Berkeley?*

I felt a harder-than-usual chomp on my nipple, and refocused my attention on the room I was in. The humans, witch, golem, cats, and baby present were politely waiting for me to have my silent conversation with Niad across town, and then report it all to them—which was stupidly inefficient. "Sorry, one more minute," I said to everyone, and then back to Niad: *We need to talk in person. And since the cats are there, it should probably be there. Can you tell Leonora I'm coming and bringing a few others? Oh—and can she invite Nora and Manka as well? They should be there.*

I shall, she said, and signed off.

Now I just had to get this whole gang across town and finesse them into our heavily protected coven house.

Following our previous logic, on the off chance that it would still do some good, we stayed off the ley lines. Christine's car was somewhere in the South Bay, and Raymond's truck was still in Mendocino, so I pulled out my cell phone and arranged for a ride share.

Leonora wasn't all that pleased to let humans into the coven house, though she graciously welcomed them once we arrived. And if either of them noticed that she welcomed Geneva and the two visiting familiars more warmly, they didn't remark on it.

She gave Petrana an even more minimally polite greeting.

Most of the coven, and the two healers, were gathered in our big front room. Jeremy was there too, standing a little off from the group, as if unsure of his own welcome. The large rug that usually sat under the sofas and easy chairs had been shunted away; the inlaid pentacle gleamed up from the floor. I felt an almost reflexive pang of alarm—was it Tuesday? Had I missed Circle? But of course not. Because the room was also filled with cats—just as Niad had said. They slept on the sofa backs; they played on the floor; they sat in the windowsills, looking out at the shaded garden. Nearly every lap contained at least one cat. I wondered how everyone's familiars were dealing with the invasion, but a glance told me the familiars were fine. Happy for the company, even.

Witch cats are generally quite social.

"We do not know why they have decided to gather here," Leonora told us, "nor even precisely how they have gotten in, though as everyone knows, cats have their ways."

"I think we need to take them to Berkeley," I said, rocking Rosemary in my lap gently. As ever, she enjoyed being in a crowd of admiring aunties. "Where their witches' bodies are. I think that's why they're here."

Leonora frowned at me, as a few of my sisters looked puzzled.

"You mentioned Berkeley a minute ago," Niad said. "But I'm

still waiting to hear how you're back in San Francisco, and then we can get to that."

Leonora nodded, so I launched into the story, catching everyone up on what had happened since we'd left for Mendocino. Including how Christine was with us, and how we'd been so abruptly returned to San Francisco.

"This is why I brought Petrana," I told Leonora, then turned to my golem. "You said that Rosemary 'led the action' to bring us home, not you. Please tell us all what you meant by that."

Petrana stepped forward from where she had been standing against the wall and faced the room. "It is as Mistress Callie says: I was left with the care of the infant Rosemary. I was feeding her an afternoon bottle when she made her intentions known to me, with some urgency."

"Intentions?" Niad snapped. "How did she—"

"The creature is explaining, Niadine," Leonora said mildly. "Please let it continue."

Petrana, unfazed of course, went on. "Rosemary can communicate mind-to-mind, in a minimal sort of way, appropriate for young witchlets, I am given to understand. She mostly communicates with her mother, naturally, but as I am a construction of her mother, animated with her power, and have been with the child since her conception, we have a communicative accord as well."

Around the room, many of my sisters, and even the healers, listened to Petrana with open-mouthed amazement. Clearly, they remembered the shambling, clumsy mud-thing I had first built, the golem who had had so much trouble understanding how to pack clothes into boxes for my move.

But Petrana had come a long way since those early days.

"I knew that she had not entirely finished her meal," Petrana went on, "but that something more urgent had come to her attention. She sent me just the emotion of alarm at first, and then sent me words, telling me to access the ley lines and bring 'Mama' and her companions back to the house, immediately. I told her that I did not have that much power or precision, but she indicated that she had all that, and more, and that I should tap into it. Before I could ask for clarification, she opened her own magical channels and I felt not just the power, but the understanding. So I looked through the line and found Mistress Callie, and brought everyone I found with her home."

Petrana closed her mouth and looked around the room, expressionless.

"But...how?" I asked, as confused as everyone else by this point. I knew Petrana was smart and capable, and I knew everyone else underestimated her, but...this was so far above and beyond both Petrana and Rosemary as to be downright baffling.

Leonora frowned. "Calendula, have you seen evidence of this sort of power in Rosemary Leonora before?"

"Well, no, but there's a lot that's odd about her..."

"This is beyond odd," Maela said quietly. "This is unprecedented. Many full-grown witches could not manage such a feat." She looked to the healers. "Nora, Manka, what do you think?"

Nora glanced at Manka, who said, "We too have noted many unusual qualities in the child and have been hoping that the passage of time would reveal more answers to us."

"But you have not seen this level of power in her, have you?" Leonora pressed them.

Again the healers shared a look. "No, we have not," Manka said.

"But we would welcome the opportunity to examine her further, once the current crisis has been resolved," Nora added.

Leonora nodded. "I concur." To me, she said, "Now tell us why you think we should take these cats to Berkeley."

"Gregorio clearly thought I'd gone to Berkeley and sabotaged something of his there," I said. "I'd done it in the in-between space instead. He doesn't realize I accessed that space and talked to the spirits of Logan and her parents there."

"And reduced his access to the supply of essence," Manka put in. "At least temporarily."

"Yes. I left Logan with the power to manipulate it herself," I said.

"Perhaps she can teach the trick to the others," Leonora said. "If the whole group of captive souls could defend themselves, that would be a devastating blow to Gregorio Andromedus."

I shook my head. "No, Gregorio cut Logan and her mother off

from the rest of them," I told her. "But at least maybe they can both work it on themselves."

"It is interesting that my father did not know you had been in the in-between space," Jeremy said, speaking up for the first time since I'd arrived. "I had always understood that sort of oversight to be unlike him."

"I was surprised too," I said, "but it was clear he thought I'd been in his creepy basement lab with the bodies, not in the place where the souls are."

He nodded. "I do not doubt you; I just thought it worth noting."

"What do you think it means?" Niad asked him.

Jeremy shrugged, looking around at the room. He seemed uncomfortable, like he wished he hadn't said anything. "As you all know, I only recently became better acquainted with my father. I grew up without him, living until last year in the Old Country. So I do not know how he has been, traditionally—how sharp, how observant. How sure of himself."

"Pretty darn sure," I said. "And awfully sharp."

"Right." He looked over at me. There was a question in his eyes, something more he wanted to say. I could see him choosing his words. "Yet when I was working with him recently, I was surprised to see him make other small mistakes, minor misjudgments. Nothing earth-shattering, but I did notice. He always laughed it off, brushed it away. Pretended that it was nothing."

"And?" Niad asked. "Everyone forgets things from time to time, drops a ball here and there." She was coaxing, I saw with interest; not challenging. Drawing him out, trying to make him feel encouraged and welcome. What *had* passed between them while we'd been gone?

"It is possible," Jeremy said slowly, "that he is not the magic wielder he once was. Not even the warlock he once was. It is also possible that the pace of his degeneration is increasing. Eight hundred—eight hundred and three, to be precise—is unusually old for our kind." He glanced at Leonora and hastily added, "Which I don't have to remind any of you about. But still." He looked back at Niad, who nodded encouragingly. "If he is losing his grip, it could explain why he has been clinging ever more forcefully to his former power, strength, and position—even to the point of violence, of crimes. I was not convinced, even as recently as a few days ago, that this was what was happening; now, I am. He must be stopped."

"And that's why I think we have to go to Berkeley," I put in.

"What's in Berkeley?" Gracie asked, from the parlor's big arched doorway.

The teenage witchlet stood hand-in-hand with Rachel, her human girlfriend. Minky, her familiar, prowled into the room, tail up, whiskers twitching. "Gracie!" I cried, rising and hefting Rose onto my hip as I hurried across the room. "Why are you here? I mean, it's great that you're here, but—"

She giggled as I folded her into my free arm for a side hug. She also didn't let go of Rachel, so it was sort of a four-way hug. Rachel and Rose were good sports about it.

"You all wanted me to come home so badly and now you don't want me here?" Gracie teased, then went on: "Actually, it was Minky's idea. Apparently there's a big thing that a bunch of cats are doing, and she wanted to be involved."

I stared at her, surprised. Behind me, Leonora said, "Come into the room, daughters, and sit down, and tell us all everything, in a sensical fashion, if you please."

More chairs had to be brought from the dining room, and the room's boundaries had to be stretched just a bit to accommodate us all, but in a few minutes, Gracie was explaining. "No, of course Minky doesn't talk to me; but I do understand what she wants and thinks about a lot more often than seems obvious at first. I mean, isn't that true for most everyone?" She looked at me. "Callie, doesn't Elnor make her thoughts known to you?"

"Well, yeah, but about food, pretty much," I said.

A few of the witches in the room smiled knowingly.

Gracie rolled her eyes. "You do spells and rituals with her. I know you do—you all do. It's what familiars are bred for."

"Gracie," my coven sister Sirianna put in, leaning forward in her chair, "while that is absolutely true, I think we're all getting the impression that you and your familiar might have a...more effective working relationship than what is common. Are you trying to tell us that you can truly communicate with Minky? That you can send thoughts and concepts back and forth, as we do with one another?"

"Not exactly," Gracie said slowly, thinking about it. "I mean, not like witch-to-witch. More like witch-to-human." She flashed a smile at Rachel. "No offense—didn't mean to compare you to a cat."

"Excuse me?" Leonora said sharply, even as Rachel gave Gracie a sweet and forgiving smile. "Witch-to-human *what*?"

"Communication," Gracie said, her smile falling away under the scrutiny of our coven mother. "You know...sending little thoughts." She shrank back into her chair. "Is that...not something normal we can do? Or should do?"

I could see Leonora gathering herself. The rest of the room had gone very still, very quiet. "It is not something known to be possible, no," Leonora said at last.

Where have I heard that *before,* I thought ruefully. *Witches don't build golems; witches don't get pregnant by accident and they* certainly *don't get pregnant by humans...oh and infants don't reach through ley space and move people hundreds of miles, just as warlocks don't trap souls in an in-between space so they can steal living essence...* It seemed a lot of impossible things were happening these days.

"Does the human send thoughts back to you?" Leonora asked. Her tone was so mild, yet even Rachel clearly understood the gravity of the question.

Fortunately, so did Gracie; she did not try to evade or downplay with her answer. "We've been trying but haven't succeeded yet. I think it's just a matter of time. We have managed to get her to do little spells and stuff."

"Little spells?" Leonora asked. "What kind of spells, precisely?"

Gracie gave a faltering smile. "Just, you know, little things, fun things. Nothing big or dangerous or scary. Making sparkles in the air with her hands; making the air cooler or warmer for a minute. Or little visual illusions." She shot me a not-quite-panicked look, then turned back to Leonora. "I thought I remembered learning that anyone can grab hold of the basic flecks of magic in the world, that you don't need to be witchkind to do that. It's just that we can do it more easily, by birth; and then we also have training on top of that."

"If you learned that," Leonora said ponderously, "it was not at this coven." Then she, too, glanced at me.

"Hey, this is all news to me," I said.

Both Christine and Raymond were following this discussion with rapt attention—because of course they were. Now Christine said, "But Callie, didn't you tell us that witches and humans were once the same species?"

"Millennia ago, yes," I said.

"So if we have common ancestry...and witchkind was self-selecting to reinforce already existing powers and abilities...it would stand to reason that humans might still have some of those abilities. And probably some more than others," she went on, looking around the room, her eyes shining. "Because some witches are stronger than others, right?"

"Absolutely," Niad said, almost managing not to preen about it.

"How do you see things magically?" Christine asked me.

"You mean our witch-sight?" I asked her. Then I glanced at Leonora—did she really want us taking up our time with this? She gave me a small nod. Okay, apparently she did. "How we can see through distances and solid objects?"

"Yeah. That."

I thought a moment. "It's kind of hard to describe, if you've never experienced it yourself. It's almost like...letting a different focus come forward?" Christine frowned, not quite getting it. "Okay," I tried, "a metaphor: you're looking at something very close, like a map in your hand. Then you refocus farther away, like you're now looking at the landscape itself, and remembering what was on the map. And you can put those things together if you want to—like if you're looking at what's inside a closed cabinet, but you also want to see the cabinet door—or you can just see them separately."

Now she nodded, slowly. "I guess that makes sense. Your eyes refocus."

"Yes," I said, "but not literally. It is obviously something physical within us, and maybe it's even resident in the eyes, at least partially, but it's not that literal refocusing."

"Do you think humans might have that thing in their eyes?"

Gracie said, "I can try practicing that with Rachel next!" The teens grinned at each other, before Gracie sobered and glanced at Leonora. "I mean, um, if that's okay?"

Leonora was sitting back now, content to let the conversation go where it would. She merely nodded again.

"I want to get back to what's most urgent right now," I said, far less content than my coven mother was. "We need to go to Berkeley, and see if that's where Gregorio took my parents and Hyacinth. That's where he's holding the bodies he's robbed of their souls. And I think we should take their familiars with us. That might be why they're here. But it would be so much easier—and better—if the familiars understood what we were doing and why." I could just see us trying to catch and transport dozens of cats against their will…that didn't work so well even with ordinary cats. "So if we can communicate with them…"

Gracie frowned, considering the question. "It's like a, what is it, catch-22 thing. Because I can communicate with Minky way better than with any other cat, because she's *my* familiar. Someone else's cat…not so much. I mean, I can try, but I don't know."

"Can you tell Minky to tell the other cats what we're up to?" Rachel asked her.

"Maybe?" Gracie looked down at Minky, who had settled on the floor by her feet, after an extended meet-and-greet with the other cats in the room, including Elnor. "Cats can be awful stubborn sometimes, even when you're pretty sure they *do* understand what you want."

No need to tell me that one. "We might as well try, at least," I said.

Gracie nodded. "Hey Minky!" she said, chirpily. "Did you enjoy making new friends?" Minky jumped up into her lap. "Do you wanna take the new friends on a little trip, to see their people? They must be missing their people, do you think?"

"We might all try this with our own familiars," Leonora said, calling Grieka to her.

The room quickly became far too noisy as the rest of my sisters followed Leonora's suggestion. Well, most of them; Niad and Fletcher eyed each other suspiciously, then she got up and went to the sideboard for a thimbleful of sherry while he went on grooming his pristine whiskers.

I got up, hefting Rosemary once more and wondering how a witch-familiar relationship could go so poorly.

"Want me to help with the kid?" Christine asked, leaping to her feet.

"Sure." I handed her over. "Come on, Elnor," I called.

Raymond and Christine came with us to the kitchen, where I sat on the window seat and tapped the bench next to me. Elnor jumped up, looking at me expectantly. Raymond pulled up a tall chair to the central island and sat; Christine walked around the room, jiggling Rosemary and humming softly to her.

It smelled good in here; how long since I'd had a meal at the coven house? It felt like it had been forever. Time had become quite unhinged in recent days, it seemed.

"This is a gorgeous room," Christine said, pausing and gazing out the windows at the view below. "In fact, this whole house is gorgeous. Hidden San Francisco."

"Yeah," I said. "I forget sometimes."

"That's what other eyes are for." She started walking again, heading off some hair-pulling by Rosemary.

"It's good to be reminded," I agreed.

Raymond said, "Why do you think Gregorio took your folks and the other witch to Berkeley?"

I sighed. "I don't, actually; it's a guess, but an educated one. Or maybe an intuitive one." I thought a moment. "It might be grasping at straws, but the fact that all the familiar-cats are gathering here—that they've been gathering at all—and that they seem to be getting ready for something...well, cats should be with their witches. I just feel like it has to mean something."

Christine frowned, still circling through the room with Rosemary. "If they're not there, then where might they be?"

"His house maybe?" I shrugged. "Or the clinic here in the city.

Or the Elders' headquarters?" I felt more and more discouraged by the moment. There was no end of places they could be...

Christine seemed to see my dismay. "I agree that Berkeley is the best place to start," she said with an encouraging smile. "Your thinking about the cats makes sense."

I nodded and turned back to Elnor, whose hopes had apparently been raised by the fact that we were in the kitchen, though she was confused that nobody was doing anything specifically food-related. "Sorry, kitten," I told her. "Our tuna supply is at our own house now."

Then, for some reason feeling even more foolish talking aloud to my cat about something important rather than teasing her about her greedy-guts appetite, I explained what I thought we needed to do—and what we needed her to do. Did I get through to her? No idea. But I went through it carefully, using both words and sending her thoughts and emotions.

By the time I'd finished, most of the rest of my sisters had done what they could too. Maybe it worked, because now the visiting familiars were more or less gathered near the center of the front room, and my sisters' cats ranged around them. It was all very friend-ly-seeming, but it still had the look of a flock of sheep, surrounded by a few sheepdogs.

Cats herding cats. Would wonders never cease?

"Calendula," Leonora said, "clearly we shall not all travel to Berkeley. I am not even convinced that you yourself should go—since you are caring for an infant."

I felt myself tighten with incipient alarm and opened my mouth to protest, but she went on.

"However, I do not believe you will settle for not going, so I will spare us all a tedious argument and at least insist that you do not bring Rosemary Leonora with you to such a dangerous place."

I again began to answer, but to my tremendous surprise, Rose—still in Christine's arms—let out a sharp yelp of protest.

The entire room turned to stare. Christine looked horrified. "I didn't—I have no idea—what is she—" Near tears, she thrust the baby at me.

I took my daughter and held her close, trying not to squeeze the very life out of her. "What is it, baby, what's the matter?" This was the child who still did not cry. She wasn't crying now, but that shout—it was beyond alarming.

"I think she's...okay now?" Raymond said uncertainly.

I loosened my grip just the tiniest bit. Indeed, Rosemary was now smiling again—and reaching for my own hair, still in its tight French braid down my back. *Luna go!* she sent me. *Rosa moon go go!*

"You...want to come along?" I asked her, then turned to Leonora. "I didn't take her to Mendocino, of course; perhaps she didn't like being left behind."

"She seemed perfectly content during your absence this morning," Petrana put in. "Until she wasn't, of course."

A few of my sisters startled at my golem's sudden return to the conversation. I was used to her statue-like qualities, though even I still found it unsettling at times. "I was gone for many hours—not just this morning, but most of the day," I said to Petrana. "And she was fine the whole time?"

"As I said, she appeared to be."

Well, maybe she was tired of being taken care of by Petrana for so long and didn't want it to happen again. Cats and babies, who could tell what they were thinking? I asked Leonora, "Well? What should we do?"

Her gaze sharpened as she looked directly at Rosemary for a long moment. Were they communicating? Or was she just thinking? At last, she said, "Take your daughter, and choose a few other companions as well. I suggest no more than five, including yourself." With a final look at Rosemary, she clarified: "Five adults."

I nodded.

Raymond, by my side, said, "Don't leave me here."

"Or me," Christine put in. "But if you need more magic users..."

"Fortunately, I am still five years shy of being an adult!" Gracie said cheerfully. "So I don't count—and neither does Rachel."

Oh Blessed Mother...

─── CHAPTER TEN ───

After much negotiation, we settled for our expedition to Berkeley on me (and Rosemary), Niad (for her strength), and Jeremy (for not only his strength, but his magical concordance with his father—and even, perhaps, some lingering trace of his father's affection for him). I tried to talk Gracie out of coming but was deflected by an epic level of sweet stubbornness, which Leonora watched with a barely concealed smile. "And we drove over in Rachel's car," Gracie pointed out, clinching the matter. "Then we only have to get one Uber."

I had never felt the coven's lack of a car so badly before.

Because we were a big crowd, as it turned out—a good many more than five. Raymond, Christine, and Rachel would come along to the campus, but *not*, I insisted, to the secret lab or any other magically altered space. They just wouldn't be able to defend themselves; it had been a mistake to take Raymond and Christine into Gregorio's house in Caspar, I now knew. We had been lucky to get away with that. I didn't want to tempt fate twice.

But they would be useful on the outside, in case we needed allies who could fly under the radar.

Petrana would come with us as well. She had proven herself indispensable when under magical attack (a few months ago, in the Old Country), and besides, she could hold the baby whenever I needed both hands. And, apparently, she could channel the baby's magic. Plus, she would never tire.

Traveling on the ley lines some thirty or forty minutes after we set out in the cars would be Manka and my coven sister Pearl. They would guide and direct the cats—if such a thing were possible. And they would be bringing their own different flavors of magic.

Because one thing we knew for certain: individually, none of us could confront Gregorio and hope to prevail. But together? We might stand a chance.

Leonora and several other San Francisco coven mothers would monitor the situation from the strongholds of their houses, where their power was deepest and most profound. Leonora had considered coming with us, but ultimately decided to remain here.

As we gathered in the front hall, Geneva, who had been listening to the proceedings with a quiet intensity, pulled me aside. "May I have a word?" she nearly whispered.

"Of course."

We stepped onto the front porch, and I eased the door closed behind us.

"Thank you," she said, her voice low. "I didn't want to step on any toes or usurp your coven's authority, but...I would like to come along as well. I have strength of my own to offer, and I think I could be helpful."

"Oh?" I asked. Not surprised, but inviting her to elaborate.

"I know we don't have experience working magic together," she said. "But...if we should find Hyacinth in this place we're going...I would like to be there."

"I understand," I said. "Hyacinth is your coven sister; it was insensitive of me not to consider that." Geneva was not an uninvolved party here. We all had someone to rescue.

And adding yet another magical user to the party couldn't hurt.

She smiled. "I'm not sure you do understand, entirely," she said. "Hyacinth is not just my coven sister. She is my particular friend."

"Ahh," I breathed, getting it the rest of the way. *Particular friend* was an old-fashioned construction, but I was familiar with it; Liza and Ruth, my own coven sisters, were particular friends, and I wasn't a hundred percent sure that Peony and Flora did not also have some sort of understanding. At least on occasion. "No, I did not understand that. Of course you can come—we do not even have to explain this to Leonora. I will just say that it is important to me that you be there."

"You may tell her," Geneva said. "It was the humans I was being discreet in front of."

"Which humans? You mean the one who arrived here with her girlfriend?" I asked, with a pointed smile. "And remember: this is San Francisco."

Geneva snorted softly. "All right, I see. I forget I am in the *enlightened* big city." Then she frowned. "I am just…worried."

I patted her arm. "Of course you are. It is alarming, what Gregorio is doing—has been doing."

"It is beyond alarming." We were silent a moment. "I will travel on the ley lines, with the cats," she added. "Chelan and Melyx should be able to help guide, assuming I got through to them. Melyx in particular will be seeking his mistress."

"Right." That would be useful.

It only remained to be seen whether the cats could be guided at all.

We were a silent group on the drive down across the city, then over the bay on the bridge. I had wanted to ride in the hired car, until wiser folk had pointed out that I'd have with me a golem, a cat, and a child who didn't need a baby seat. Tough to explain away—any of those things, much less all three. So we'd sent Raymond, Christine, and Jeremy with the unsuspecting human driver.

I sat in the back seat of Rachel's car, with Elnor next to me and Rosemary in my lap. "Keep the baby low enough so that no cops can see her," Gracie's girlfriend had requested, before we set out. "We don't wanna get pulled over."

I had promised.

Niad sat in the back with us, glancing at Elnor with something that might have been wistful envy, though she'd have hidden it if she'd known I was looking. Fletcher had gone with the cats, on the ley lines. At least he had deigned to join the party at all.

Petrana was stretched out in the trunk. I knew it wouldn't bother her, but it still felt wrong to shut her in there.

I stared out the window at the bay below us. Night was falling; it had been a long day. Hard to believe it had begun with a drive up the coast with Raymond...that felt like days ago now.

Hard to imagine how much we still had ahead of us.

We were again on the "no ætheric communication" protocol, leaving those who stayed behind in the coven house to send up more blankets of chatter to other covens near and far. Several of my sisters were in fact deep in discussions with Sapphire's cattery coven; the story they were telling was that the cats were becoming a problem for everyone, and the cattery needed to come up with some mechanism for controlling and containing them.

No witch would believe such a thing, but a warlock just might. It was the way Gregorio would think to solve the problem, after all.

Rachel signaled and pulled off onto University Avenue. Rosemary squirmed in my lap, trying to sit a little taller to see out the window; I kept easing her back down. It didn't help that Elnor, on the seat beside us, kept squirming as well, trying to claim her own space (and also see out). Niad pretended not to notice any of this.

It was fully dark by the time we approached the university. "Where's this lot again?" Rachel asked, breaking the silence.

"Around behind the campus—turn left here," I told her. "It should have lots of space this time of day." At least, I hoped so; I still wanted to use as little magic as possible, till we knew what we would find at the library building. I'd already texted Raymond, telling him where to direct their driver.

I needn't have bothered with my subterfuge; as soon as the Uber driver pulled away, I felt the gentle *push* in the air that signified a ley line opening, and the space around all of us was filled with dozens and dozens of cats, and the three witches they had come with.

"Good lord," Christine said in surprise, as they popped into view. "Aren't you afraid someone will see you?"

"We looked ahead," Manka informed her.

Geneva nodded. "We found only you here, so that seemed like a good omen. Besides, this was where the cats wanted to be."

"I didn't even know there was a ley line that led here," I said. I'd worked at this university for decades and had always taken the major line that led to a portal in a junk shop run by the Elders.

Pearl followed my gaze around as Niad stretched her legs and readjusted her already-perfect hair. "It looks like a nice campus," Pearl remarked. "I always meant to visit it someday."

"So, what's the plan?" Raymond asked, shifting nervously from foot to foot.

"You are still not coming inside the building," I told him. "That building way down there, specifically," I added, pointing at the massive Doe Library in the center of campus. The cats were already flooding toward it, not even looking both ways before they crossed the street.

"I know, I know..." Raymond said, though his expression, and the way he oh-so-carefully avoided even glancing in Jeremy's direction, conveyed just the opposite. "I just, uh, wondered how close you wanted us. Should we stay by the car for a quick getaway, or closer to the building so we can help if you need us?"

Rachel, and Gracie with her, were listening with interest. "Maybe a little bit of each?" Rachel asked. "Christine and I can stay by my car, and Raymond can get closer to the building? At least get partway onto campus?"

She was wise, this girl, I realized. But of course Gracie would make a good choice in a partner. She might be a dramatic and emotional witchlet, but she knew what was important in life.

"You got your cell phone, right?" Raymond asked me.

I smiled and patted my pocket. "You know I do."

"If we don't want the cats to get inside without us..." Niad said pointedly.

"Right." Even Elnor was just about straining at the leash to join the others—imaginary though the leash might be. I looked down at her. "Kitten, can you persuade your friends to hang on just another moment till we get organized?"

"Actually, I like their momentum," Manka said, and began striding after the clowder. Geneva gave me a quick glance and then followed her.

I sighed. "Okay then. Petrana, will you hold the baby, and stay close to me?"

"Yes, Mistress Callie. Of course."

Jeremy fell into step beside me as we crossed the street and entered the campus. "I do not detect my father's presence anywhere in the region," he said quietly. "Though we know he can mask it, of course."

"Like he did earlier today," I said. "I think we can assume nothing, and try to be ready for anything." Empty words, those felt like. Even though I'd anticipated a trap, I certainly had been caught off guard when he'd slapped the hold-spell on me in Caspar.

But could he really capture all of us, and the cats too, before we could mount our attack?

We had to gamble that he could not. What other choice did we have?

The campus was shadowy in the fading light, and largely deserted. I had always liked the university when it felt like it belonged to us — denizens of the night, however much we also moved comfortably about during the day. *Cal would be a great place without all these students and faculty,* we used to joke back in the happier, olden days. Back when I was an aspiring research biologist studying under the eminent Dr. Gregorio Andromedus.

"I am still feeling quite abashed at having so utterly misjudged my own father," Jeremy went on, keeping his voice down. Ahead of us, Manka, Gracie, and Geneva kept up with the cats; behind us were Niad and Pearl, talking in equally low tones. To my right, nearly invisible in the dark, Petrana walked, carrying Rosemary. Raymond trailed behind us all, having promised to go no farther than the edge of the Hearst Mining Building. "I just...I have no excuse for it," Jeremy went on.

"Don't be so hard on yourself." I kept my eyes ahead of me, feeling awkward. "I know him far better than you do, and he took me in just as completely." A few steps later, I added, "And my parents as well, it seems."

"I always wanted him to be proud of me." It shouldn't have been possible for an elegant sixty-eight-year-old warlock to sound like an unhappy child, but Jeremy did. "Everything I have done in life, even long before I moved to San Francisco to join him, I have done with the intention, the hope, of pleasing him." Then he glanced over at me. "Well, nearly everything."

I laughed softly. "Even you and me, though, if we're honest. Yes, we got together because we wanted to—but it was clear to both of us that *he* wanted it as well."

"I wonder if he still wants it," Jeremy said, almost too softly to hear.

"Does it matter?" I said, more sharply than I'd intended. "I'm quite finished with making any personal life choices based on what Gregorio Andromedus wants or doesn't want. In fact, if I learn he *does* want something, then I'm against it. No matter what."

"My apologies." Jeremy stared straight ahead. "That was insensitive and inappropriate of me. I only meant..." He shook his head. "I don't know what I meant."

"I'm sorry too," I said, much more softly. "I didn't mean to snap. This is hard for all of us."

"It is. It is indeed."

Is it going to be too hard for him to move against his father? I wondered, and not for the first time. When it came right down to it, would Jeremy falter, or stand with us? I could not know...not until it was too late to change course.

But I would be keeping an eye on him.

We turned the last corner of the winding campus road, and the library building came into full view. The cats practically ran up the big front steps, crowding around the double doors as if they couldn't find a dozen other, more subtle ways into the building.

Manka, Gracie, and Geneva had nearly kept pace with them; they caught up a moment later, and Jeremy and I, and Petrana with Rose, were with them a minute after that.

"It's closed!" Gracie exclaimed, looking at a notice on the door. "I thought it closed at nine!"

I peered at the sign. "Natural gas leak, huh? How convenient. We'll have the place to ourselves then."

Jeremy looked as suspicious as I felt. "Do you think that he somehow…"

"I'm sure of it," I said, even as I sent my magical senses into the building, checking for traces of activity, Gregorio's presence, anything. "Yet how unlike him to send a bunch of innocent humans away, out of harm's way." At this, I glanced behind us, seeing no sign of Raymond. Good.

Pearl and Niad joined us. "Yes, that seems oddly considerate of him," Niad said with a frown. "Though he does like to keep everyone off balance, hm?"

"Or he could just be trying to minimize distractions," Pearl said. "If he is starting to lose his hold on his power, a bunch of humans running around might be more than he wants to deal with."

"Well, we could stand here all night wondering about it, or we could go in," I said.

Gracie laughed. "I vote we go in!"

It was the work of a moment to spell the locks and gain entry. It took only a minute or two longer to cross the wide, empty lobby and find our way to the faux "broom closet" that led to the lower floors. The mob of cats continued letting us open all the doors for them, rushing through only after we did. I wondered about it. Were they conserving their powers? Did they know something we didn't about the risks involved?

Elnor kept close to me but also, I noticed, to Minky and Willson — Gracie's and Logan's familiars. She and Willson were old friends; she had no such history with Minky, who was barely out of kittenhood.

Minky, of course, was already proving to be an extraordinary cat, as her connection with her witch showed. And she had unlocked the cat portal in my house for Gracie and Rachel.

Fletcher and Pearl's familiar, Grayson, lost themselves in the larger group of cats.

With every door and passageway we opened, I kept not just a close eye on the familiars, but also on my daughter. I had still not figured out what happened earlier today. I did not distrust Petrana, of course—I didn't know if she was even capable of lying to me, even if she should somehow, against all logic, develop the desire to do so—but it was also so patently impossible for a three-month-old, even a very unusual one, to reach hundreds of miles away, break a powerful warlock's hold-spell, and bring a handful of witches, humans, and cats to herself.

And yet. Apparently, that was what had happened.

I wasn't *afraid* of my daughter. Of course not.

I just…wished I understood better what was actually going on here.

She seemed delighted with our progress into the basement of the library building. Though she kept utterly silent while we went, as if understanding our need for stealth.

"This is it," I said, at the last door. "It looks like the end of the line, but there's a whole room…"

"I sense it," Pearl whispered. Jeremy nodded. At our feet, all around us, cats nosed forward, nudging one another side, eager to enter the room.

I took a deep breath. "Okay, everyone. As we discussed." I wished the hall were wider, that we could spread out more—make Gregorio have to work at smiting us all—but it was what it was. I began to hone and focus my magic, then glanced around at my companions.

"Ready," Manka whispered, and then everyone else echoed in turn.

"Do it," I said to Jeremy.

He reached out and broke the spell locking the door. Then he put his hand on the doorknob, waited a half-moment, and opened it.

It swung open; we all stepped in, as we'd planned. I held a powerful charm ready to fling at Gregorio Andromedus and braced myself for whatever he'd fling back at us—a hold-spell, a counter-charm, whatever.

But we stepped into the stillness of an unoccupied room.

"Make sure," I whispered, as my companions and I all scanned the space, with both eyes and magic.

After a minute, Niad said, "He's not here."

"No," Jeremy agreed.

Of course the room was not, in fact, unoccupied. Instead, as we stepped farther in, I saw the same creepy, heartbreaking sight I'd seen last fall—only with even more inert bodies on cots now. They were crammed into every available bit of space, and still and silent as the dead. The same machines rimmed the room, pushed even farther back against the walls. Many of the machines hummed or emitted low lights, though a lot of these were even dustier than I'd remembered. The Enchin Aberra, however, the one with the bell jar, gleamed darkly from its place a few paces in. It looked perfectly clean.

"Oh Blessed Mother," Geneva moaned. "This is...this is a terrible thing."

"Indeed it is," Niad said soberly. Gracie looked like she wanted to cry; Manka seemed as though she might faint.

Jeremy just stood, staring wide-eyed. After a long moment, he shook his head and closed his eyes. "I didn't...he showed me a treatment ward, with recuperating patients...not this...this..."

Pearl just bit her lip and walked into the room, looking down at all the bodies, whispering a name when she saw a face she recognized. It seemed that she was purposely gazing upon every body, giving it the reverent attention that it deserved.

I stood watching all my companions for a moment before beginning to search. I looked at each cot, drawing ever more deeply into the enormous room.

But my parents were not here.

I went through a second time, more slowly, to be sure. No Mom. No Dad.

I stifled my grief and glanced around. The others were still moving through the room, taking it in, absorbing what they were seeing here. After a minute, I walked over to the Enchin Aberra and put a hand on it. "This one," I whispered to Petrana, who had kept close beside me, Rosemary still in her arms. "He's touched this one recently." I wondered how much time we'd missed him by.

Was this the machine he thought I'd messed with, that he came back and "fixed"? Was it the one that extracted the souls themselves? I wished I had learned more in the Old Country, but all my investigations had ceased when the Grand Laurel Mellenoc warlocks had sucked my memories out of my mind.

I turned around and faced the room once more. The cats had wasted no time finding their witches, jumping up on their cots, purring and rubbing against them. Of course, the bodies made no responses; their souls were elsewhere. But it was good to know the cats still felt a connection to the bodies.

My companions had spread even farther apart by now. I had told everyone what we would find here, of course, but no one else had seen it for themselves. It was a lot to come to grips with. Even Niad looked moved, as she stared down at an older witch I didn't know. Was that a tear in the corner of her eye?

I turned my head away, leaving Niad to her private moment, and examined more of the bodies myself, petting a few cats as I went.

Ultimately, I found my way to the back of the vast, gloomy room, where Logan's body lay. Willson of course was up on her cot, sitting on her feet. He was purring, though he was clearly not content or relaxed. Cats can purr when they're distressed. Elnor sat up there with him, grooming him on his shoulder and back.

"Good kitty," I whispered, petting her. "Nice kitty, so nice of you to take care of your friend." Then I sat on the corner of the cot myself, and brushed Logan's hair out of her face. Her skin wasn't warm, but it wasn't cold either; no spark of life met my fingers, but the clamminess of death wasn't present.

How did this place connect with the in-between place?

How long would it take us to find the answer?

Only now did I admit to myself that I'd been hoping the cats would be more help with this. Since they'd found the portal in my house to begin with, wouldn't they find it here as well? But they were only sitting with their mistresses.

Not that I could begrudge them that. Some of them had been separated for quite a long time now.

Niad looked up from her friend, or auntie, or whoever the older witch was. She straightened and looked around, then caught my eye and walked over to me. Jeremy, noticing, came up as well.

"I did not see your mother or father here," Niad said. "Nor Hyacinth."

"No," I said quietly.

Jeremy looked sympathetic.

"So, what's our plan?" Niad asked, after a moment.

On to the next place, I supposed. We had agreed with Leonora that we would try Gregorio's house after this room, though now I wondered if there might be more East Bay places to explore first. Perhaps that field where Jeremy and I had done the cautery on Flavius? But that was just a public park. "We should ask Leonora—" I started, but then caught myself as the oddest sensation ran through me. Niad and Jeremy stared back at me. "Did you feel that?" I asked them.

Niad nodded; Jeremy said, "It felt like…I thought my throat was closing down, but it didn't."

"It was a magical ripple of some kind," Niad said.

I looked at Petrana, still holding Rosemary; they both looked back at me. "Did you sense that?" I asked Petrana.

"I did not, and it doesn't seem that Mistress Rosemary did either."

I had to agree; Rose looked curious and alert, but content.

Geneva and Pearl hurried over to us; Gracie was right behind them. Manka joined us a moment later. "What was that?" Gracie asked, sounding very frightened.

"We don't know," I said, giving Jeremy a hard look. "Did that feel like your father's magic?"

Unfair of me, perhaps; as I'd only recently realized, I likely knew Gregorio's magical signature far better than his son did. And yet, I had never sensed anything quite like that, and I did not have a good feeling about this.

"I don't know," he said, looking worried. "I still don't detect his presence."

All around us, the cats remained with their witches' bodies, though those nearest to us were looking at us, as if trying to figure out what we were so anxious about. So…they hadn't felt the ripple either? Golems and cats and babies were immune?

"I think we should leave," Gracie said.

Geneva shook her head sadly. "Yes. Hyacinth is not here."

"Nor are my parents, nor Gregorio," I told her. "He *was* here, but I can't tell if it was before or after we saw him in Caspar."

"So can we *leave*?" Gracie asked, sounding younger with every word.

"Yes," I said.

"What about the cats?" Geneva asked.

I looked around. "They seem to be fine here," I said. "They weren't exactly part of our plan of attack. I think this is where they belong."

We were already heading for the door before I finished speaking. Our feet apparently didn't need convincing.

Jeremy reached the door first and rattled the handle. "It's locked!"

"Well, spell it unlocked!" Niad snapped.

"I did," he replied, equally testily. "Would you like to try?"

She nearly muscled him out of the way, but she had no better luck. "Blessed Mother!" she swore, and wheeled around to face us. "Now we know what that was: the monster has locked us in here with the dead."

They're not dead, I didn't say, realizing how unhelpful such pedantry would be at this moment. "Let me try," I said instead.

But the door didn't obey me any more than it did them.

"We're trapped!" Gracie sobbed, sinking to the floor and dropping her face into her hands.

Pearl sat beside her and put an arm around the witchlet's shoulders. "It's all right, dear, don't panic. We'll figure out what's going on and how to fix it."

I sure hoped she was right. "Well, I guess we don't have to keep wondering whether he knows we're here or not," I said.

Niad shot me a dark look but didn't say anything.

Geneva, looking pale and frightened in the gloom, said, "I assume there are no other exits from this room?"

"I don't think so," I said. "But we should look."

Nobody pointed out the obvious: as Gregorio had locked us in here magically, he would not have overlooked a back door.

Nonetheless, we rushed around the huge room, inspecting every corner, sending magical probes and battering rams at the walls, the ceiling, the floor—everywhere. In a minute, we were back by the front door again.

"We should have left a witch outside!" Gracie wailed now, sinking to the floor beside the door. "Why did we leave only humans out there—we can't even let them know what's happening, and that they should get help!"

"I tried contacting Leonora," Niad said. "But I got nothing—no response."

"And I tried to reach Nora," Manka said. "Our communications are blocked as well."

"Because of course they are," I muttered, then felt a sudden flash of hope. "Oh, duh! My cell phone!" How clever of us to have humans on our team! I dug my phone out of my pocket and called Raymond. It didn't ring. I pulled it away from my ear and looked at it. No service—because we were underground, of course.

Stupid worthless technology.

I settled to the floor beside Gracie, resisting the urge to hurl my phone at the wall. *Can we even still talk to each other?* I sent Niad.

Apparently, she answered.

Well, at least there was that. Small favors. *Very* small favors.

Elnor came up and nudged her way into my lap. I pulled her tight and squeezed her for a moment. She tolerated it, or even perhaps appreciated it. Manka sat down near us; Pearl leaned against the wall. Everyone tried the door, one by one. I guess we all had to see for ourselves.

But it was hopeless.

—— CHAPTER ELEVEN ——

We sat in the gloom, huddled by the locked door. Trapped. No one spoke for a time, until Pearl asked, "Who has tried contacting Gregorio? Perhaps he will respond to a direct appeal."

"I called to him," Jeremy said. "No response, no sense even that my communication went through."

"I suppose I should try," I said with a sigh. "It does seem to be me he's focused on; maybe he's waiting to hear from me." Though he didn't usually wait—his style was more to bust into my mind as soon as I'd fallen asleep, or to pounce on me when I was looking for my mom in his creepy vacation house. Even so, I sent an inquiry, and then another. They went out into the void without result.

"Nope," I said.

Above me, Petrana stood tirelessly, holding Rosemary, who also seemed just completely unfazed by the situation. Ah, to be so young and innocent. *What do you think, youngling?* I asked my daughter silently. *Are we in trouble here or what?*

Or what, she answered.

I huffed a small chuckle, though there was nothing funny about it. No, my daughter wasn't giving me a snarky-but-serious answer. She was just echoing my words, like she loved doing.

I gave Elnor one last squeeze, then set her down and heaved

myself to my feet again. "Well," I said to the group, "I guess I might as well investigate the machinery."

Niad looked up at me, bright-eyed. "Of course. They all must do something. Callie, why didn't you immediately start on that? You're the scientist."

"None of these machines have anything to do with the science I do," I told her, though I walked over to one anyway and brushed off its sign. "And I doubt any of them unlock the door. This is Gregorio's creepy secret evil research, remember?"

She shrugged, but at least she refrained from saying something inane like *Science is science*. Anyway, she wasn't entirely wrong; I knew at least the broad outlines of what Gregorio had done to these witches and warlocks, even if I didn't understand the mechanisms behind it. And I was the only one who had been to the in-between space and contacted some of the missing souls.

What I didn't know was whether any of these devices could help us with our current situation, of course. But doing something, anything, seemed far preferable to sitting by the door, despairing.

I looked over the first few machines, but they were so dusty and so bereft of any sign of recent use that I had to conclude that, if Gregorio had ever used them, he had long since abandoned them for newer models. Many of the newer-seeming machines were further back in the room, except for the nearby Enchin Aberra. "This is the one I felt a recent trace of his essence on," I told the group, approaching the bell jar machine. "You all should feel free to poke around as well. Let me know if there's something you want me to take a closer look at."

"All right," Geneva said, getting to her feet, followed by the rest of the group.

Jeremy gave a squat, brick-red machine a long look. "Should we refrain from touching them? I mean, could we trigger something unwanted?"

"Maybe?" I said. "Though honestly, and I'm almost afraid of saying this out loud because I know what the answer is—can we really make things a whole lot worse for ourselves?" Niad shot me one of her patented *How do I tolerate such idiocy* looks, but bit her lip. "I mean, yes, I suppose it's possible that we could hit the one button that would trigger a soul being sucked out of a body and all our essence harvested, but I kind of doubt that that's just one machine. If it's anything like the rest of Gregorio's work, it's a process involving a series of steps, with maybe a spell or incantation on top of it. Besides," I went on, "if it were just one machine that did it, then why are there so many here?"

"So if we turn something on, we should turn it off again before turning on the next one," Geneva said.

"That seems prudent."

"And if you don't have to touch a machine to get a sense of it," Manka put in, "then by all means, do not touch it."

We spread out once again, as everyone poked their way through the room, reading signs and sending magical probes, flipping switches and pushing buttons, trying to make any sense of what we were surrounded by.

I was still puzzling over the Enchin Aberra, which remained just as opaque to me as it ever had (other than filling me with a sense of nameless dread—bell jars are just plain creepy, if you ask me), when Niad sidled back over to me. "I wanted to see what you think about something," she said, quietly.

"Oh?"

"Over here."

I followed her to a small, unlabeled device sitting on a tabletop about halfway into the room. "I didn't want to get everyone's hopes up—or scare them—but I'm sensing something odd about this one," she said.

I walked around the table, looking at the device from all sides. It was roughly the size and shape of a Lendora assayer, which we used upstairs in the lab (or, well, we used to, when the lab upstairs was still a place where I did research, and not the cover for an evil warlock's secret evil schemes of evilness). The Lendora assayer separated the first level of inert coating from some of the muscle cells we worked with, allowing the more sensitive probes easier access to the relevant matter underneath. This machine, however, seemed strangely backward. Or, maybe sideways; I could see where the material would be added in the collection chamber at the top, but the series of apertures along the side made no sense to me. Anyway, being unlabeled, there was no hint as to its purpose or operation. Perhaps its similarity in appearance to the Lendora was a meaningless coincidence.

"What seems odd to you about it?" I asked Niad.

She pointed to the side openings, specifically the one closest to the back of the machine. "I was looking for an on/off button and brushed just the tip of my finger along there. It gave me the strongest sense—almost a compulsion—that I should stick my finger into that hole."

I looked at her. "Do not stick your finger into that hole."

Niad actually gave me a gentle smile. "Do not worry, dear sister of mine. I have no plans to do anything of the sort. But I do wonder if arming machines with such compulsions is a normal thing in science, or is it unusual?"

"I have never heard of anything like that being added to any kind of device or machine." I walked around the table again, studying the thing, this time adding a little magical query, particularly at the apertures. Yes, I could see a tiny glow within, deep inside the machine. But what did it do? Was it something that the researcher added their own magic to, as a catalyst or accelerant; or was it a trap, luring in innocent subjects, victims? Was this how he caught some of these witches and warlocks? "We can try some experiments, sticking inanimate objects in, sending a blade of magic in. Stuff like that. See if anything happens."

"Need help?"

"Sure—or at least, stand by in case I need rescuing."

I tried a magical probe, a piece of metal piping Niad found on a nearby shelf, half a dozen other things. Nothing happened, until I blew a sharp breath into the last hole, triggering the compulsion Niad had experienced.

"Ugh," I said, jerking back and grabbing my index finger protectively. "That's…compelling. And so clearly a bad idea. But I have no clue what this could be for—or if there's any way it can be useful to us." I stood frowning at the device. "I feel like we should move on, maybe come back to this if we don't have luck elsewhere."

She nodded. "We should warn the others to stay away from it."

"Good idea." But rather than raise my voice in this unsettling room, I sent an ætheric message to our companions.

Understood, Manka answered at once; the others chimed in as well.

Twenty or so uneventful minutes later, I was beginning to look at a large machine near the back left-hand wall when Jeremy came up to me. I realized he had been sticking close for a while, without being obtrusive about it. "Any luck?" he asked.

"Not so far." I pushed out a sigh. "What a jumble."

Now he glanced around. "Where's Rosemary?"

"Oh, Petrana has her, right he—" I said, turning, but they weren't there. "They were right beside me a moment ago." My heart pounded. "Petrana!"

"Here we are, Mistress Callie," Petrana said, stepping out from behind the next large machine over. "Rosemary wanted to look back here. I didn't mean to alarm you."

"Oh Blessed Mother." I put a hand on my chest and leaned against the wall. "Say something next time, okay?"

"Of course," Petrana said. "My apologies."

"Why did she want to look back there?"

"I do not know."

I stepped over to look at the machine, Jeremy beside me. Its label read:

Grand Laurel Mellenoc

Enchin Gnosphorus

Zchellenin

"Gnosphorus?" I asked, brushing cobwebs off the label. "What does that mean?"

Jeremy frowned. "The root has to do with knowledge, though the word itself doesn't actually mean anything in that precise form. Many of the other machines seem to have similar nearly-nonsense names."

One by one, the others wandered up to join us.

"Knowledge," Pearl said. "Knowledge of what?"

Jeremy shrugged, as puzzled as the rest of us.

"What did you want to see back there, daughter mine?" I asked Rosemary. "Do you want to show Mommy?"

Petrana handed her over, and I took her behind the machine. She smiled and looked around and pulled at my hair and blew bubbles, and gave me absolutely zero clue what might be of interest. Elnor sniffed at the floor, and the wall behind it; I looked the thing over from top to bottom; nothing.

Back in front of the machine, I handed the baby back to Petrana, then explored and poked and prodded at the thing, as did several others, but it yielded no secrets.

"Is anyone having any luck at all?" I asked, looking at my companions.

Shrugs, frowns, and shaken heads all around.

"I'm scared," Gracie said in a small voice. "And kinda tired."

"Maybe we could use a break," Manka said kindly.

By unspoken agreement, we went back to the door before sitting down to rest. Several of us tried it yet again. It did not open.

I leaned my head against the wall and closed my eyes, trying to remember how long it had been since I'd last slept. Yes, witches could go days and days without sleep. No, we could not go forever without it.

I felt someone sit down next to me. I opened my eyes and turned my head to see; it was Jeremy.

"If you want a nap, I'll keep watch, and wake you if anything changes," he said.

"Do I look that tired?"

He smiled. "You look as tired as we all feel. Gracie is already out." He nodded toward the other side of the door, where the witchlet was curled up, her head in Pearl's lap, Minky cradled in her arms. Grayson snuggled against Pearl, also sacked out. Even Fletcher was sitting near Niad; they both looked utterly spent.

"We can all sleep," I pointed out. "Petrana can watch for us."

"Ah. Right."

I caught a whiff of Jeremy's clean scent, and a compulsion nearly as strong as the one produced by the mystery device flooded my weary senses. How comfortable, how sweet it would be to lie down just as

Gracie was, snuggle up to Jeremy, rest my head in his lap...to feel his gentle hands in my hair, smoothing it, soothing me.... I drew in a quiet breath, settling my heart, stilling my face. Trying desperately not to let any of those impossible emotions show.

I did not know what our future might be—if anything. I did not know if we would ever escape this terrible room, before his father came back to finish us off. But I did know that cuddling up to him now would be a very bad idea.

"Rest well," I said.

He gave me one last glance, then leaned back against the wall and closed his eyes.

The sound of babbling awakened me.

"I am sorry, Mistress Callie, Master Jeremy; I did try to keep her quiet."

I blinked and looked around, completely confused—it took me a moment to remember even where we were, and why. Petrana walked toward us, Rosemary in her arms; the golem had been near the back of the cavernous room.

"What's going on?" I asked.

Petrana came closer. Rosemary chirped and giggled and made nonsense words; slowly, the rest of our party woke up too.

"She slept a few hours, but then she woke up and started making conversation," Petrana said, drawing closer. "So I carried her as far away from you all as possible, so you would not be awakened. But you were awakened after all."

"That's all right," I said, rubbing my eyes, and trying to work the crick out of my neck. "What time is it?" I'd been so deeply under, I'd come unmoored from my sense of time.

"Nearly midnight," Jeremy said.

"Yikes," I said, but then I felt it too. "She's probably hungry, that's why she's so restless." I got to my feet and stretched, then reached out for my baby. "Are you hungry, sweet pea? Did you think we would never wake up?"

My butt was sore from sleeping seated on a hard floor, and my body ached from leaning against a hard wall. I walked around, letting the blood come back into my limbs as I gently bounced the baby, looking for somewhere more comfortable to nurse her. Ha. No such luck, of course. Unless I wanted to relocate one of the bodies on their cots, which—no thank you very much.

With a sigh, I returned to my position on the floor and unbuttoned my blouse.

Rosemary suckled a bit, but quickly grew bored and restless. *Time,* she sent me, letting go of the nipple and letting milk dribble down my boob.

"Time?" I asked her. "It's the middle of the night."

Time, she said again, and gave me her toothless smile. *Time. Place. Luna.*

"Oh my darling," I whispered, rocking her. "I cannot wait until you can communicate more clearly. I wish I could understand you better." But then of course she would be a bigger girl, and I would lose this adorable infant, who I could contain so easily in my arms…

Why did nobody ever tell me that having a child would be so bittersweet?

"If I may, Mistress Callie," Petrana said, unusually diffidently (at least for these days).

I hauled myself to my feet once more and buttoned up, wishing I had a towel or even a rag. "What is it?"

Niad and Jeremy, who had been talking with Geneva by the door, turned at my tone.

"I believe I understand more of what Mistress Rosemary is thinking," my golem said to me. "She is interested and engaged here; distressed, of course, at our frustration about being locked in, worried about her maternal grandparents, and unhappy about the plight of these witches and sad for their bereft familiars; but my strong sense is that she is hopeful that we are well on our way to finding solutions for all these challenges. And she's particularly excited right now."

I stared back at her, unsure what to make of any of that.

"How do you know this?" Niad asked her, as she and Jeremy stepped over, followed by the others.

"Just what is going on with my daughter all of a sudden?" I asked, even as I knew there was nothing sudden about this…she had been not precisely of this world since before she was born. But she was becoming undeniably weirder and weirder lately.

"I think she has found the way to the souls of these witches and warlocks, and even perhaps a way out," Petrana said. "And I think she is telling me that the way is back here."

"Back…in the back of the room?"

"I believe so. She does not give me any more words than she gives you, Mistress Callie, but the emotions she sends are particularly strong. That is the other reason I walked with her back there. She was quite eager that I do so."

After exchanging puzzled yet hopeful glances, we all followed my golem to the other side of the room.

"Where?" I asked, staring at the blank spot of wall that my daughter, still in my arms, pointed at. "We've already been through this entire room, every inch of it."

Minky ran in front of Gracie, stepped into the blank space, and promptly vanished.

"Noooo!" Gracie howled. "Minky!"

I handed Rosemary to the first pair of arms that presented themselves—Jeremy's, as it happened—and bent down, running my hands all along the wall where the kitten had disappeared. "Minky!" I called, much more softly than Gracie. Pearl was trying to soothe the witchlet, and having a smidgen of success.

"Where did she go?" Niad asked, crouching down beside me. She too touched the wall thoroughly; I could feel her sending her strong magic into it, probing, searching for any unseen portal or soft place.

I was reminded, forcefully, of my experience with the cat portal in my closet. "Elnor," I called. "Come help us here, kitty?"

My familiar dutifully sniffed at the wall, as did Grayson, but it did not open for them. Or for any of the rest of us.

Gracie was now sniffling quietly in Pearl's arms. "Where did she go?" she asked. "How do we get her back?"

Niad leaned back on her heels and looked up at my golem. "What does Rosemary say about this?"

Petrana shook her head. "As I said, she doesn't really *say* anything about anything," she said. Before Niad could protest, she went on: "And she isn't really giving me any kind of hint about this, either."

"But you just finished telling us that you understand a lot more of what she's thinking," I said. "And she led you back here, and gave you all those hints. She knows *something*; I even believe she's trying to tell us something. So what is it?"

"I have told you everything I have gleaned from her," Petrana said. "Again, it is not words; just ideas, senses. Emotions. There is something here. Clearly, this is true; the cat went somewhere. And Mistress Rosemary is not distressed. Quite the opposite: she still seems happy and excited."

I looked up at Jeremy, holding the baby. Rosemary, wearing a bright smile, stared wide-eyed around the room, as interested as ever in her surroundings—and giving us no hint as to what we should be doing about any of it.

I stood up and went to them. Rosemary blew a milky spit-bubble at me.

"Come on, sweetie, what do we do now?" I crooned to her.

Now, she sent me. *Place.*

"Place? This place? That place?" I pointed at the blank spot on the wall. "The place where Minky went?"

Gracie, on the floor beside the wall, had stopped crying. She still looked very distressed, but she had pulled herself together. "Minky," she whispered. "Come back to your mistress now, you're scaring me."

I put a gentle hand on her shoulder. "She'll be back," I promised, even though I had resolved never to lie to her.

A moment later, I felt the quiet turn of midnight, and the shifting of the entire world's energy around us. Minky popped back out of the wall and into Gracie's arms.

I took a deep, grateful breath, even as I tried to figure out what this new feeling around me was. It felt familiar, but I could not quite place it.

"Where were you?" Gracie said to her cat, holding her tightly. Minky did not protest. "Where *were* you?" Gracie pressed.

"I hope she was in the in-between space," I said. "But if that's the way for us to go, I don't know how to…"

I trailed off as the wall's solidity faded, and a denizen of the Beyond stepped out.

── CHAPTER TWELVE ──

P errine!" Niad said, as Pearl gasped. I just sat there, stunned.
A petite, dark-haired witch with sharp features, old-fashioned clothing, and a centuries-out-of-date hairstyle stood before us—well, mostly; she was still insubstantial, not precisely on this physical realm. So that was the feeling I'd sensed: Beyond energy, and us not in our trances, or on our pentacle.

Nothing was as it used to be.

Perrine smiled. "Greetings, daughters and pupil of Leonora's coven," she said, and her voice was more here than not. Even her body seemed to sharpen in focus, until she was very nearly all the way here. "Greetings, daughter of Magenta's coven; son of the warlock Gregorio Andromedus; and good healer. Greetings, creature of mud and magic; and greetings to all our feline friends." Her smile widened. "And most especial greetings, dear Luna Amadora. How we have missed you in our realm."

In Jeremy's arms, Rosemary gave a great, delighted squeal. My mouth fell open in shock. What was she...?

"Sadly, as I explained the last time we spoke," Perrine went on, "events have overtaken us. They move faster all the time. We must travel at once. Come!" She raised a delicate hand and swept it toward us in a peremptory manner, and before anyone could react, we were brought through the portal and into ley space.

I felt a sharp *twang* as the spell that had been holding us captive in the room snapped under Perrine's Beyonder magic, tingling along my skin and my magical channels before falling away. Beside me, I thought I heard one or two of my companions groan or sigh; they clearly felt it too.

We were not on any ley line that I knew. In fact, I wasn't even sure we were on a line at all; the space around us felt large and empty, though I knew it was not the in-between space either. I had no more than a moment to wonder about it before we emerged back into the physical realm, in a darkened room in a house somewhere...in San Francisco...I knew this space...

"Oh Blessed Mother," Pearl moaned. "We're here."

She'd brought us to his actual *house*! *Inside* his house! Perrine stood calmly before us, a half-smile on her face.

"What was that you said a minute ago about *Luna* somebody?" I asked her.

"Hearken to me, all of you," Perrine said, the smile vanishing as a note of strong coven-mother authority came into her voice. She gazed around at us all. "Our window is small, and fast closing. The warlock Gregorio Andromedus has spread his energies between here and his north coast stronghold, and they are made thin by these efforts; he will work hard to close these gaps. Having to trap you in Berkeley was an expenditure he did not anticipate, one which you must take advantage of. We will continue to help from our side as we can, but the barriers are powerful and unpredictable. Midnight is a more reliable moment, though if we find others, we will use them. Be prepared. Be strong, be observant, and be decisive. Strike where you can, and take care of yourselves.

"And take heart. We love you all, and we know that you can do this. I have brought you to the seat of his power and must step back from you now; I have several other critical tasks to perform in the scant minutes before the path narrows. We have come too far to turn back. We *will* defeat him—together."

And step back she did—she took a literal backward step and was gone.

I exhaled a shaky sigh and looked around. We seemed to be in a small sitting room, sparsely furnished. And yes, Perrine had brought us all through—five witches, a warlock, a witchlet, a golem, our seven cats…and…a reincarnated Beyonder? Taking the physical form of an infant…*my* infant daughter?

I stepped over to Jeremy, who stood, stunned, by the wall. "May I?"

"What? Oh! Of course." He handed me my daughter.

I pulled her close, trying to look into her eyes, into her face. But she was wriggly and gleeful, and would not meet my eye.

Luna? I sent her. *Are you really…?*

Mama! she sent, sounding cheerful.

"Rachel's still in Berkeley!" Gracie cried. "The old witch left the humans behind!"

"They'll be fine," Niad said authoritatively. "I've already called to Leonora about them—our communication capacity has been restored."

Gracie went limp with relief. "Is she going to go get them?"

"She can send somebody over on the ley lines to tell them to drive back to San Francisco," Niad assured her. "Or Callie can call Raymond, it doesn't matter. What's critical right now is to figure out where we are *precisely* in Gregorio's house, and even more importantly, where *he* is." She glanced around, clearly looking with witch-sight. "I do not recognize this room from any of the times I have visited here."

I felt the critical thing right now was *Who in the several worlds is this creature I gave birth to*, but Niad wasn't wrong. For once, I was glad she was being so assertive and sharp. My brain seemed to be caught in a spin cycle.

I tried to refocus, looking around. I did not recognize this room either, though it reminded me a bit of the inner rooms I'd visited at Gregorio's last party, when I'd stumbled across the original core of the house while looking for the bathroom. The furniture at least seemed to be of the same vintage as those old spaces.

"I don't sense my father in the house," Jeremy said, "though we all know how little that means. I imagine he has been cloaking his presence reflexively for some time now."

I nodded; it would only make sense. Though if Perrine was right…

"He might be running out of energy for the cloaking, if he's having to do too many things at once. Can anyone tell if he's in the city, or up in Mendocino County?"

"I'll call to Mother Magenta," Geneva said.

I opened my witch-sight as well and scanned the house. Yes, the room we were in was just down a short hallway from the weird little kitchen where Gregorio did his home spellwork; and no, he did not seem to be in the house. I stretched my sight wider, seeking his essence in the city, in Berkeley, and beyond.

"Magenta says she does detect his presence in Caspar," Geneva announced a moment later. "She is not sure whether to believe it; it is so strong, she suspects it to be a decoy."

"Maybe," I said. "The phrase 'trust, but verify' comes to mind right about now."

Niad smiled. "Just so."

"Someone is in the house, however," Manka put in. "I detect a presence, far below." She paused. "No, two presences."

Below? We were on the original ground floor, though the house was built on a steep hillside. Did she mean closer to the street? I cast my witch-sight down, finding nothing in the area around the stairs, what would have passed for "front yard" in a more normal dwelling. I shifted my sight downward. Beneath the ground, under the floor under our feet, was a dug-out basement. Most of it was unused, or filled with dusty boxes, but one labyrinthine room...

Pearl said softly, "Is that...a dungeon?"

Gracie stifled a snicker, then looked mortified. I gave her a gentle smile. "I see it too," I said. "It certainly does look like a dungeon. But, why?"

"Look at the back," Niad said, her voice grim. "The very back, behind the false wall."

"Sebastian," I whispered. "Oh Blessed Mother."

"And he's not alone," she said.

Sebastian sat cross-legged on the floor in the back of the space, much like how he'd sat in mid-air in Gregorio's Caspar place. He seemed awake and alert, but also...just completely wrong. It was rather gloomy in there, so it was hard to see his precise expression, but I knew that I had never seen such a look on my friend's face. He twitched, he gleamed with perspiration, he blinked rapidly; he was not at all right.

Making matters worse, Flavius Winterheart was in the dungeon-room as well. He seemed just as unconscious as he had been in the Mendocino coven, only now he was curled up on a hard stone floor at Sebastian's feet.

How did they get here?

I wanted to run down and rescue them both right away—get Sebastian out of this place, get the ring's tainted effects out of his head, do whatever we could to get him back before things got even worse. Get Flavius restored to health.

"We need to know how—and when—he got out of our coven house," Geneva pointed out. "I will call to Magenta again."

Manka nodded. "I would like a more thorough search of this house," she said. "And perhaps we can bolster our own defenses."

"We can't ward his house," I said.

"Especially not if we're trying to lure him here," Niad said, refraining from rolling her eyes.

I huffed out a breath. "Exactly. But even if we wanted to, we couldn't. He's lived here for so many years, and he's modified every bit of the place with so much of his own personal magic over that time."

"I think what Manka meant was that was we should cloak *ourselves* in defensive and deflective spells," Pearl said, gently. "Use his tricks against him."

Manka nodded. "Yes."

"I hope all the familiar cats are all right," Gracie said softly. "We just left them in that awful place."

"They're where they need to be," I assured her. "With their witches."

"And they are not at all helpless," Manka added. "I have the strong sense that their part of the struggle, at least, is going just as it should."

Geneva looked up from the wooden chair she had taken. She was pale. "Magenta says that to the best of her knowledge, Sebastian Fallon is still there, still held in the, er, guest room. And that no one has been seen to leave the room that Flavius Winterheart was in. She is going to check on them both right now, in person."

"So which Sebastian-and-Flavius are real and which Sebastian-and-Flavius are the illusion?" Niad mused, quietly.

Geneva just shook her head.

"I am willing to walk through this house," Jeremy said. "I agree with Manka; we should be sure of who is and is not here."

"Yes, but I don't believe any of us should venture off alone," Manka said. "Do take at least one other person with you."

"You could take me," Petrana offered. "I cannot be hurt in any meaningful sense, and I could perhaps be very helpful."

I looked at her, surprised as ever by her growing initiative. A part of me wanted to keep her close—to protect me? So I could protect her? So there would be someone to hold the baby?—but I realized the wisdom of her words. "Yes, that is a good plan," I said. "The rest of us can go to the basement."

"Should we not wait until the house is searched? Perhaps we should all do that first, together," Pearl said, frowning.

"Mother Perrine said we needed to work quickly," I pointed out. "This is a big house, which will take a while to search. Six of us, and our cats, should be plenty to take care of whatever nastiness we find in the basement." *I hope.*

Oh, Sebastian, I thought, looking down at him again. His position was unchanged, as was his expression. *What has that ring done to you?*

"All right," Pearl said, still sounding reluctant.

Niad had been gazing at the floor; now she looked up and focused on us. "I've been conferring with Leonora. She agrees we should split up as discussed. She and the other coven mothers are continuing to watch us; they will come if they find us in danger."

Jeremy nodded. "Good. Shall we?" he said to Petrana; they left the room. I heard their footsteps for a minute, then a door closed and they were beyond earshot.

As I turned back to suggest that we get moving, Geneva drew in a breath, sounding even more shocked and dismayed than before. "Magenta says the mad warlock is no longer in the guest room, and the injured man is gone as well." All heads snapped to her as she went on. "And...the ring is no longer in the dragon box."

"What does that mean?" Manka asked, very stern. "What is a dragon box?"

"It...it was supposed to be impossible to break. We wove different magics in—nobody even knows the entire recipe, the spell. Well, except for Magenta." Geneva shivered. "She is very upset right now. And scared."

"I can imagine," Pearl said. "It is a very upsetting world we are living in at the moment, full of confusing happenings and impossible-seeming realities." She seemed to steel herself. "All we can do is keep working together, as Mother Perrine has counseled, and trust that we will prevail in the outcome."

Working together... I thought. *Working together with the freakin' Beyond.*

"Yes," I said aloud, and gave Pearl what I hoped was a brave smile. "Good point."

We have cleared the first floor, Jeremy reported to me—and to the others, from the looks on their faces. *We have found nobody here. Now we move to the second floor.*

Thank you, I sent. *Keep being careful.*

He sent me a chuckle, privately. *Thank you, Callie, I will.*

"I guess we should go to the creepy basement dungeon place now?" Gracie asked. She was holding Minky very tightly.

"I think so," I said.

"Should we—" Niad started, and then laughed and cut herself off. "I was going to say, should you bring Rosemary or would it be wiser to leave her behind with someone, but she's probably better equipped than any of us to navigate—all of this."

"I know," I said. "I'm trying not to think about—where my mind wants to go, and I just can't yet—but you're right." I shook my head. "It's hard not to think of her as an innocent helpless infant. Whatever is going on...whatever she is...this is going to take some getting used to."

Point, Rosemary sent to me.

Point? Fair point? That was the point? Or maybe she was just talking about her own chubby little hand, pointing at the doorway?

Whichever it was, we followed.

After covering each other with some solid protection spells, we set out, though it took some exploring and several false starts, even with our witch-sight, to find the way down to the basement. I'd known that a lot of this house was magically constructed, but I hadn't realized how incredibly convoluted it was.

Almost as if it were designed to be confusing.

Along our way, Jeremy sent two more updates, reporting that he and Petrana had found no one else in the rest of the house, and further—though there was no way of knowing if this was just another false trail—that it seemed as though no one had been here for at least several days. We told him to join us downstairs.

Now we stood before the dungeon door. "Wow, that's tacky," Niad said.

Gracie snorted. "It looks like a prop from a cheesy horror movie."

They weren't wrong: the door appeared at first glance to be heavy and solid, made from rough wooden planks and reinforced with iron bands. It was rounded, rimmed with stone, and had a big keyhole set in a heavy iron plate.

But at second glance... "Not even a horror movie; it looks like something out of a video game," I said.

Gracie raised a hand to tap on the stone.

"Hold on," I said quickly, "let's not touch it yet."

She lowered her hand; everyone looked at me. On my hip, Rosemary studied the door, eyes wide, though she was silent—both aloud and internally.

"Something that looks *this* fake—that has to mean something," I went on.

"Maybe no one was ever supposed to see it?" Geneva asked.

I shook my head. "No. Gregorio does nothing that no one is supposed to see—not like this. He saves that for his terrible crimes, but even those, he spins them so he can pretend they mean something else. So he can brag about them. So everyone can know what a powerful warlock he is, and how lucky we are to have him here to take care of us all."

"You're not wrong about that," Niad said slowly. "This is supposed to look fake. In order that we don't sense what's real about it, perhaps?" She took a large step back, then lifted her hands and narrowed her eyes, focusing not just her witch-sight, but also a deeper spell of magical seeing.

Manka watched her a moment, then pulled one of her divination powders out of a pocket of her tunic. She sprinkled some into her palm, closed her hand around it, and stood silently. After another minute, she opened her hand, spilling none of the powder, and pressed her palms together.

Geneva watched both witches with interest. "Do you mind if I try something?"

"Not at all," I said. "We should do everything we can. We're all in this together."

She gave me a faint smile, then crouched down, calling Chelan to her, as well as Hyacinth's familiar Melyx. Putting a hand on each cat's back, she stared straight at the door, unmoving.

As I was trying to figure out how I could help, I heard steps on the stairs above: Jeremy and Petrana rejoining us. In a moment, Jeremy turned the corner and stopped.

"Oh," he said, staring at the dungeon door. "I've never been down here before. How…unsubtle."

"Do you know why it looks like this?" I asked him quietly, shifting the baby from one hip to the other.

He shook his head and took a few steps closer. "No, but you're right to be cautious. It is…quite a departure from the style of the rest of the house."

"That's what I thought too." Indeed it was: Gregorio's tastes, at least here in his city house, ran rather more to elegant little antique Chinese tables, delicate vases from esteemed Old Country artists, and exquisite paintings.

"There it is," Niad announced, dropping her hands. "In the frame, not the door: a particularly nasty little charm."

"Ahh," Manka said, a moment later. She opened her palms. They were clean and dry, no trace of her powder remaining. "Yes, I see it." Shaking her head and frowning, she added quietly, "How did he even *get* marchiona in San Francisco?"

Geneva nodded. "That's...impressive."

Jeremy looked where Niad indicated. "Oh, interesting." He turned to us. "I might be able to defuse that. Would you like me to try?"

"Please," I said, "if you can safely."

He gave a half-smile. "That's what I meant. Don't worry, I'm still being careful."

"Can any of us help?" Gracie asked, politely.

Jeremy shook his head, now smiling down at the witchlet. "I do not believe so, Graciela, but thank you. No, this is my father's magic; because I am of his blood, I stand the best chance of being able to unmake it. Besides," he added, glancing around at the rest of us, "he recently taught me some methods that are rather similar to what I am seeing here—if I am understanding this, that is."

"I imagine that he did not anticipate that his own instruction would be used against him," Pearl said wryly.

"No, I expect not." Jeremy took a step forward, still keeping well back from the door.

We had heard nothing from within, the whole time we'd been standing here. A glance through with witch-sight revealed that Sebastian and Flavius were still there. Sebastian was still immobile... still staring straight ahead with that look on his face. Flavius was still inert.

I shivered, and withdrew my sight from the room.

"If I do manage to release this charm," Jeremy said, "we should be prepared for whatever Dr. Fallon might do. We do not know if he came here willingly and sits behind this door for his own protection; or whether he was sent here by my father and is imprisoned there."

"I know," I said. "He is not himself—he might very well be ready to attack us." I shook my head. "Though my heart just doesn't want to believe it. Not Sebastian. He would never hurt me—would never hurt anyone. Not willingly."

"I understand," Jeremy said softly. "I know he is a particular friend of yours."

I widened my eyes at the words. *No, Sebastian and I never...* Then I realized that Jeremy would likely not be privy to witches' code, and that he only just meant that we were, you know, *friends* friends. Buddies. "Right. So. Gregorio could easily have planted him here, assuming that I would want to rush in there and rescue my completely not evil or crazy friend."

"Either way, we must all be ready for whatever he does when I open this door. This could even be my father in disguise."

We all shivered as we considered this. "Right," I said after a minute. "So let's be ready, as we were in Berkeley."

Everyone stood by, at full alert. "Okay," Jeremy said. "Here we go."

"Are you looking for me?"

We all whirled around. Sebastian was now standing behind us, grinning like a maniac; his eyes glittered, and his hair was pasted to his forehead.

"Because it's not polite to talk about people behind their backs."

Jeremy grabbed me and practically thrust me behind him as he drew us back toward the dungeon door—away from Sebastian. Rosemary, still in my arms, held perfectly still. The others, even Petrana, backed away from Sebastian as well. The cats hissed and growled, drawing close to their mistresses, baring their sharp teeth.

I flicked my witch-sight gaze backward, into the dungeon; only Flavius remained. Okay then. "Sebastian," I said, stepping out from behind Jeremy. My arms trembled; wow my daughter was suddenly heavy. "What is happening?"

His grin did not falter. "We are defeating the evil wicked warlock! Right here in his very house! Oh, what a wonderful turn of events!"

He's not even talking like himself, Jeremy sent me. *He sounds like he's reading lines.*

I nodded and glanced around at the others. Everyone was waiting for my lead; even Niad looked unsettled. *Oh Blessed Mother, don't stop being bossy now,* I thought. What to do?

Well, I had to do something, and quickly. "I'm glad you still want to defeat him," I said carefully. "So do we—that's why we're all here!" Jeremy glanced at me, and noted my shakiness; he reached out, silently offering to take the baby. I handed her to him gratefully. "Maybe we could talk about how to do this, though?" I forced my face into what I hoped was a friendly smile, though it probably came out as more of a grimace.

"Of course!" Sebastian moved a little, side to side, as if he wanted to hop from foot to foot but somehow realized that that was not quite the right thing to do. "We just—you know—defeat him!"

"I do not know," I said slowly. "So...can I ask you a few questions about that?"

His gaze darted around the room. My heart pounded as I watched him, searching for any sign of my sweet, caring friend. Oh, I hoped we could get Sebastian back. He looked at me again. "Yes, Callie, you can ask me questions." He suddenly giggled. "I might even answer them!"

Okay, well, that was better than nothing. "First, tell me more about how you got here. Can you do that?"

He frowned, which was at least better than that crazed grin or the creepy giggle, but it still wasn't my friend. "I...stepped away. I needed to be here." He was not wearing the ring, but his right hand strayed toward his waist—toward his pocket? I needed to keep the ring out of his hands.

"And you brought Flavius Winterheart with you?" I asked, keeping my voice calm and gentle. So far, the others just stood behind and beside me, continuing to let me take the lead. I could feel them holding their power; I had to trust in that. Elnor leaned against my leg. My daughter remained perfectly still and silent in Jeremy's arms.

Sebastian smiled weakly. "I put his magic back in him," he said, sounding almost sullen, or perhaps just confused. "He used to be a warlock until you burned his magic out of him."

I nodded. "Yes, I did—Jeremy and I did. You remember that we thought we had good reasons for what we did, but we were wrong." I took a tiny step forward, trying not to look threatening at all, wondering if there would be any way to get the ring away from him. Wondering if I dared, if it would not just do me terrible harm instead. "Can you tell me how you put his magic back? I did not think such a thing was possible."

"So many more things are possible than we ever knew!" Sebastian's smile grew, too wide, but his eyes were still desperate, searching. Was I seeing the real Sebastian peering out? Oh, I wished I had any idea how to handle this. "If we only reach for the power that is available to all of us." Again, his hand strayed toward his waist; again, it stopped before he pulled out the ring.

"Can you unmake the charm in the doorframe here so we can get Flavius out?" I asked, more to divert him than anything else.

Sebastian shook his head. "No, Callie. Only its maker can unmake it."

I affected a puzzled look. "But you just told me that so many things are possible. I thought maybe this would be."

"Why do you want the charm gone? I'm out here."

"For Flavius," I said, patiently. "I would like it if Manka could take a look at him." I quickly glanced at Manka, who nodded. "He seems to be unconscious; we are wondering if he's all right. And I'm still confused about how you put his magic back, and I would love to look at him myself, to see more."

Sebastian pondered this. At least his hand kept still this time. "He's fine," he said, after a long moment. "He's…reabsorbing his magic. It might take a while." Now he sounded tentative.

"All the more reason to let us look at him, hmm?" I took another minuscule step forward. "See if he's okay? He's been out of it for quite some time, hasn't he?"

"He was awake for a…" Sebastian started, then stopped, frowning at the door behind me. "Didn't Jeremy say he could unmake the door charm?"

"I said I was willing to try," Jeremy said, "but if we don't need to, that would be best. You stepped right past it just now—not to mention you stepped into the room when you came here. Didn't you?"

"I did." His frown deepened; he looked petulant. "Oh but it

is so icky down here, so cold and...stony. Let's go upstairs to Dr. Andromedus's nice sitting room."

I stared back at him, trying to think fast. I didn't like it much down here either, but that wasn't the point. Upstairs, many of the rooms were laced with Gregorio's magic, if not entirely constructed with it; I couldn't remember how much of his sitting room was mundane material and how much was illusion. Down here, though, seemed to be almost entirely magic, including the ugly charm in the dungeon door's frame. On balance, upstairs seemed like a better bet, even though it was clearly what Sebastian wanted.

Then again, as long as Sebastian was at least acting like he was on our side, we should encourage that.

The bigger question was, where would be the best place to face Gregorio? *Upstairs,* my gut answered me, at once. *Not here, not underground, not in a magical construct of his design.*

"That sounds like that might be a good idea, Sebastian," I said, hedging. "Can you tell us why you were down here, though, if it was so icky?"

He laughed, spun on his heel, and started for the door. "Not talking here!" he called over his shoulder, in a sing-song voice. "Talking upstairs!"

"Let's bring Flavius with us!" I called after him.

"Nope! He needs to rest! He stays there!" He trotted out of the room and headed for the stairs.

I turned to the others and let out a shaky breath. "Wow, that's... really unsettling."

"Tell me about it," Niad said, shrugging her shoulders to release tension.

"The ring's poisonous effects are running deep in him," Manka said sadly. "I hope we can free him from it; I hope that he hasn't spent too much time in proximity to that terrible device."

"Me too," I said. "He's a good warlock, a good man...gentle and kind."

Geneva's eyes widened. "If you say so."

"He is," I insisted. "This ring..."

"Nothing of its ilk should ever have been allowed to be created,"

Manka said. She turned and looked at the dungeon door, frowning. "I mislike leaving Dr. Winterheart down here. Jeremiah, *do* you think you can unspell this door?"

"I do not know, but I would like to try." He handed Rosemary back to me, then stood back and opened his arms to his sides, closing his eyes.

We all moved a step or two away from him, watching carefully. I could see the strain on his face as he worked, but could not detect what sort of magic he was performing.

After nearly a minute, he dropped his arms and sighed heavily. "I cannot." Beads of sweat had formed on his forehead. "I…thought it was something, but it is not that."

Can't you try again? I wanted to ask, but I knew he would have if he could. And besides, Sebastian had marched out of here and demanded we follow nearly five minutes ago. "We should join Sebastian," I said instead, "before he gets impatient and does something weird. Something *else* weird." *Or falls into Gregorio's clutches*, I added silently.

"Yes," Niad said. "We can come back for Flavius."

"We *will* come back for him," I said.

— CHAPTER THIRTEEN —

I n the large formal sitting room at the front of Gregorio's house,
we arranged ourselves in a ghastly charade of a cozy little gathering. At least the room was big enough that we could spread
out, and we kept our protection spells around us.

I was further grateful that Sebastian didn't insist on us all having
tea or cocktails—I wasn't sure I could consume anything right now.
Though he did stride around the room as if he owned the place.

I sat in a large, upholstered chair, holding Rosemary, who still
looked around with deep, intense interest—not just at Sebastian,
though certainly at him. She gazed around the entire room, and
everyone in it, taking it all in. Communicating nothing.

Petrana stood at my shoulder and Elnor sat at my feet; Jeremy
sat in a matching chair on the far side of the fireplace from mine;
the rest of the witches took couches and other soft chairs. Everyone
watched Sebastian warily as he stepped away from gazing out the
front window and smiled happily at us.

"There! That's better, isn't it?"

"Sit down," I said, gesturing at another chair not far from me.
"You must be exhausted, after all you've been through."

He laughed eerily; it sounded nothing like his old laugh. "Oh
Callie. You're so kind. Do you know how long it's been since I've
slept? I don't need to rest at all anymore!" He shook his head. "If

I'd only known…if only Dr. Andromedus had brought me into the secrets of his research sooner…"

This could not be just the ring, I thought. I'd worn that ring for months, and though it had clearly monitored me, and prevented me from removing it (to the point of blowing up Petrana when I'd tried), it had never done anything like this.

Of course, I hadn't put it on intending to gain power; I had thought I was being gifted an important family heirloom in recognition of my carrying Gregorio's grandchild. But then Sebastian hadn't had evil intentions to begin with either…though he had always been worryingly attracted to learning more about the ring.

"What other secrets of his are you privy to?" I asked. "What has he told you?"

Sebastian smiled down at me, as though I were a student who had gotten the right answer. "I know lots of his secrets! But best of all, none of them are things that he told me—they are things I figured out for myself!" His hand again went to his jeans pocket, without reaching in. I glanced quickly at Jeremy, making sure he noticed too. Jeremy nodded back. "I know that this house is the locus of his power," Sebastian went on. "Despite the lab at Berkeley, the clinic downtown, his north coast house, or any of his other places—everything important, everything *real*, is done here. Which is why *we* need to be here." His grin widened.

"We are here," I pointed out, not adding, *And we already know that; that's why we came.* "Do please sit down; you're making us all nervous, pacing around like that."

He gave a dramatic sigh but then did take the chair I'd indicated. Where he proceeded to fidget so incessantly, I quickly regretted my words. He looked like a meth addict at the end of a binge.

I hoped we could save my friend before the crash…I hoped there was any saving him.

"How are you planning to defeat him?" I asked, still trying to act calm, relaxed. Unafraid. Gregorio was almost certainly spying on him—and by extension us—through the ring. *This is what we're doing here*, I reminded myself, yet again. *This is the plan.*

Oh, but it terrified me.

I needed to keep Sebastian talking. Keep him focused. Try to talk him into letting us help him…and getting that be-damned ring away from him in the process.

"I will meet him in single combat," Sebastian said, sitting up tall and thrusting out his chest. "He does not even suspect how strong I have become; he cannot, or he would have never let me go when we met earlier."

"Sebastian," I said gently, "don't you remember how we talked about working *together* to solve this problem? First just you and me, and we made great progress, but now I have gathered a whole community." I gestured at the room around me, and then was about to mention Perrine and the Beyond, but in case Gregorio didn't know of their involvement already, I held that back. "The covens, the healers, us researchers—together, we are far stronger than any one warlock—you, or Gregorio, or anyone. Together, we will remove this threat in our midst." I, too, sat up, just a bit, stirred by my own words.

Because they were true. I suddenly understood this more deeply than ever before—in my gut, even more than in my mind. All the witches and warlocks—the humans—the cats—and yes, even denizens from the Beyond—we brought so much to this struggle, far more than any individual could.

But Sebastian just shook his head. "I can do it!" he cried, suddenly shrill. "I'm tired of seeing everyone I care about getting hurt! It's time to stop him, and *I can do that!*"

"Dr. Fallon," Manka said, leaning forward and bringing the full weight of her gentle "healer voice" to bear. "We do not begin to doubt your strength, your kindness, or your bravery. But Calendula is correct: Dr. Andromedus has isolated himself thoroughly. He is entirely without allies, and yet, he is immensely powerful and unthinkingly crafty. He preys on our weaknesses and seeks to isolate us, so as to defeat us one by one. He *wants* you to step forward, to push us all aside, to face him alone—so that he may cut you down."

Sebastian leapt to his feet, furious. "I can do it! I can send him from our midst!" Then he threw his head back and yelled, "Gregorio Andromedus, I call you to me! Come here and face me, *now!*"

"Your wish is my command," said a smirking Gregorio, appearing in the center of the room. No matter how much I'd been expecting it, no matter that we'd intended to confront him here, I still felt a rush of panic in his presence. "I cannot believe you have learned so little from me, that you would imagine I would permit you to visit violence upon me in my own home." As he spoke, he waved a desultory hand at Sebastian, who immediately fell under Gregorio's hold-spell, his hand frozen halfway to his pocket.

The hand continued moving past Sebastian, even as we all started to leap to our feet, to combine our spells and whip our power into a weapon with which to smite the ancient warlock. He froze us all with that casual motion.

Stop...underestimating...him...

Then Gregorio turned and looked around the room. "Well now, what is this?" he said. "Welcome to my home, I suppose, though I see you felt you needed no invitation."

My heart careened in my chest. He must have sensed my fear, because he turned the full weight of his gaze upon me.

"Calendula Isadora," he said, drawing out my name. "Why, I shall even permit you to rise in my presence. Under your own power... such as it is." He flicked his fingers, and I felt the freeze-spell release me. In my arms, Rosemary stirred—so he'd freed her too.

Interesting.

As I stood, Jeremy sent me, *I would take her again, but I cannot.*

I shook my head. *That's all right.* Whoever my daughter really was and however she came to be here, we would face this monster together. She stared at him, eyes still wide, gaze steady.

Gregorio gave her a long look, his smile falling away. Then he looked back up at me. "Before you can ask your tiresome questions yet again, let me alleviate your curiosity on this point at least."

He opened his hands and spread his arms at his sides—the same gesture Jeremy had done downstairs shortly ago. In the blink of an eye, my mother and my father stood to either side of the ancient warlock. Though I was relieved beyond measure to see them, they both looked...diminished. Almost smaller; or was it that Gregorio grew in stature, beside them?

"You look like the freakin' Devil card," I spat at Gregorio, almost before I'd realized I was going to say it.

He blinked and took a half-step back, then raised his right hand and lowered the left one mockingly. The only things missing were the horns and the hairy goat-legs. "Like this? You mean the *tarot* card? Is that the filth you speak of?" He chuckled, without humor, and folded his arms across his chest. "I would expect no less at this point, given the unwise and unnatural roads you have gone down."

I opened my mouth to protest, or question, but he went on.

"Yet Belladonna and Lucas are not little imps, are they? They are just poor unfortunate souls, caught up in events much larger than themselves. Never understanding their proper places in the world—not until it was far too late, at any rate."

For someone who apparently held the tarot in such contempt, he was awfully familiar with its iconography, I thought.

I shot a quick glance around the room. My companions were all still thoroughly spelled. Unless that was a knowing gleam in Niad's eye? She was turned toward me, and the look on her face seemed suffused with meaning.

Had she been able to contact Leonora? I did not dare to ask, or to try to do so myself. If our coven mother had been monitoring us here, she already knew what was happening anyway.

I turned from Niad to my parents, meeting Mom's eyes. She looked back at me with fierce intelligence and determination, but did not budge, clearly frozen as well. I gave her a slow blink and turned to Dad. He only looked sorrowful, and older than I'd ever seen him.

Gregorio was waiting for a response from me. "Okay, so what are their proper places?" I asked, refraining from pointing out that when you freeze someone and move them around like a puppet, you can put them any place you like. "And why don't they understand them?"

The ancient warlock gave me a patient, tolerant smile. "Lucas Grandion," he said, gracing my father with a really good imitation of a fond glance before turning back to me. "My oldest, dearest friend; my greatest supporter, through good times and hard times, both in the Old Country and here in this new settlement—even to the degree of following me here and making a new life when our time there drew to an end. Lucas, my disciple, my student, my other half in so many ways…the rest of me."

Gregorio's fond look turned icy. "Lucas failed to comprehend that his deepest and most important bond was always, and ever, to be with me. Of course he could have other associates, other companions, even others close to his heart; but his primary loyalty was to me. Did you not swear it to me, those many hundreds of years ago, Lucas?" His gaze upon my father was terrible in its woundedness, its sorrow. Its raw pain. "As I swore it to you.

"And yet. When you proposed to sign a contract with the young witch Belladonna Isis, you hid your innermost heart from me. You spoke to me of her beauty, her kindness, her gentle and agreeable nature. You spoke of her line's great fertility, and your desire to beget a child with her; a child who you would bring into our work, a child who would be a new student for us, learning our science and expanding it to unforeseen new breakthroughs, bringing her unique witchly perspectives and powers.

"You did not tell me that you had fallen in *love* with Belladonna Isis.

"You did not tell me that you would renew this contract, when its initial term was up; that you would seek to spend ever more time with her over the years, not less, as is the normal way of things; that you would put her interests above mine. Above *ours*.

"Lucas Grandion, you betrayed me."

I stared at the tableau before me, as frozen as if I were still spelled. What a…monstrous ego.

Gregorio Andromedus turned to my mother. "And you, Belladonna Isis. Witch who will not keep a familiar, witch who failed to return to her coven as promised. Temptress who stole the heart of my dearest friend. And mother of Calendula Isadora, who you secretly have trained in the ways of that filth, the human fake-magic, the tarot." He could not quite mask his sneer.

"Belladonna, you hide behind your weak, innocent, pleasant demeanor, your pretty face, your gentle ways. You fooled me for far too long. I did not see your contract renewal coming; and even then, you and Lucas together persuaded me that it was entirely innocent, that you merely wanted more time to enjoy each other's company, that you wished to try for another child—another child to serve me! All while you were plotting and scheming, teaching Calendula Isadora to make her own decisions, to follow her own whims and wild desires—even to the building of a monstrous mud-creature!"

Now wait just a minute here, I thought. Mom had only recently gotten serious about trying to teach me tarot—though all my life, she had encouraged me to grow, to learn, to be my best self. And Gregorio had always seemed very impressed with Petrana—positively so, I'd thought.

Speaking of which, where *was* Petrana? She had come upstairs with us, she had stood beside my chair when I'd sat down…was she still in the room? I hadn't seen her when I'd glanced around a minute ago. Had Gregorio frozen her too? *Could* he freeze a golem not of his own making? Oh, no doubt. But I didn't dare look for her now, in case Gregorio was moved to wonder where she was as well.

So I kept my mouth shut and my eyes on Gregorio.

"It is my own failing that I did not see what was happening for far too long," he went on, glancing around the room to take in his captive audience; he knew he held the spotlight, if only because they couldn't take their eyes from him. "My own fault that I trusted too much—trusted Lucas, trusted Belladonna. Trusted Calendula. I imagined that everyone understood what I have always, since my earliest days, been trying to do for witchkind: strengthen us, protect us, improve us."

His angry eyes bored into me; I stared back at him, hardly having to fake my fear. "Recent events, alas, have opened my eyes. Have revealed to me just how much trouble you all have created for me—particularly you, Calendula Isadora. Forcing me to scramble about like a freshly-minted intern just to keep my crucial research from being shattered irrevocably, rather than forging new frontiers at its cutting edge."

My stare turned into a glare, and I was suddenly unable to keep my silence a moment longer. "What do you *want*, Gregorio? Really, what do you want? I'm sorry, but the world is changing, and my parents ought to be able to love each other if they want to. Making my dad swear fealty to you for all his days was *never* okay—and it's certainly not okay now. But you know what's a *whole lot more* not okay than *any* of that? Preying on witches and warlocks to harvest their essence for your own personal use!"

Arms still crossed, he gazed down at me sternly for a long moment. Then he shook his head and blinked, as if sad. "It is not for one such as you to ask me what I want, Calendula, but I will answer you all the same. I will answer you all." He glanced pointedly around the room, at all my still and silent companions. His gaze, heavy with disappointment, lingered on Jeremy. In my arms, Rosemary stirred ever so gently, never taking her eyes off him.

"I had imagined it was clear, but apparently I need to state it yet again. What I 'want' is nothing less than a return to the way things have always been—the way they ought to be. The way they were designed to be. Warlocks build their power over the centuries and protect witches. Witches live together in covens, preserving our heritage and our culture, and bearing us children when the occasion presents itself. All of witchkind accepts the direction and guidance of the Convocation of Elders, with advice and counsel from the collected coven mothers. And, when the time comes, we move to the Beyond to continue our journeys."

"You are hundreds of years overdue to move to the Beyond, Gregorio Andromedus," I growled. "Is that what you're using all the stolen essence for—not just strengthening yourself, but keeping yourself here, where you no longer belong? Listen to yourself! You're not even making sense. You lecture me, lecture us all, on *the way things should be*—and then turn around and break the rules and traditions yourself!"

"Because I am above the rules!" he thundered. I startled at his sudden shout, but Rosemary remained still. I imagined I could feel her strength, her resolve, pouring into me. "I *make* the rules, I do not follow them! I will move to the Beyond only when *all* my work on *this* plane is finished!"

I narrowed my eyes at him, my anger continuing to burn away my fear. "You are not the king of all witchkind. You are not even the king of San Francisco witchkind. You're just a crazy old warlock who has stuck around far past his sell-by date and is wreaking all kinds of terrible, selfish, deadly havoc on the rest of us. And when anyone dares challenge you, dares to speak the truth to you, you suck their memories out of their heads and kill anyone trying to help them. Or you divide their bodies from their souls and steal their essence. Or you cauterize their magic right out of them—or let them steal a ring that twists their minds and fills their heads with lies. Or you freeze them with a spell—you silence them!" I waved my arm, indicating my companions. "I don't even know why you unfroze me. It would make it easier to lecture me if I stood here silently, wouldn't it?"

"It most certainly would," he sneered. "Is that what you want? Do not try me, Calendula Isadora. I would not hesitate to do so, but I imagined you wanted a *dialogue*. I thought you wanted *answers*."

I wasn't the one who called you here, I thought. *Sebastian was, and you froze him without a thought.* So there was some other reason he held back... In my arms, Rosemary shifted again, just a tiny bit. Not enough to be observed, just enough for me to feel her.

Rosemary, who had been uncomfortable in Gregorio's presence since the day she was born. No, not just uncomfortable: downright freaked out.

Rosemary, whom Gregorio had never managed to hold—never even managed to touch. Not even in the days when I thought he was her loving grandfather. Not even on her very first day.

Rosemary...who, if what Mother Perrine had said was true, was a reincarnated soul from the Beyond.

Are you protecting me somehow? I thought, but kept the words in my own mind, not daring to send them to my daughter. But what else could it be?

My mind spun as so many other mysterious messages began to make more sense. *We have sent you help*, Perrine had said, when she'd visited our coven in Circle. *But we did not correctly predict the urgency of the timing, so that help is thus far limited... Believe the youngsters, even unto the youngest among you.*

Rosemary. She was the youngest among us, by far. Not Gracie, or the other students.

And then there were all her "Luna" babblings. Heck, even

Geneva's shop in Mendocino, The Empress and The Moon—did it all carry meaning?

Gregorio would not, *could* not, touch Rosemary.

All this flashed through my mind in an instant. "I do want answers," I said, "but it's just plain weird to be standing in a room of frozen people, talking in front of them like they're not even here. Are you so afraid of my parents, my coven sisters, a witchlet, *your own son*, that you cannot let them think and speak and breathe freely?"

A flash of something crossed Gregorio's face, there and gone in an instant. Fear, anger, pique? Then his condescending smile returned. "Of course not. I fear nothing, not even discourtesy—though that distresses me, particularly in my own home. I will consider releasing your companions, if they will assure us they will act in a civilized manner." He cast a glance at Sebastian, whose face was frozen in a rictus that pained me to see. "About him, however, I feel no such compunctions. He is not himself, and shall remain bound until he can be conveyed to a…secure location."

Wow, something Gregorio and I agreed upon: Sebastian was absolutely not himself. I tried to stifle my surge of excitement at the thought that Gregorio might unfreeze everyone…it wouldn't help us attack him. He'd be ready for that. What I needed to do was draw this out, to buy time. "Release my parents," I demanded instead. "Despite what you think, they have done you no harm."

Then I looked at Niad, trying to convey *I have a plan* without actually sending the words. Which was harder than you might think.

"You do not command me, Calendula Isadora," Gregorio said, frowning. Then he lowered his hands and pointed an index finger at each of my parents. "But, because I respect you, and them, despite everything, I shall undo my spell upon them, as a gesture of generosity and goodwill." He flicked his fingers again, and both Mom and Dad relaxed with a sigh. Mom wavered on her feet; Dad hurried to her, not even glancing at Gregorio, whose frown deepened.

"Bella," my dad whispered. "Please, sit down." He nodded at a small chair in the corner and tried to lead her to it, but she shook her head.

"I'm fine," she said softly, with a brave smile as she squeezed his hand. "Thank you, Lucas." She took a step away from Gregorio, though, drawing Dad with her.

Gregorio turned back to me. Before he could say anything obnoxious like *Are you happy now?*, I spoke.

"That's a great start," I said, trying for a tone of strength, but managing something more like snotty. "How about the others now?"

"I told you that I would consider—" he started, but then everything happened at once.

— CHAPTER FOURTEEN —

Petrana stepped heavily into the room, lumbering like she hadn't since her earliest days. She carried a huge platter of cheese and crackers and sliced fruit. "Here are the refreshments you requested, Mistress Callie," she boomed out in a machine-like monotone.

Gregorio, startled into silence, wheeled to her—just in time to miss seeing Perrine step out of a wrinkle of air behind him. Leonora followed on her heels.

"What in the—" Gregorio said, as Perrine snapped her fingers, releasing everyone in the room from Gregorio's spell—including Sebastian.

"Ahhh!" Sebastian cried, thrusting his hand into his pocket and coming out with the ring.

"No!" I yelled, and leapt for him, but I had a baby in my arms, and since I wasn't going to let go of her, there wasn't a whole lot I could do.

Gregorio recovered from his shock and turned back to face me, but Petrana was still coming straight for him with a heavy platter of snacks. "Stop that thing!" Gregorio snarled.

"The ring!" I shrieked. "Leonora, get the ring from Sebastian!"

My coven mother turned to him, but Sebastian danced away.

The room, not all that large to begin with, was now a crowded, chaotic scramble. Niad darted behind me and whipped up a powerful spell, but I couldn't tell if she was trying to trap Sebastian or Gregorio—they were both wild cards, and both needed stopping. Geneva and Gracie were both shouting incantations. Manka was chanting; Jeremy was yelling; cats were yowling.

Petrana plowed straight into Gregorio, knocking him sideways toward my mother, just as Sebastian shoved the ring at his own finger.

"NO!" I screamed again, as my mother—

Noooooo!

—as my mother reached out, snatched the ring from Sebastian, and slipped it into her mouth, swallowing it.

Before I could fully register what she had done, she stepped forward and wrapped her arms around Gregorio. With a small, sad smile, she pulled him close, firmly but gently. "Time to go," she whispered, and closed her eyes.

The room darkened; a high keening sound filled the air, as an unseen wind moved about us all; the cats hissed, I howled, and Rosemary shrieked (with fear? with triumph? with shock?); Perrine chanted words in the ancient language; my father cried out in grief; and Gregorio and my mother vanished from this plane.

I felt it. I knew she was gone; I knew she had gone all the way Beyond, and had taken Gregorio Andromedus with her.

"Belladonna!" my father cried, his voice drenched in despair. He felt it, too. He knew. "No!"

"Noooo!" I cried. "Mother!" My knees buckled under me, and I was on the floor.

Mama, Rosemary said in my mind, though I was not comforted. I wanted to lie in a puddle on the floor and cry forever—I wanted to reach into the hole in the universe and pull my mother back—I wanted to kick and scream and fight—

The high keening sound grew louder, until it was an earth-shaking rumbling. "What *is* that?!" Gracie yelled.

"The house is collapsing!" Niad screamed, and I opened my eyes just in time to dodge a chunk of plaster falling from the ceiling. "His magic went with him! We have to get out of here!"

The building crumbled beneath and above and all around us, all the years of magical intervention that Gregorio had laid along the rafters and beams and bricks vanishing, leaving behind a rotten, hundred-year-old structure. Holes opened in the floor, windows shattered, walls became bare ribs laced with dust and spiders. A brick hit me in the face, giving me a sharp stab of pain. A panicked Elnor hissed and clawed at Petrana, who was trying to pick her up. The floor slanted at a crazy angle; my chair fell through it; the rest of the furniture, as well as the tray of cheese and crackers, slid toward what remained of the far wall. Jeremy lay blinking in the corner, seemingly stunned, though I could see no obvious injury. Sebastian lay motionless at my father's feet; my father's pained face was impossible for me to look at.

I didn't know what the others were doing, because the floor was now falling apart, too. I scrambled to hold on with one hand, clutching Rosemary with the other.

"Come on!" yelled Niad. "Along the ley line!"

"We have to carry them!" I yelled back, pointing to Jeremy and Sebastian. *At least them*, I thought, still not knowing where everyone was. And then I remembered: "Flavius!" I shouted, to no one, to anyone.

"Got him," Pearl said, and vanished. Geneva followed her.

"I've got this one," Manka said, picking up Jeremy.

Leonora simply reached down and scooped up Sebastian. He lay limp in her arms, his face relaxed and peaceful again.

The floorboard underneath me gave; I stabilized myself with magic, searching for the nearest ley line. Had Niad found one? There used to be one that led into this house, but had it been real, or had it vanished with Gregorio and the rest of his twisted magic?

"Here!" Perrine called, and she pushed open a passageway. It had more than a whiff of the Beyond to it. I felt a brief, erratic surge of hope, which she must have seen in my face. "No, Calendula," she said to me, almost too softly to hear. "She's not there."

I gulped back a sob. "Okay." I started to step onto the line, then turned and said, "Follow me. We'll go to my house."

"No, ours," Dad said, stepping past me. "Everyone, now."

I did as he ordered.

Rosemary and I emerged in the large formal living room of my parents' elegant Pacific Heights home. Dad was already there, sitting in his easy chair, his shoulders slumped and his face in his hands. I wanted to go to him, to comfort him—but I also wanted him to comfort me, to hold me and tell me Mom wasn't gone, that he was going to go fetch her back, that he was going to make it all right.

But none of those things could happen, because things were not all right, and they weren't going to be. And because Petrana popped out of the ley line just behind me a moment later, a spitting Elnor still in her arms. She set my familiar on the floor; Elnor stalked about, tail high and fluffy, fuzzy face filled with indignation. Until she sneezed.

Everyone else stumbled out behind them—Manka holding a woozy Jeremy, Leonora holding the unconscious Sebastian, then Niad and Gracie and all the rest of the cats.

Geneva and Pearl followed a minute after that, my coven sister carrying the still-unconscious Flavius.

"Oh thank the Blessed Mother," I said. "I thought maybe the door charm..."

Geneva nodded. "I guess it fell apart with the rest of the house. We found him on the bare earth, behind the house."

Pearl laid him gently down on a long sofa before an elegant coffee table.

Manka put Jeremy on a second long sofa, set a hand on his forehead, and nodded. "He will recover."

"Did he get hit by something?" I said, feeling my own face. It stung, and my hand came away bloody.

"You're bleeding," Niad told me, quite unnecessarily. But then she pulled out a handkerchief and handed it to me. I took it gratefully, and made a terrible mess of it.

Manka said, "His father planted many spells within him, but without Gregorio's active reinforcement of them, they will shrivel and die in time."

I shivered as I finished wiping my face. "Poor Jeremy." He'd only ever wanted his father's love. Instead, he got this.

"Where is Mother Perrine?" Leonora asked. She had set Sebastian down on the banquette seat built underneath the front window. "I thought she was with us."

"Where's *Rachel*?" Gracie asked, her voice high with anxiety. "Are the humans back from Berkeley yet? Are they okay?"

Oh—Raymond and Christine—and of course Rachel. Where were they? I sent my senses around looking for them, but human energy doesn't shine as brightly as the witchly kind does, and without a direction to help guide me...

"They will be along," came Perrine's voice as she stepped off another ley line, this one exuding even more familiar energy...

"Callie!" came a beloved voice, and then Logan was in the room with us. Logan, entirely herself, body and soul together, Willson in her arms. "Callie!"

"Logan!" I cried, and tried to pull my friend into my own arms, but of course I was still holding Rosemary, and Logan held her cat. It was an awkward embrace until Logan set Willson down and reached for Rose.

"Who is this lovely child?" Logan asked, beaming as I handed Rose to her—I almost had no choice in the matter, as my daughter was eager to wriggle into my best friend's arms.

"Uh, remember how I told you there was so much you didn't know..." I started.

Logan looked at me, wide-eyed. "Callie, really? Did you have a *baby*?"

"I did. This is Rosemary Leonora."

"Rosemary! Such a gorgeous name. It suits her." She jiggled the delighted baby. "With who?" Logan asked me. "Who is your father, sweet child?" she crooned down at Rose.

"That's, um, kind of a long story..." I said, wishing I had even a clue what to do right now. Or even what emotion I should be feeling, because I was basically deluged with all of them—grief, joy, relief, sorrow, and probably half a dozen others I hadn't even had time to notice in all the commotion.

"The humans are on their way," Leonora said, looking up from speaking with Perrine. "They were nearly to the warlock's house, and now they are driving here, in their automobile. They are unharmed."

Gracie nodded, looking fretful but mostly mollified.

"Humans?" Logan asked, sounding confused. She glanced around the room and spotted Jeremy. "Oh!" she said, her face flaming with sudden color, her delight deepening. And then, "Oh, he's hurt!"

I took Rose back from her, grateful for the distraction. "Manka says he will be all right."

Logan rushed over and bent down beside him. I turned away, feeling like a jerk for not telling her...anything...but when had I been supposed to?

And did it even matter? Jeremy and I were no longer together. If he and Logan wanted to resume where they had left off, who was I to stand in the way?

The pathway that Perrine had come through was still open, still exuding energy. A witch stepped through, one I didn't know; she blinked and looked around, her relieved smile growing. Another witch came through behind her, and then a warlock. In moments, the room was flooded with folks—more trapped souls reunited with their bodies. I recognized a few of them, but most were strangers. Because of course, Gregorio had mostly preyed on the unattached, the loners. People who were less likely to be missed.

"Hyacinth!" Geneva cried, pulling the older witch into her arms.

And then came Logan's parents, who embraced her and Rosemary and me in rapid succession. The cats poured in with their witches, and quickly all became noise and happy turmoil...except not happy, not at all happy. Not everyone.

Not me.

And not my father. I found myself beside him. He was still slumped in his chair, so I crouched down and put a hand on his arm.

"I...I cannot believe she would do such a thing," he muttered, seemingly unaware of the burbling chaos around us. "Why would she do that?"

I stood up and pulled on his hand, drawing him to his feet and leading him into the small passageway between this room and the kitchen. The butler's pantry, where I had sat what felt like a thousand years ago, at my parents' Yule party. Last month.

Dad sank onto the little bench there. I sat next to him.

"I don't know," I said to him quietly. "I can't really believe it either, though I saw it and I felt it. She went Beyond."

"She was far, far too young." His voice trembled with emotion. "She had many hundreds of years ahead of her. Years we could have spent together."

"She saved us all," I said, woodenly. "She took the ring, and she took Gregorio through." I knew this and he knew this, and yet I still had to say it aloud. "She saved witchkind."

"Perhaps there is a way we can retrieve her?" Dad said, suddenly looking up with hope in his eyes. Because apparently we *both* had to follow the whole process.

I shook my head sadly. She could be reincarnated into a vessel on this plane, as my daughter apparently had been; but such things were quite rare, and would not satisfy him anyway. "She wouldn't be Belladonna anymore," I said. "Not the witch you knew." I did not know who Luna Amadora had been when she was a witch living her first life here, but she was probably not a redheaded half-human hybrid who never cried.

"Then I shall join her there."

I choked back a sob. "Please, no, Dad," I begged. "I can't lose *both* of you at once."

"I cannot live without her."

"Don't do anything now," I said. "Let's...talk about this more, later. When the shock isn't so immediate."

"I cannot promise anything," my father whispered. "But I shall try. For your sake."

I nodded and wrapped my arms around him, pulling him close. We sat in communal grief for a long while. Eventually, I felt another presence join us, and looked up.

It was Perrine, looking slightly less substantial than she had before. Was she leaving us?

"My time here is drawing to a close," she said, answering my unasked question. "I want to express my condolences and gratitude to both of you before I return to the Beyond. It was not our intention that Belladonna Isis complete the work that we had begun. She took that on of her own accord, in a decision of the moment. We will welcome her in our midst with great love and honor, for she has done more than nearly anyone else to heal all our worlds."

I blinked up at her. "Why did it have to be her?" I asked, piteously.

Perrine smiled sadly at me. "It did not have to be, but it was. She showed quick thinking and tremendous bravery. Gregorio Andromedus never suspected she would do such a thing, likely because she herself did not know it until she acted."

My father shook his head. "He always underestimated her. He never saw her strength, her courage. He never understood why I loved her."

Perrine faded a little more. I could see, through her form, a hint of the wall behind her. "There is a consolation, and though it is a small one at the moment, you may find it comforting over time." She gave a small smile. "If I may?"

I nodded, though I didn't know what she was asking, exactly.

She lifted her hands and a second later, Rosemary was in her arms, looking at me and Dad contentedly.

"The wise old crone Luna Amadora, who moved Beyond centuries ago," Perrine said, her words holding an air of formality now even greater than her usual archaic speech patterns, though she glanced fondly at my baby as she spoke her original name, "volunteered to travel back to this plane to incarnate as the newborn witchlet Rosemary Leonora, to guide the necessary efforts here to defeat the warlock Gregorio Andromedus. Unfortunately, as time passes differently between one plane and the next, and it is never certain where a soul will land, we sent her forth without sufficient time to come of age and into her full mental and magical capacities. In addition, as I mentioned to your coven, the warlock Gregorio Andromedus may have learned of our efforts and hastened his wicked work. We regret that Luna Amadora was not able to assist your efforts more capably."

I wanted to somehow defend my daughter. She'd helped plenty, all along the way. And hadn't she saved a whole group of us from Gregorio just yesterday, reaching through ley space and bringing us back here from hundreds of miles away? But I kept my mouth shut and nodded.

"Because she had intended to spend many decades back on this plane in the performing of the task that brought her here," Perrine continued, "Luna Amadora has formally requested to remain here, if this meets with your approval, Calendula Isadora. She would like to explore more thoroughly the capabilities and personality of her Rosemary Leonora incarnation, particularly her hybrid parentage. And she most especially would like to be raised by you, her mother, Calendula Isadora—even though she did not ask your permission before incarnating as your daughter, as is not only customary but has always been our law."

"Uh, of course, yes," I said, suddenly terrified at the thought of losing my daughter as well as my mother, and maybe even my father, all in the same moment. It hadn't even occurred to me that Rose might leave me! "Of course she can stay!"

"We thank you, but please do think carefully before you give your answer," Perrine said, her voice gentle. In her arms, Rosemary's eyes were wide and steady upon me. "It was a large deception we placed upon you, however noble were our reasons: for if you did not know this thing, that knowledge could not be taken from you—as so much other knowledge has been, along the way."

Like the warlocks who stole my memories in the Old Country—at Gregorio's bidding. Or whatever Gregorio learned from me during the months I wore his be-damned ring. I tried to do as Perrine asked, I tried to carefully consider the question—but all I wanted to do was reach out and snatch Rosemary from her, to hold her tight and never let her go. "I...I think I understand why this happened, why you did this," I said, after a minute. "But I love Rosemary—I mean, Luna— and I just cannot imagine letting her go. Especially..." I glanced at my father, silent next to me, and then took a deep breath, forcing down the sob that wanted to escape from me. "Especially after just losing Mom."

Perrine nodded gravely. "We understand, and we appreciate what you are suffering right now."

Mama, Rosemary sent me, and reached out her chubby little arms.

I took her and managed not to squeeze her too hard. *Oh, Rose*, I sent her. *You're still my baby daughter, aren't you?*

"She is Rosemary Leonora," Perrine said, after glancing at my daughter. "But she is also Luna Amadora. She asks to be called Rosemary Luna Leonora in this incarnation, to honor who she is and who she is going to be, as well as who she was. If that meets with your approval?"

"Of course!" I blurted, still trying to wrap my head around the fact of there being such an old soul in this tiny body. "I mean, she's the one driving this—she and those of you in the Beyond."

Perrine smiled as she shook her head. "But she is not, and we are not," she said gently. "That is the purpose of revealing all this to you. When Luna Amadora made the decision to undertake this journey, she set down large portions of who she was in order to inhabit a new life—quite literally: there is not enough room in an infant's brain for an adult to reside. Not even magical adults, in magical infant brains. As she grows, she will inhabit the body you and her human father have created for her, and become—something else. A third thing; a hybrid-hybrid. Part witch, part human; part old, part new; all herself." Perrine's smile grew, even as her form faded just a bit more. "She may be a trial to you, as she grows. There has never been such a one as her; there will be no one to advise you on her particularities and peculiarities. You must truly understand what you are agreeing to—as much as any of us *can* understand—before you give your assent."

"And if I don't agree?" I asked. "Would she go back to the Beyond?" *Could Mom come back in her place then after all?* I thought wildly, even though I knew she couldn't; even though I had just told Dad that it wouldn't work, it wouldn't help.

Brains are stupid.

Perrine probably couldn't read my mind, but she seemed to know every nuance of my thoughts. "She would return to the Beyond, yes, and you would have no daughter. Your mother Belladonna Isis will remain with us on our plane no matter your decision."

I sniffled and looked down at Rosemary. *Of course I'm not going to let you go, sweet pea*, I thought to her. *I'm just sorry you won't know your granny. She was a wonderful witch—a wonderful mother.*

Rosemary looked up at me gravely. A single tear formed in the corner of her eye.

Somehow, that was what undid me. I burst out sobbing, leaking tears all over my daughter. After a minute, my father pulled us both into his arms and wept with us.

A long while later, when we regained something of our composure, I wiped my eyes and looked up. Mother Perrine was gone.

My father cleared his throat. "We have many guests," he said, "and I have no partner to help me look after them. I hate to ask…"

"Dad, please," I said, getting to my feet and hefting Rosemary onto my hip. The hubbub of the crowded room next to us seemed to only be growing louder, and more joyous. "I will help in any way I can—we need to find out where all these folk came from initially, and how to get them back there."

"If they have a 'there' to get back to," he said, frowning. "I saw Augustus and Lorenna in their midst; they were taken from the Old Country decades ago. I am quite certain they do not wish to return there, even if their dwelling were still unoccupied, which I doubt."

"Right, uh, hmm." This didn't seem like a huge problem to me—couldn't they just stay with Logan?—but I took his larger point. We had a lot of misplaced people all at once, from who knew where. And we didn't know what condition their minds might be in. Logan seemed pretty much herself, when I'd talked to her in the in-between space, but was she entirely restored back on this plane? Or had what Gregorio taken from them all been a permanent reduction?

Too many questions, and we weren't going to answer them hiding in the butler's pantry.

"Let's go see to your guests," I said to my father.

"Our guests," he corrected, and put a gentle arm on my shoulder as he ushered us out.

—— CHAPTER FIFTEEN ——

Back in the main room, however, there wasn't a whole lot for us to do. Niad, bless her shriveled little heart, had channeled her inner bossypants and arranged for big platters of food and copious drink to be procured from somewhere; Leonora was organizing Gracie and several of my coven sisters to speak to every returned witch and warlock, welcoming them back, taking down their names and personal details. "Oh good," she said when she saw us. "Lucas, you have many unused bedrooms on the second floor; I would like to place some of the weaker returned ones in those, if I may."

She didn't couch it as a question. My father quickly agreed.

Manka was examining as many returnees as she could, and Nora had arrived as well, looking at others.

I didn't see Jeremy, or Sebastian, or Flavius. Perhaps they had already been moved to the bedrooms?

"I do not see that there is much for us to do," my father said to me quietly, as we stood watching this bustle of activity.

"No, I—" I started, and then noticed the two people standing in a quiet corner, looking lost and a little frightened. "Yes, actually, come with me."

Dad followed me through the crowded room to the window seat at the front of the house. Christine looked up; her frown lines quickly vanished. "Callie, oh!" she said, leaping to her feet. "They said you were okay, but nobody knew where you were exactly, and…"

I hugged her, and then she took the baby from me as Raymond got up and crushed the very breath out of me. "Oh jeez Callie," he said into my ear, his voice husky. "I mean, jeez."

"I'm fine." *Well, not really, but…* I squeezed him in return and then drew back to look into his eyes. "Are *you* guys all right?" I asked.

Christine just shook her head, and stroked Rose's curls. She looked even paler than usual.

"I am now," Raymond said. "But *jeez.*"

"What happened? Oh—sorry, this is my father, Lucas. Dad, this is Raymond, and his sister Christine."

My father politely shook their hands and formally welcomed them to his home, and didn't even send me a silent message asking *So this is your baby's human father?*, which I appreciated.

"One of your sisters came and told us you were gone, and that we should drive back to the city, maybe help there," Raymond said. "We got to the address where she said, and there was just a big smokin' crater in the ground!"

"Not that we saw it exactly," Christine said. "Mostly we just saw dozens of police cars and ambulances and yellow crime scene tape."

"I saw enough smoke," Raymond grumbled. "And I heard those cops talking."

Christine swallowed audibly. "It was terrifying. We didn't understand. We thought you'd…"

"I see. I'm so sorry, you guys; I wish I could have told you what happened, but…"

"After we got here, Niadine told us about your mother," Christine said, more quietly.

I brushed away another rush of tears; my father turned his head aside for a moment.

"Oh, I mean, and your wife," Christine added, to my dad. "We're *so* sorry for your loss."

"Thank you," I said. "I…I don't think I really believe it yet."

"Neither do I," said my father, recovering his composure. He glanced behind us, but still looked lost. As if he couldn't decide whether mingling with a bunch of happy rescued souls or talking with a couple of humans was more impossible.

I put a hand on his arm. "Dad, maybe you should go, um, upstairs and see whether Leonora needs any help figuring out the guest rooms?" *And maybe take a little time for yourself?* I added ætherically.

He nodded. "Good idea, I shall." He inclined his head to Raymond and Christine. "It was a pleasure meeting you both." Then he left us.

I sat on the window seat beside Christine; Raymond crowded next to me. He seemed to want to hold my hand or wrap me in his arms or something. He settled for kind of leaning against me, and making goofy smiling faces at Rosemary, who blew spit bubbles at him.

"I'm sorry I couldn't get word to you guys," I told them, once more. "I wish there was a way to communicate with you like witch-kind does to each other."

"I thought you might call," Raymond said.

"I tried, from the library basement, but there was no service. Then when we got to Gregorio's house, things, well, got pretty crazy."

"A lot of things have been crazy lately," Christine said.

Understatement of the century.

"So, what happens now?" Raymond asked. "The bad guy's all defeated and everyone, um, everyone who's still here, is okay now?"

I gave him a weak smile. "Honestly, sweetheart, I have no idea what happens now, or if folks are okay." I gestured to the busy room. "I think everyone's trying to figure that out."

As if to underscore my words, the front door opened and in walked Sapphire, along with a half-dozen witches from her cattery coven, laden with grocery bags. "Where are the hungry cats?" Sapphire cried. "We're here to help!"

"I know how to feed cats," Christine said, suddenly smiling. She handed Rosemary to me. "I'm going to make myself useful."

By the end of the day, we had all made ourselves useful—even Rosemary, whose contribution was bringing smiles to the faces of witches who were not depleted enough to require medical care from the healers, but who were too wiped out or lost to retake charge of their own lives just yet.

Many of the witches and all of the warlocks (there being far fewer of them) had found their way somewhere—even a temporary somewhere, on their way to figuring out where they were going to end up. Sometimes this came with tearful reunions with loved ones who had thought they were lost forever; others made their way back to quiet, solitary existences with their cats. A few elected to move forward to the Beyond, mostly those who had been trapped the longest. "I do not feel as though I belong here anymore," a soft-spoken crone with many long grey braids confided to me. She had no familiar with her; the cat had probably already long since gone ahead. "This world is not my world."

Every one of those who remained was grateful to our little makeshift team of rescuers and insisted on thanking me profusely, even though I explained again and again that I was just part of a whole group of folks who had helped, and that we couldn't have done any of it without the direct assistance of some pretty powerful entities from the Beyond. "I mean, Perrine literally walked in there and set you all free, remember?" I found myself saying more than once.

Staying busy helped keep the worst of the grief at bay. I was able to be distracted for whole minutes at a time as I refilled food platters, cleared dishes into the kitchen (which Petrana had commandeered and was washing up like, well, like a super helpful and tireless golem), scritched cats, and exchanged quiet words with grateful folk.

For most of the afternoon, Logan was never far from my side, though we didn't have much chance to talk. My heart was torn asunder by the loss of my mom, but seeing Logan's bright blue eyes under her blond bangs put balm on that wound.

"I am so sorry I was such a bubblehead when I first got here," she said to me now, as we stood by the fireplace. Someone had lit a fire, which emanated a cheerful warmth and threatened to make me remember how little sleep I'd gotten in the past few days. "If I had known about your mom…"

"But you didn't, and I am still overjoyed to have you back," I said to her. "As I told you hours ago, more than once."

She leaned over and put her arm around me, pulling me into a side hug. I rested my head on her shoulder.

"And then Jeremy…" She sighed. "I talked to him. I know… what happened."

I turned and looked at her; she gave me a shy smile, then cast her eyes down.

"I'm *such* a bubblehead," she said.

"You are *not* a bubblehead. You've been effectively dead for nearly a year. Of course you wouldn't have known about anything that happened while you were gone." I shrugged. "And I don't know… what he and I are. If anything."

"Callie, he told me you guys were about to sign a contract."

"But only because you weren't in the picture. And that was all before…" I shook my head. "Logan, you and he had something real—you were just getting started. I think you should give that a chance."

"I don't know if that's what he wants," she said, very quietly.

"You can't—"

"I know, I know," she said, trying to sound brave. "I know it's too soon for any of us to know about anything, but I'm just so…" She held my gaze. "I feel like the worst friend in the whole wide world, only thinking about myself. But I'm just such a jumble inside—so happy to be back, so sad for your mom, so excited to have my parents back here, and that you have a daughter, so confused about how that all happened…"

"That doesn't sound like 'thinking only of yourself' to me," I said with a smile. "And I'm a jumble inside too. I think probably everyone is. Jeremy too."

She shrugged. "Yeah." Then she smiled back at me. "Callie, I knew you'd come to save us. I mean, yes, I heard you about Perrine; but you were the one who came to us first. And you were the one who figured out how we could control Gregorio's taking our essence."

"But that didn't help," I protested. "He figured it out and we had to turn that off. He even took your father away as punishment."

Her smile grew. "Yes, and no."

"What do you mean?"

"Yes, we had to undo what you'd done—and it was scary when he took Dad—but once you showed me how it worked, Mom and I were able to work on it ourselves, quietly. We learned so much, Callie. We manipulated our own energy, and that of each other; we even made changes to the space around us. Not just the illusions I used to play with, but real changes." Her face glowed with pleasure. "We found our way back to the others and were starting to teach them how to work it when Mother Perrine showed up—and with all our cats!" She reached down and petted Willson, curled at her feet and purring loudly. "This is the first day of the rest of my life. And I am so grateful for it, and for *you*," she said, straightening up and looking into my eyes. "Thank you."

I nodded, feeling far too many emotions to even put into words. I had my best friend back. I'd lost my mother. We'd defeated Gregorio, and saved witchkind.

I'd lost my mother.

I hugged Logan, hard, and whispered, "You're welcome."

Late in the evening, Raymond found me in the kitchen. "So, um, I think Christine and I are gonna head out, if you don't need anything more?"

"Oh gosh, you've both done so much," I said, rushing over and pulling him into a hug. "'Thank you' seems completely inadequate, but, well, thank you."

He squeezed me back and stroked my hair. I inhaled the scent of him, losing myself for a moment in the comforting familiarity of his arms.

"You're welcome, Callie," he whispered into my ear. "You're always welcome."

I nodded against his shoulder, blinking back yet more tears.

After a long moment, he released me. "Call me soon?"

"I will," I promised.

I walked him to the front door and said goodbye to Christine. She too offered to help more—"though I do need to get back to work tomorrow," she added—and I assured her that we had it handled.

It seemed as though half of San Francisco's witchkind had passed through this house today. Amazingly, almost nobody had blinked at sharing the work with humans.

After they'd gone, I went back into the kitchen, but Petrana, Sirianna, Geneva, and Hyacinth had finished the cleanup. "Go rest, Callie," Siri insisted. "Your dad went to his room an hour ago. We've got this."

"I...okay. I will." I knew I was exhausted—beyond exhausted. But I wasn't quite done yet.

I had left the baby with Logan and her parents a while ago. Now I checked on them, and they insisted they were intending to kidnap her and never return her to me. "She is the sweetest thing ever," Lorenna said, her eyes shining with joy.

"So well behaved," Augustus agreed.

Logan just beamed at me, and her parents, and my baby.

So I made my way upstairs—not to the second floor, where my parents' bedroom and the big formal guest rooms were, but to the third floor. A former attic or perhaps servants' quarters, this floor had several small rooms, including my own childhood bedroom (by my own insistent choice), and it was where I still felt most at home in this big formal house.

It was also where the healers had put both Jeremy and Sebastian. After some discussion, Nora and Manka had agreed that Manka would take Flavius, along with some of the most profoundly afflicted returned witches, to their home for deeper healing, but anyone who didn't need such critical care was being stashed here under Nora's watchful eye.

I met Nora at the doorway of the first room at the top of the stairs. I sent my senses inside and saw Sebastian asleep.

"How is he?" I asked quietly.

She frowned, thinking. "He is quite weakened—the ring had worked its way deeply into his psyche—but I believe he shall make a full, or nearly full, recovery. Fortunately, he is young, and his personality is generally positive and upbeat."

"He's a good warlock," I said. "A good man."

Nora nodded. "Intelligent and empathetic, and he was only using the device to try to do good in the world, by defeating evil." She gave a small, wry smile. "Despite all cautions to the contrary."

"I told him, like, a million times to not touch that thing," I said. "I wish I'd never given it to him, but I didn't know what else to do… it came off me after I'd given birth, and I just didn't know who I could trust with it." I looked the healer in the eye while I made this admission, painful though it was. Why hadn't I trusted her or Manka with it? I couldn't articulate it, exactly; Sebastian was not only my friend, but we were already working on trying to untangle all the mysteries together. And he was a warlock; I had felt he might have a better handle on a warlock-created device.

It had been the wrong choice, clearly. I was just glad it hadn't been a fatal one for my friend.

"May I see him?" I asked Nora.

"Yes, though you won't get much sense out of him, if he even wakes up."

I nodded and pushed the door open quietly. Elnor snaked in ahead of me, nose busy as ever. She did the room's corners and then approached the bed, sniffing at Sebastian.

"How does his essence seem, kitten?" I asked her.

She turned her yellow eyes to me and then continued sniffing the blankets.

I pulled up a chair and set it by the bed, then sat down. Sebastian looked even paler than Christine had when she'd arrived earlier, and even more diminished, though part of that had to be because he was sound asleep. His hair was matted to his forehead with sweat, but his features were at peace. "Hey," I whispered, resisting the urge to touch him. Sleep was restorative, and probably the best thing for him; I didn't want to interrupt that.

He slept on.

I sat by him for a while, then told myself I'd have to be content with what I'd seen the moment my mother had taken the ring—that moment of clarity in Sebastian's eyes, before all the rest of the hell had broken loose and everything had gone so terribly, grievously wrong.

And I would have to be content with Nora's prognosis. Sebastian would heal.

I rose quietly and let myself out, then stood in the familiar hallway, seeking the room Jeremy rested in.

The healers had put him just next to my old bedroom. Did they know? I hadn't had much call for healer attention when I was a witchlet; I didn't think they'd ever visited me in this house. In any event, the room he was in was a small but cozy one, tucked under the eaves on the north side of the house. Its small windows let in a peekaboo view of one of the towers of the Golden Gate Bridge, but only if you leaned into the deep sill and craned your neck around a little.

I didn't do any of that, just stepped in and looked at the green-eyed warlock resting on the single bed.

"Calendula," he said, and pushed himself up on his elbows.

"Don't get up," I said, walking over to the bed. "I just wanted to see how you're doing—I know you need more rest."

He blinked at me but lay back on his pillows. "I'm…quite exhausted, you're right."

"They told me your father put a bunch of spells in you, but that they'll slowly leach away, and you'll be your old self after a while."

He sighed and shook his head, though not in denial of my words. "I should have known," he said quietly. "What a fool I was."

"How could you have known? We all were fooled by—"

"No, I *really* should have known," he cut me off, suddenly bitter. "All the work he and I did together—even the work he helped me with in modifying my study in your house—every time I would cast a spell, he'd be right there with me, reinforcing the spell, altering it slightly, showing me a better, stronger, more efficient way to do things." He exhaled through his nose. "I never even thought to examine the magic he put in me while he did that. I was just so happy that my father was finally paying attention to me—was finally *parenting* me—I didn't question a bit of it. I never even wondered why he called me to San Francisco in the first place. And I call myself intelligent!" He turned his face away from me, glaring at the wall.

I sat down on the bed beside him; Elnor jumped up as well and climbed up him to sniff in his face. Jeremy couldn't help but smile at her as he scritched her ears.

"Please don't do this to yourself," I said to Jeremy. "We all should have known, and we didn't, and we do now, and we will build a better world going forward. Okay?"

"If I had asked more questions, better questions, and asked them sooner, your mother would still be here with us," he said, very quietly.

I bit my lip, ready for more tears to come, but I seemed to be out of them at the moment. Instead, I just gazed back at him.

"I am sorry, Callie," he whispered.

I reached out and took his hand. It was cool, and a little clammy. "I am sorry, too," I said.

He nodded, squeezed my hand, then let it go. "Logan came to see me."

"Yes," I said. "She told me."

"Did she tell you that I shared everything that has passed between us?"

"Yes."

He watched me. "I really don't know what to think. About, well, any of it."

"We have time to figure it out," I said softly. "I don't think I can... think about any of that right now, though."

"Of course not." He took my hand again, and we were silent together.

I sat with him until he drifted off into a restless sleep. Then I left him and stood a long moment in the hallway, wishing I could just go crawl into my own teenage bed and hide under the covers until my mom called me down to dinner.

But my narrow childhood bed was in the coven house now, and my mother was in the Beyond, so I took a deep breath and—despite what I'd promised Siri, despite how tired I was—went back down to see what else I could be helpful with.

The next few days were a confusing blur. There was still some work to do getting the returned witches settled, but there were plenty of hands available for it, so there wasn't a lot for me personally to handle. Plus, everyone kept telling me to take care of myself. *Go home and rest, Callie. You've suffered a terrible loss. We've got this.*

I knew they meant well, and I did certainly catch up on that missing sleep. But the fact of the matter was, when I was at home, I was alone—except for my golem and my cat and my baby, of course. Which, as much as I loved them all, they also didn't need me to do a lot.

My cell phone was functional and fully charged, but I didn't call Raymond. Not just yet. I wasn't even entirely sure why. I just... wasn't ready.

Mostly, I grieved.

I did visit Dad twice, thinking there would be comfort in our shared grief. The first time, he had clearly made an effort to welcome me, to acknowledge how much we had both lost. But it was so obvious that he felt his loss was far greater than mine.

And could I blame him? I had lost my mother, far too young, yes; but it is the way of things that one's parents go Beyond before us. He, on the other hand, had lost his partner, the love of his life. His other half.

The second time I went to the house, he met me at the door, looking all of his six hundred-plus years. "I am sorry, Calendula, but I just cannot...see you right now," he said. He closed his eyes and turned away for a moment. "You look so much like her."

I burst into tears. "Oh Dad."

He shook his head and looked back at me. "I do love you, my daughter. And for your sake, I promise not to do anything...drastic... at least not for a time. But I have not yet managed to convince myself that I should not join her."

I nodded, weeping, and fled back home on the ley line.

— CHAPTER SIXTEEN —

I was at home when Nora called to me. *If it is not too much of a burden right now, Calendula, may we ask your assistance with something?*

Oh, anything, I answered at once. *I'm just moping around the house here.*

A pause. *I am sorry to hear that, but glad to have your help.*

I'll be right over. Then I added, *Just me?*

Yes, please, though you may bring Rosemary if you need.

I left the baby with Petrana and headed over, stepping off the ley line down the block from the healers' house, then walking up to their door. Nora met me before I could knock, and welcomed me inside.

She led me down a hall and into the treatment area. "Oh!" I said, stopping in surprise.

"Hey," Sebastian said. He sat in a wooden chair, looking weak but entirely himself, I was delighted to see.

I rushed over to him and took his hand. "How are you feeling?"

He smiled and looked abashed. "Better every day, if you're asking about how I am physically." I raised an eyebrow, inviting him to go on. "I also feel pretty foolish."

"I told you not to play with that ring. But do you listen? No, you don't," I chided him, but I couldn't stop grinning. I was just so happy to have my friend back.

Behind me, Nora cleared her throat, and then Manka stepped

into the room. "He is recovering, though a bit more slowly than we would have liked to see," Manka said. "Which is why we'd like your help with what we must do next."

I turned to the healers, puzzled. "What can I do?"

"Come this way, both of you."

Manka led us to another patient room, where Flavius Winterheart lay on a cot.

"Is he *still* unconscious?" I asked, aghast. It had been over a week!

"By design," Nora said. "Every time we've tried to awaken him, we have found…" She bit her lip and shook her head. "Something strange and wrong, and quite foreign to our scrying."

Again, I wasn't sure how I could help. "I'm not a healer," I said. "But…?"

"But you do have experience with burning away magical essence inside a body. Inside *this* body, specifically," Manka said gravely.

"Oh. Oh, no," I said, backing away from Flavius. "No, don't make me do a cautery again—not now, not to him!"

Sebastian put a gentle hand on my arm. "It's not a cautery, it won't be the same. And I'll do it with you. I…I put magic into him, but magic that doesn't belong. But I'm not strong enough to undo what I did." He looked at me beseechingly; his face was so full of pain, and guilt, and sorrow. "Callie, I did this to him, and I need to make it right. We've tried, but it doesn't work with me alone, and the healers aren't getting a handle on it either. We thought…since you'd done work in his channels before, maybe you could at least try? With me?"

I looked down at the unconscious Flavius. What this poor man had been through… And at my hands, however unwittingly; and then at Sebastian's, even more unwittingly (for Sebastian had surely been out of his wits). "I can try," I said. "Though I haven't any idea how."

"That, we have worked out," Sebastian said, looking relieved. "Just sit down here beside him, and I'll talk you through it."

"We will all talk you through it," Nora added, putting a hand on my shoulder. As ever, her touch was so soothing, so reassuring. "You feel rested, which is good. Would you like any nourishment before we get started? You should be at your full strength, to make up for Sebastian's impairment."

"I had lunch not long ago," I told her. "I'm good."

We started with me just exploring his channels without attempting to do anything to them. Taking his measure. At first, I didn't find anything there. I could see where Jeremy and I had burned the magic out of him, but not where anything had been put back in…wait…

"Ugh," I said, recoiling as I yanked my hands from Flavius.

Sebastian looked at me apologetically. "You see it, then."

"I certainly do." I looked up at the healers. "Was this same sort of energy inside Sebastian as well?"

"Similar, though not precisely the same," Manka said.

"No wonder you were not yourself," I said to my friend.

He looked even more abashed. "I…don't remember a whole lot of it. I just remember feeling powerful, and, well, *right*. Powerfully good, I mean."

"That is not how it looked from out here," I said, dryly.

"Believe me, I do get that now."

I shrugged my shoulders, hard, trying to shake off the icky feeling. "All right, I see what's going on in there. So, what do we do about it?"

Sebastian glanced up at Manka, who explained. "You two will, as it were, walk through the channels together. Sebastian will find everywhere that he pushed the energy; you will loosen it and ease it out of there. We managed to handle some of it, but, well, you are more powerful than either of us, Calendula, and as we said, you've worked in his body before." She looked at Nora, who nodded. "We will both be here as backup, but if the two of you can do the working, that will be cleanest, and have the greatest chance of success. Does this make sense to you?"

"Mostly, I think," I said. "If I need to stop before we're done, is that going to be okay? Or would it ruin the process?"

"You can take breaks," Nora said. "It would be best if the breaks came after you push a piece out, rather than loosening it and leaving it to flow within."

"Right. Got it." I looked at Sebastian. "I guess I'm ready, whenever you are?"

"No time like the present." He gave me his familiar grin again, and that was so comforting, I suddenly knew it was going to be all right.

And it was, almost completely. We stumbled a bit at first, but then we found our stride. The healers were correct: this was not at all like a cautery. It was a gentle, healing process. The feeling of the nasty power within Flavius was disgusting, but loosening and removing it was deeply satisfying. It was like pulling weeds, if the weeds were also scorpions, and poison, and despair.

"Who creates such a terrible piece of work?" I asked, during one break. Nora massaged my hands, sending gentle healing energy along with her touch.

"That's a rhetorical question, right?" Sebastian asked. "We all know where it came from."

I shuddered. "To think I wore that ring for months and months…" I said, and not for the first time.

"Clearly it was able to take on many different aspects," Manka said. "Gold, being so inert and so malleable, could carry a variety of spells for a variety of purposes. You believe that Dr. Andromedus gave it to you so he could monitor and manipulate you; but that does not mean it didn't contain other, more insidious energies." She gave Sebastian a significant look. "Energies set to be released when someone tried to wield the ring's power against its maker, for example."

"Yes, I know, I know," he said softly, but he was smiling. "Shall we start again?" he asked me.

"Yes, I'm ready." Nora released my hands; I stretched my fingers, then made fists. "Yep: good to go."

It took the better part of an hour, and I did start to get hungry by the end, but then at last, we removed the last of the evil energy that flowed through Flavius's channels. Sebastian and I made one more trip through to be sure. "He's clean," I said.

Sebastian nodded and leaned back. "I think so."

Both healers came to check for themselves before concurring. "Good work," Manka said at last. "Are you sure you have no interest in studying the healing arts, Calendula?"

I smiled at them both. "I think my efforts are better spent at the lab bench. I have a terrible bedside manner."

The healers chuckled politely, rather than contradicting me.

"But in all honesty," I went on, more serious now, "I have decided not to rule anything out at this point. I'm...taking some time right now to figure out what my life really should look like."

"That is wise," Manka said. "You have been through a tremendous upheaval, and a profound loss."

"Yes." I nodded. "But not just that: I've had to start rethinking everything I thought I knew—about the world, about witchkind, about myself. About my daughter; about my family, my coven, my career, my magic. So, I don't *think* I want to become a healer...but it would be beyond foolish to say I'll never change my mind." I thought a moment, then added, "Or my heart. But I don't actually feel a heart-draw toward healing either."

Nora and Manka both nodded slowly, watching me with odd expressions...was that pride? Nora just said, "Well, you know where to find us if that happens."

"I do." Suddenly awkward, I glanced down at Flavius. He didn't look outwardly changed, but I could sense the energy shift within him.

Manka followed my gaze, then turned to Nora. "Let us remove the spell of sleeping upon him and welcome him back to the world."

A minute later, he shifted and rubbed his eyes. "Am I...where am I?" he asked blearily.

Nora leaned over him. "You are in the healers' home, and you have been cleansed of the poison-magic that was put inside you."

He blinked, confused, then spotted Sebastian and his eyes widened. "You!"

Sebastian lowered his head. "I am cleansed as well, my friend. And I apologize most profoundly for what I did to you. I was not myself, which is no excuse, but it is the reason."

"I..." Flavius shook his head, still looking uncertain and a bit frightened. "We're healed? Both of us?"

"Yes, you are," Manka said.

"Not only that," Nora added, "but the warlock Gregorio

Andromedus has been removed from this plane of existence. He has been taken to the Beyond and shall not trouble us here any longer."

"Uh…wow, that's great!" He struggled to sit up a bit in the bed, but he was very weakened. "That's wonderful! How did it happen?"

I blinked back the threat of tears and stepped toward the room's door. "If you guys don't need me anymore…"

"Of course," Nora said softly, touching my shoulder. "Go, nourish yourself and get some more rest. We will tell the story."

"Thank you," I whispered.

Sebastian caught up to me at the front door. "Do you want company, or to be alone?"

I smiled weakly at him. "Alone for right now, I think; but I have missed my friend very much, and I would love to hang out…soon."

He pulled me in for a quick hug. "Just say the word, and I will be there."

Back home, Petrana met me at the door. "Shall I make you a grilled cheese sandwich?"

"I…" I stared at her. "Yes. A thousand times yes. That's exactly what I want, and I had no idea until this moment."

She gave me a small smile and headed to the kitchen.

Five minutes later, I sat at the kitchen table, my face and fingers greasy with butter as Petrana stood at the stove, grilling a second sandwich. Rosemary was down for a nap; Elnor was lurking around my ankles, clearly hoping that I wouldn't be able to stuff the entire second grilled cheese inside me.

I gave it about fifty-fifty odds, myself. Maybe sixty-forty, in my favor.

Petrana brought me the second sandwich. I took a delicious, gooey bite, then said, "How did you know I was hungry?"

She gave the golem-equivalent of a shrug. "I felt it, Mistress."

"But you don't feel, per se…" I started. "Do you?"

"I do not feel physical sensations or emotions in the way that you do, to the best of my understanding. But you are my maker, and your magic animates me. We have done many workings together, and you have taught me all that I know of the world and how it operates, and particularly how magical beings function. Further, I knew that you had been called to the healers' home to help them with something; it was easy to guess that it was likely something involving magic, and that it would probably be taxing, would drain your energy. Energy, which is replenished by food, particularly high-calorie food. In addition, I know that there is an emotional component to food. Grilled cheese sandwiches are both caloric and emotionally nourishing. But I didn't know for certain that you would want one, so that is why I asked."

I just stared at her as she laid this all out. Then I took another emotionally nourishing bite of my sandwich and said, "You are showing so much more initiative all the time, Petrana."

"Is that a good thing? Is that what you want of me?"

"Blessed Mother, yes," I said quickly. "I'm just…surprised, I guess; or not surprised exactly, but I don't really understand how it all works." I shook my head in wonder. "Do not for a minute think I am complaining. If you hadn't gone after Gregorio with a snack plate, I don't think we would have defeated him and sent him Beyond."

She gazed back at me. "That was not entirely successful, as you well know. I did not intend for the confrontation to cause your mother to be taken with him."

"I know. Nobody intended that—except maybe Gregorio himself, if he'd been able to finesse it that way. No, that was a decision she made herself, in the spur of the moment—but that moment only happened because you created it. You saved witchkind, Petrana."

"Not alone, by a large measure," she said evenly. I knew this wasn't modesty, false or otherwise; my golem wouldn't possess that emotion any more than she would any of the others. "We all saved witchkind, your mother more than most, but it was us all working together that brought it about."

"Yes," I said slowly, then took another bite. At my feet, Elnor began to look a little more concerned. "All of us. Witches, warlocks. Humans and cats and Beyonders. Oldsters and youngsters. And a golem," I added with a smile.

"And your golem," she agreed, giving just the slightest emphasis to the *your*.

"And my golem." I chewed in silence, thinking it over. "You're Rosemary's golem too, though, aren't you?"

"What do you mean?"

"She worked through you to bring us back from Caspar. As happy as I am that it happened, I've never quite understood *how* it did."

"I do not know either, more than I have already told you. You needed help, and quickly; she knew that, and then I knew that, and then she made it so." She paused a moment. "She is a creature of the Beyond, however much of that power she had to set aside to return here. The Beyond is not like this plane."

"No, it is not," I agreed. In a corner of my awareness, I sensed Rosemary upstairs in her cradle, stirring. But she did not awaken. I returned my attention to the kitchen. "I asked you once, 'What do you want?' You explained to me then, that as a creature of my making and not a living being, you did not want, could not want."

"Yes, that is true."

"But is it?" I pressed. "Is it still true, I mean? You've grown in so many other ways. Do you still want nothing?"

"I want to serve you, my mistress," she said. "That is my purpose: the purpose for which you created me. I do not have feelings as you do, but I do know that when I am helpful to you, it gives me a greater sense of rightness than if I were to go against your wishes, or to be a trial to you." A ghost of a smile. "Not that I would have any way of being able to go against your wishes, you understand. But as a thought experiment, I can see that that would be undesirable to me."

As a thought experiment. Since when did golems run thought experiments? "I am glad to hear that, and it does make sense," I said. "But…" I stopped, trying to figure out how to articulate my question. "Because you are growing and evolving, it seems plausible to me that that might change somewhere along the way. That you might begin to want something that was not just to do with me—something for yourself."

"I suppose anything is possible, though I do not anticipate it," she said.

I nodded. "Well. In case it does, I want you to promise me to tell me about it."

"Of course, Mistress," she said at once.

"I mean it. Don't just be obedient, or worry that you will annoy or inconvenience me," I insisted. "I want to hear about it, okay?"

"Yes, Mistress," she said, more slowly, gazing back at me. "One item does occur to me," she added, after a long moment.

"Yes?"

"Golems are, to my understanding, intended to be temporary creations. Built for a specific purpose, then unmade when that purpose is done."

"That is what I have heard as well," I said. She was going somewhere with this. And never ceasing to impress me.

She nodded. "And of course, as my creator, you have the full and unquestioned rights to determine my existence or non-existence."

"Okay," I agreed.

"Should I become less useful to you, or a burden in any way, you should give no thought to the question of unmaking me. I will have served my purpose, and that will be as it should be."

I nodded, telling myself to let her get it out in her own way. "All right."

"However." She continued to gaze at me. "All else being equal, and assuming that I do remain useful to you, I find that I should prefer to remain in existence."

Good job, Petrana! I thought, and gave her a warm smile. "I, too, should prefer that you remain in existence," I assured her. "It is my intention to keep you so."

"Thank you, Mistress Callie," she said, formally.

"You are most welcome. Thank *you*." Then I took the final bite of my sandwich. Before Elnor could object, I said to Petrana, "Go ahead and grill one more, and put half of it on a dish for this poor neglected cat before she starves to death."

"Yes, Mistress Callie," she said, with a definite smile.

— CHAPTER SEVENTEEN —

Witchkind funeral practices, like so many other of our rites and customs, differ from humankind ones. Mostly this is because we do not die, per se; we move to the Beyond, and even this is most usually voluntary, and planned well in advance. So we do not generally gather to mourn a loss, but rather to recognize the accomplishments and gifts of the one who is planning to move on.

"Planning to": because the usual practice is to celebrate the life *before* the witch or warlock leaves, with a smaller, more private ceremony after the departed has gone to the Beyond (often coinciding, in the case of a coven, with our first contact with our late sister).

Of course, unexpected passage does occasionally happen even in witchkind, whether by accident or violence, illness or suicide. When that occurs, if the departed was a warlock, or an "important," more public-facing witch such as a coven mother or, say, the consort of an Elder, the Convocation of Elders holds a formal ritual of memorial and honor, with speeches and catering and the like. When a more private witch moves on, her friends and loved ones gather in the manner that feels best to them.

All of which is to say that we were all at something of a loss in planning my mother's funeral.

First of all, of course, the Convocation of Elders itself was in disarray. Gregorio had been its leader; my father was the second-most senior member. Most of the Elders had revered Gregorio, or had at least acted as though they did; it was impossible to tell if any of them suspected what he had been up to. Certainly, every last warlock among them professed shock, dismay, and horror when the truth came out, and distanced themselves from their late leader, while casting aspersions on one another.

I didn't want anything to do with any of them, and thankfully, neither did my father. Unfortunately, my father's deep grieving meant that he was too undone to even tell me what he wanted to do about a service for Mom.

Not that I was in much better shape. Most of the time, all I really wanted to do was curl up and hide—sleep, take care of my daughter and my cat, and recover from all that had happened. I'd put off Sebastian when he'd contacted me offering to get together a few days after we'd healed Flavius, and I had even brushed aside several of Logan's attempts to reach out, making what even I knew were poor excuses. I missed my friends, and was so unspeakably grateful that they were returned to me, but…I didn't know how to be with them. It all just made me feel exhausted.

But we needed to do something—I *wanted* to do something to publicly remember Mother. A memorial service was an important step in saying goodbye: with community, with ritual, with loved ones. It was a comfort to those left behind.

It felt like a step was missing, each day that went by and we had not gathered to remember my mother.

Oddly, this differed from how it had felt to me during the long months that Logan was gone. That had been sad, but also mysterious, and not without hope. Particularly when I began to unravel the mystery, and it seemed at least possible that she might return.

Mom was not returning. She had not contacted me from the Beyond yet, and she might never; but I knew she was there. Perrine and later Nementhe had confirmed it.

So I intended to plan something, and dithered, and set it aside, and went back to bed…until Leonora called to me one day and summoned me (gently, but firmly) to the coven house.

"What are your plans for the remembrance for Belladonna Isis?"

she asked. We were seated in the second parlor, along with several of my sisters—Sirianna, Pearl, Peony, and of course Niad. "I have heard nothing from the Elders, and people are beginning to wonder."

"I...I don't know," I said. "I can't think about it without getting overwhelmed." Tears stung my eyes, for the millionth time. "The Elders are worthless. And Dad is...even more lost than me." And I didn't want to push him. I wanted him to stick around. Selfish of me, perhaps, but...there we were.

"Oh, daughter," Leonora said softly, looking surprised, even shocked. Then she actually rose from her chair and came to me. I got up and stepped into her embrace. She held me a long time, rocking slightly. "Oh, daughter," she said again, after a long moment. "I should not have left you to bear this alone so long. I imagined that if you needed us, you would come to us." She pulled back and gave me a sad smile. "Logandina Fleur told me that she had spoken to you of the remembrance, and you assured her that you were handling it. But you do have your streak of independence, so naturally you would think you were alone in this."

"I...um..." I couldn't very well deny it, could I? "Logan came to you?"

"Yes, she did, because you are *not* alone," she said firmly. "She is your dear friend, and we are your family, and we *all* love you." My sisters echoed her, even Niad. "I am your mother as well," Leonora went on, "and I care deeply for your happiness."

"Thank you," I sniffled, wondering what happiness would even feel like.

"I was honoring your independence, and I see what a mistake that was. Of course you are lost. Now, sit down and let us come up with a plan together."

It did not take long, once fully functioning brains were added to the mix. Leonora and my sisters told me I didn't have to do anything at all except say yes or no to their proposed details; they would handle it all.

"Logandina has offered to help with anything too," Sirianna said to me. "But she...didn't want to keep pestering you."

Oh, Logan. "I missed her so much, but I feel…just helpless right now," I admitted. "Like I'm no kind of friend."

Sirianna gave me a gentle smile. "She understands."

Does she? I felt awful.

My sisters and Leonora made short work of the memorial arrangements. A call was put in to Mom's old coven mother, Isadora, and the service was soon scheduled for the following Tuesday at midnight, at her house.

I feared that Dad would not even want to accompany me to the memorial, but he put on his soberest dark suit and a deep red tie, and came for me at eleven thirty. He did not bring his car, as I'd thought he might, but instead escorted me on the ley lines to Isadora's lovely coven house, high in the hills north of the Berkeley campus. I debated whether to bring Rosemary, but finally left her at home in Petrana's care.

Most everyone was gathered by the time we got there. Isadora had cleared the downstairs of her house, stretching rooms and tucking furniture away to create a large open space. Witches and warlocks sipped tea or small cocktails and nibbled cookies, but the mood was quiet, not festive.

I wondered how many of the guests here had even really known my mother. Certainly, everyone had met her—she was the consort of an important Elder, and she and my father had thrown politically strategic parties all the time—but she had kept her circle of intimates small. Still, I was pleased at the large turnout. It felt right.

Isadora and Leonora led the ritual together. On the stroke of midnight, the lights dimmed and we all sank to the floor where we stood. Dad, who had stuck close beside me, reached out and took my hand, squeezing it gently. Niad sat on my other side, and she took my other hand. I wasn't entirely sure how to feel about that, so I just accepted it.

There would be no Circle this evening, nothing so witch-centric as that; but there would also be no grand speeches like the warlocks favored. This was a hybrid service, for a hybrid group of mourners, in these odd and uncertain times.

Once we were seated and still, the two coven mothers chanted us into a light trance, and then each spoke of her personal knowledge of and affection for my mother. Leonora talked of Mom's gentleness and her kind and generous spirit, and of the strong and amazing daughter she had raised, before entrusting her (me!) to Leonora's coven. She praised Mom's seemingly effortless balance of remaining in my life as an involved and loving mother, while ceding any important authority to my coven mother.

It was *such* a Leonora thing to say, I thought.

Isadora spoke of my mom when she was younger, before I had ever known her, obviously. But even then, it seemed she'd had a quiet nature, and was content to work on collaborative projects in the house, and to study the tarot. She was a good cook, though never flashy or show-offish about her talent. She was always happy to teach others anything she had to share, and equally happy to learn from her sisters and friends as well.

The descriptions of her reminded me of Logan, in a way I had never quite put together before. No wonder we had become such close friends as witchlets. Still in my light trance, I let my gaze roam around the room, finding Logan and her parents near the open French doors at the back of the house. We had not yet spoken this evening—Dad and I had not been here long before the ceremony started—but it warmed my heart to see her.

I caught her eye; she smiled back at me, her eyes filled with love and sympathy.

Jeremy stood near Logan—not right next to her, but close enough to not seem random. Had they come together? He gave me a nod and a gentle smile. I nodded back, and returned my full attention to the service.

After both coven mothers spoke, they invited others to share their memories of my mother. A number of them did, painting a deeper, richer, fuller picture of her. Nearly everyone lamented her early leaving of this plane, and thanked her for her astonishing sacrifice, a gift that had saved us all.

Part of me felt comforted by this, and part of me felt angered. What about Dad and me? We didn't ask to give her up! *We* didn't choose to make that sacrifice!

And yet...it hadn't been our choice to make. Mom owned her own life, and she chose to take one huge, profound action that changed the world for so much the better, for so many of us. Would Dad and I be so selfish as to wish for her back, and Gregorio still among us, preying on the weaker members of our numbers, spreading evil among us all?

I sighed, and relaxed into the trance, letting the emotions and love that surrounded me soothe and comfort me. And by the time the last person finished speaking, I could feel Mom's presence settling over the room. She did not speak; I didn't even see her face; but I knew she was there. She touched our hearts from the Beyond, and I felt a tiny bit of the pain and anger and grief leaving me.

Mom, I will miss you forever, I thought. *But I am so grateful that I had you for a mother as long as I did.*

I slept soundly that night, without dreams.

When I woke late the next morning, I felt a small shift inside. My grief was still heavy, the loss was still achingly fresh; but the simplest tasks no longer seemed impossible.

I had lost Mom, but I had regained Logan. So why did I keep pushing her away?

I was up and dressed before I'd quite realized what I intended to do, and I was on the ley line, Rosemary strapped in her carrier on my back, before I could lose my momentum.

We emerged at the end of Logan's block. Rose giggled as she breathed the fresh city air, and her fingers grabbed for my braids. I let her yank on them, still feeling a little uncertain about treating an eminent Beyonder witch like an infant.

I knew I would have to get over that, or my child would grow up to be a horror. But all in good time.

We approached Logan's building; I sent my senses into it as usual, then paused, surprised. Had another magic user moved in? I felt Logan's presence, and that of her neighbor, the witch from New

Orleans I'd not yet met; but I also felt then a third—no, third and *fourth* set of energies.

Interesting. If magic users occupied even just a few more apartments, the balance of the building would likely tip. Humans would find it uncomfortable there and would move out.

Still, it was mostly human-occupied for now, so I rang the bell for Logan's apartment, though I sent her an ætheric message at the same time: *Logan, it's Callie.*

Come on up! she sent, and the door buzzed.

I took the stairs to the top floor and walked down the hall to her apartment. The door was open. "Callie!" Logan pulled me into a hug, disengaging before Rosemary could reach for her hair. She was already on to the ways of my daughter. "Come on in—can I make you some tea?"

"Sure," I said, looking around. Her apartment was warm and inviting, as it had always been—cheery pictures on the walls, a scent of toast and marmalade in the air, Willson curled up on the sofa—but there was something more here. It felt…more like a home, I thought. Not that it hadn't before, but there was a new element now.

She brought two steaming cups from her small kitchen and handed me one, taking hers to the couch. Willson stretched and snuggled against her.

I unstrapped Rosemary and took the guest chair across from the coffee table, settling the baby on my lap. When she was arranged, I looked up and smiled at my best friend and her familiar.

Logan sipped her tea and set it down. "That was a lovely service last night," she said.

"It was. Thank you for reaching out to Leonora."

She frowned slightly. "I wasn't sure…I didn't want to overstep."

"No—Logan, you *couldn't* overstep, not even if you tried." I swallowed a lump in my throat. "I'm just sorry I've been so—well, lost. I've been no kind of friend to you."

Her eyes widened and she shook her head. "Callie! You've just lost your mother. Believe me, I know…I know what that's like."

I started to answer, and then suddenly realized whose the extra energies were. "Are your folks here?" I looked around again, but it was a small apartment; unless they were hiding in her bedroom closet, I wasn't sure where they might be.

Now she grinned. "Yes, but no! They've been staying with me while they figure out what they want to do. Karina, in the apartment next door, is traveling for a few months, so they just started subletting it! It's wonderful to have them so close…" Her smile fell. "Oh Callie, how insensitive of me, I didn't mean to—"

I hefted Rosemary and rose from my chair, rushing to sit beside Logan on the couch, where I pulled her into another strong hug. "Logan, don't. Your parents have been lost to you for decades, and you finally have them back—here, on *this* plane. That is nothing but good. I can be sad for my mom and happy for you at the same time." And it was true, I realized. I might not have been able to honestly say this before last night, but now, my heart had eased open a bit.

She hugged me back; I could feel her tears against my cheek. "I'm still so sorry for you."

"I understand. And thank you."

We sat holding each other, the baby sort of in both of our laps (and miraculously not pulling anyone's hair) for a long moment. On Logan's other side, Willson leaned into her and purred. Finally, I pulled back gently and smiled at her. "I missed you so much."

She studied my face. "I missed you, too. But like I said, I always knew you would come and rescue us."

"You had more faith in me than I did."

"Well, someone had to," she said, teasingly. Then she grew more serious. "So, I think I know the big things that happened while I was gone, but what *else* went on? I see the Calico Café has a new owner, and Muni is cutting their budget again. And Niad seems to have undergone a personality transplant."

I snorted at this. "Not exactly, but yes, I think she and I have come to a new level of understanding."

Logan picked up her tea and sipped it, her eyes shining. "Tell me *everything*."

I did what I could. Three hours later, I took my nap-ready baby home, feeling as though a vital piece of my world had grown just a little bit warmer. Softer. More accessible.

A few days after my visit to Logan, I did finally call Raymond. He didn't pick up but called me back within the hour. "Sorry—band practice," he said, sounding slightly out of breath. "Didn't even hear it ring."

"That's okay," I said. "You get to have a life. I'm sorry I didn't call sooner."

"That's okay," he said. "How are you doing?"

"I'm all right," I said, truthfully. "We had my mom's memorial service last week, which helped. It gets a little easier every day, though a huge part of me still can't quite believe she's gone."

"I can't even think about what that must feel like, to lose your mother," he said quietly. "Our mom...she's something special."

"I would like to meet her someday," I said.

He paused, then said, "Really?"

"Yeah, really." I chuckled. "Is that so surprising?"

"Well, um, Callie, you know—I just don't know what's surprising or not anymore, I guess." He exhaled. "Everything I thought I knew isn't the way I thought it was."

"Me too, actually." In the awkward silence that followed, I said, "So—do you want to get together and talk about it?"

"Love to," he said, with no hesitation whatsoever.

"Great. What's your schedule look like?"

"Um." I heard him shuffle through what sounded like a pile of papers. "Actually, sucky, for the next few days. We've got a gig down in Half Moon Bay, and then two nights in Santa Cruz right after that. I won't be back till after the weekend."

For a moment, I was tempted to invite myself along—I hadn't heard his band play in far too long. But...no. Too soon, and everything was still too uncertain. And it wouldn't be like we'd have much time to talk anyway, while he was performing—or setting up, or tearing down, or partying with the band, or sleeping it off. Not to mention now I had a baby to add to the mix. "After the weekend will be fine. Call me when you get back?"

"You bet!"

"All right. Talk to you soon, and good luck with the gigs."

"Thanks!"

Sebastian and I were having a picnic at Ocean Beach when Jeremy called to me. *May I speak with you about something, Calendula?*

Sure, I sent back. *What is it?*

I would prefer to do this in person, if I may. Are you available?

I glanced over at Sebastian, who was building a sandcastle for Rosemary down by the water, and using hardly any magic at all. She was delighted, smiling brightly and making incoherent babbling sounds at him. Occasionally, she batted at the castle, toppling turrets and filling the moat. Sebastian just laughed and started over. *I'm not home right now,* I sent Jeremy, *but I should be back within the hour.*

Do not rush, he sent. *I could come at cocktail hour, if that is better for you?*

That is, I said. *Six, then?*

I'll be there. Shall I bring anything?

Not unless you want something other than Bulgarian frog brandy.

He sent a chuckle. *That sounds delightful. See you then.*

I got up and walked over to the castle-building (and -breaking) duo. "Jeremy wants to come and talk to me," I told my friend.

Sebastian shielded his eyes from the sun as he looked up at me. "Oh? What about, do you think?"

"I don't know. I haven't talked to him much since…since it all fell out. He was pretty upset with himself, for not seeing what his dad had been up to. Even though I told him not to beat himself up over it."

"Well, I can understand how he feels," Sebastian said.

I shrugged. "Me too. But still, not helpful."

"Nope." He grabbed a handful of wet sand and dribbled it over the latest tower, making it an inch taller. "Do you need to go now?"

"No, this evening. I have time to help you shore up your defenses against the Mighty Baby from the Beyond." I bent down and picked up my own handful of sand, shaping it into a brick which I added to the castle's front wall.

"She is pretty mighty, I have to say."

"She's no match for us," I vowed.

I was *almost* right; or, okay, well, I was actually totally wrong: *we* were no match for *her*. In one bold move, she kicked her little foot and brought down my wall even as she swung her tiny fist at Sebastian's tower.

"There will be no keeping the barbarian hordes out now," Sebastian sighed.

"Alas."

Back home, I nursed Rosemary and put her down for a nap, fed Elnor her late-mid-afternoon tuna snack, then took a shower. After I was clean, I stood before my closet, wondering what to wear for Jeremy's visit. Did he think this was a date? No, likely not; if he'd intended that, he'd have asked me out. He was old-fashioned that way.

I still didn't know quite how I felt about Jeremy. I had been furious with him when I'd learned how egregiously his father had been controlling and manipulating me—and when I'd thought that Jeremy was in on the program, I had wanted him entirely out of my life. Later, when it became clear that he had been as deceived and wronged as I had been, I felt for him…but I still felt confused and uncertain about *us*.

We had been real, once. The feelings that had grown between us, as we together mourned our loss of Logan, hadn't been Gregorio's doing—no matter how much the old warlock might have also wanted us to form a union, for whatever creepy reasons of his own. No, those feelings were all ours.

Jeremy was a gorgeous, intelligent, powerful, sensitive warlock: definitely excellent relationship material, by any standards. And according to Raymond, at least, Jeremy still wanted me. Was that what he was coming over to discuss?

Was I ready to even think about such things? I hadn't even gotten together with Raymond yet. Speaking of complicated questions.

But first: what to wear? I finally settled on dark, loose-fitting fancy pants and a silky blouse in a bright but complementary color. Elegant-ish, but casual. I considered going even more casual and staying barefoot, but decided that suggested a level of intimacy that I wasn't at all prepared to offer.

I reached down for some comfy sandals. "So what will I tell him if he asks to start over?" I said aloud to my bedroom mirror.

I felt the familiar pang of dismay and sadness that I wasn't able to talk about this with Logan…then the newly familiar realization that I *was*, in fact, able to…followed quickly by the thought, *Yes, but not about* this.

Or could I? Maybe we should all talk together? What was gained by talking behind one another's backs?

Logan, I sent, *I need to talk to you. Are you busy right now?*

Not at all.

Come over?

I'll be right there, she sent.

In a minute, she was standing beside me. "Are we going somewhere?" she asked, looking me up and down. "I didn't dress up."

"Jeremy is coming here in an hour to talk to me. I thought you should be here too."

Her eyes widened. "Really? What about?"

"He didn't say, but I imagine he is going to ask me where we are. Him and me, with each other. But you're part of this too."

"I am not!" she said, shaking her head. "You're the one who had the actual relationship with him. You were about to sign a contract together!"

"Yeah, but I *didn't* sign it. And you were seeing him first. I never even considered dating him till after you were gone—I *had* a boyfriend."

"It doesn't matter. We'd gone to lunch, like, twice." But her cheeks were pinkening. "You were *much* more serious."

"Logan, *that* doesn't matter. You still like him. Maybe more than like him. And I…don't know how I feel about him."

She started to protest again, then stopped. "It's so weird," she said softly, after a minute. "I know almost a year has gone by for you all out here, but for me—despite the time I spent in limbo, because I experienced that too—but, out here, it's like it was all just the other day. Like, it feels like last week that you moved into this house. And that I had lunch with Jeremy." She gave me a tentative smile. "Yeah, I do still like him. But so what? He's obviously moved on."

"We don't know that," I said, despite what I suspected. "Let's let him tell us what he's thinking and feeling, instead of deciding it for him."

She sat down on my bed and frowned, thinking. "Okay, I guess I do agree with that. But I don't think I should be here."

"Why not?"

She gave me a pointed look. "Callie, he called you, he's coming to see you. He didn't call me."

"Well, we don't need to ambush him—we'd let him know you were here."

She shook her head. "I don't know."

I went and sat beside her. "Like I said, he didn't say why he's coming. It could be something else entirely." And even if it wasn't, his feelings weren't the only ones that mattered here—not by a long shot. "I'm not sure if I could ever truly trust him again, all the way down," I told Logan. "I have a lot of...stuff to work through in my own heart first."

She turned to me, her bright blue eyes earnest. "So meet with him. Alone. Listen to him, and be as honest with him as you can right now. Then tell me how it went, and we'll take it from there. Fair?"

"I don't know," I said. "It doesn't feel fair. You were there first."

She smiled and rolled her eyes. "I told you that doesn't matter. It feels fair to *me*, so you'll just have to live with it."

I smiled back at her. "When did you get so bossy?"

"When an evil warlock felt entitled to just grab my life force and use it for his own selfish purposes," she said wryly. "I think we all learned a little bit about taking care of ourselves, out there in limbo-land."

Interesting, I thought.

"Anyway," she went on brightly, "those clothes are all wrong." She got up and walked back over to my closet, then reached in and started flipping through items. "Take them off immediately."

I snorted. "Yes ma'am."

She pulled out a few things and tossed them over her shoulder behind her. I caught them before they could hit the floor. "Seriously?" I said, holding up the little black cocktail dress with the deep plunging neckline. "Not this."

"I'm not choosing anything yet, I'm just exploring possibilities," she said. "Seeing what you have. I'm grabbing what grabs me, and when I'm done in here, we'll talk. Then we'll choose."

"Yes ma'am," I said again, and stopped protesting.

In the end, she dressed me in something so similar to what I'd chosen—flowy pants, nice blouse, but in different colors—that I suspected she'd made me change arbitrarily, just because she could.

It was *so* nice to have my best friend back in my life.

"Good luck," she said at the front door, leaning in and pecking me on the cheek, "be true to yourself, and keep me posted. I'll be waiting with bated breath."

"I will call you as soon as he leaves."

"Even if that's tomorrow morning?" She gave me a really convincing wicked grin.

I rolled my eyes. "It won't be tomorrow morning."

"If you say so."

On the front porch, she glanced up and down the block, then stepped straight onto a ley line and was gone.

I had only about ten minutes till Jeremy was due. I used it to fuss around in the front parlor, rearranging throw pillows, then putting them back where they'd been originally. You know, useful stuff.

He arrived right on time. I welcomed him in and ushered him into the front parlor. "Brandy?" I asked.

"Yes please." He smiled up at me.

I turned to Petrana, waiting in the doorway. She nodded to indicate she'd heard him, and asked me, "Smoldering Dragonfly?"

"Sounds great."

I sat down in the comfy chair that matched the one he sat in, angled to face it, with a small table between us. "How are you feeling?" I asked him.

"Better all the time," he said. "I don't always feel the spells drying up, but I can tell when another one leaves me. The healers say they are mostly gone, and that the rest are so weak, they might as well be."

"That's good," I said. "You look good—healthy, I mean." I smiled, kicking myself internally. Would he think I was flirting with him?

"And how are *you* feeling?" he asked, gently. "Your mother's service was very nice."

"Thank you." I considered my answer for a moment. "Better all the time as well, I think. It was good to have the service. Not as painful as I thought it might be."

Petrana returned with our drinks, almost too quickly to have walked the distance from here to the kitchen and back, much less made or conjured two cocktails. Jeremy raised an eyebrow but thanked her politely.

She withdrew, and we toasted. "To your continued improving health," I said.

"And to yours."

We sipped. "Where is Rosemary?" he asked, setting his drink on the table.

"Napping; she'll wake up soon. Petrana will get her."

"Ah."

I took another sip and set my own glass down, looking up at Jeremy. This was his meeting: I'd let him start it.

"Right," he said, looking briefly uncomfortable. "I...probably should have reached out sooner, but I've been doing a lot of thinking, and wanted to figure a few things out before I spoke with you."

"And you've been healing as well," I blurted, immediately forgetting my own resolve of a moment ago. "Sorry, didn't mean to interrupt."

But he gave me a kind smile. "You didn't interrupt. This is a conversation. We are both allowed to speak."

I smiled back at him. "Thanks. But, um, you first."

"All right." He took a healthy measure of his brandy, held it in his mouth for a moment, then swallowed. "We talked briefly at, ah, your father's house," he began. I nodded. "I still feel as though I should have known more about what *my* father was engaged in, but I did not, and much harm came of it. I cannot do anything about changing the past, but perhaps I can help shape the future."

"I hope we all can," I said.

"Of course." He toyed with his glass, caught himself, and put his hands in his lap. "That is a good point: we all can, and I hope that we all will, in the ways best suited to our own experiences and strengths."

I nodded again, resisting the urge to play with my own drink as I waited for him to get to his point.

"With that in mind, I have realized that the way I can best help witchkind move forward and heal the damage that my father has done is to return to the Old Country."

My mouth fell open. "What?"

He leaned forward, warming to his topic as he talked. "The warlocks who run the Grand Laurel Merenoc were deeply involved in my father's 'research,' and they have remained untouched by what your mother did to him here in San Francisco. He was their leader, yes, but they are neither fools nor powerless; they will regroup, and they will continue their ugly work. Unless someone stops them." He sat up a little straighter. "I aim to stop them."

"By yourself?"

"Perhaps not." He glanced away, then back at me. "But I don't know for certain about that just yet."

Was he going to ask me to go with him? All the reasons why I had to stay here flooded into my mind—I wasn't ready, I didn't know what I wanted, Logan had just returned to me, I had a baby—but he went on.

"You seem surprised," he said. "And I understand that. When we spoke earlier, I felt angry and lost. I no longer feel that way: I have a direction, and I am eager to get moving on it. The longer I wait, the more time they have to build more terrible machines, to do more egregious damage. I cannot let them do that."

"It's not that," I said. "I am surprised, yes, but—well—I thought you loved San Francisco. And, um, this wasn't what I thought you wanted to talk to me about." I felt my cheeks flaming. "I thought you…" I trailed off, more awkward than ever.

His face softened; his eyes were so kind, and so lovely, as he gazed at me earnestly. Reading my thoughts on my face. "Calendula… Callie…I care so deeply about you," he said. "My feelings for you, for *us*, have been complicated at times, but they have always been warm and loving."

I just stared back at him. This sounded like...like a breakup? "Logan still likes you," I said, still desperately trying to find my way in this conversation.

He blinked, then took a sip of his brandy. "I am so relieved that she is back and in such good health," he said. "She is a special witch, kind and good-hearted and joyous. I will always be grateful I met her."

So... "Who are you thinking might go to the Old Country with you?"

He looked thoughtful. "It is not yet decided, and I do not know if I am at liberty to say, but I shall entrust you with this if you promise to keep it to yourself."

"I promise."

"Niadine Laurette has expressed interest in accompanying me."

"*Niad?*" I gasped.

He nodded. "Again, she has not made her decision, and she has not yet spoken with your coven mother about this, so do please keep this quiet until she does—*if* she does. But she has a number of questions about her own origins—questions she and I have in common—and this has kindled a desire to learn more about witchkind in general, at its source." He smiled. "And, she is one of the most powerful witches I know, second only to you. She would be a formidable ally to me."

"She would," I said, my mind racing as my whole sense of the world reordered itself. "This all does make a kind of crazy sense," I said slowly, after a minute.

"Thank you," he said, still smiling, "for understanding." He leaned forward again, this time reaching out a hand for mine. I took it. "Callie, I meant what I said a moment ago. I do care about you, tremendously. But our lives are long; neither of us have even completed our first century. My hope is that I will find a way to aid in the healing of witchkind—to atone for my part in the damaging of it—however that may unfold, and then, who knows what may happen? I do love San Francisco, you are not wrong. And you, I believe, thoroughly enjoyed your trip to the Old Country. Our paths will likely cross again. In fact, I fervently hope they do."

I felt a tear forming at the corner of my eye. *Wait!* I wanted to shout. *You can't just leave!* But...did I want him to stay just because he wanted to go? Or because of what we'd had? What we might have someday? He was right: barring something unforeseen, we would have ample opportunity to explore our connection later.

It wasn't like he was human, with their short lives.

I took my hand back and brushed away the tear. "I hope so too," I said. "Jeremy, you are a good warlock."

His smile was warm and loving. "And you are one of the best witches I have ever met. I am honored to have shared even a small portion of your life with you." Then he winked. "So far."

— CHAPTER EIGHTEEN —

Raymond didn't wait to call me until he got home from his short road trip; he called late at night, after the second gig. "I didn't wake you, did I?"

"No," I said, smiling into the phone even though he couldn't see it. I was in the front room on the second floor of my house…the room that had, briefly, been Jeremy's study. I had been standing in the middle of the space, considering turning it back into a cozy reading room, even though I'd never really used it that way. This was an awfully big house for one witch (and one witchlet and a golem and a cat).

"Oh good. I knew you stay up late, so I thought I'd try."

"I do. What's up?"

"I'll be home on Tuesday, probably mid-afternoon. Wanna get together then?"

"Sure." I had no commitments on Tuesday until, hmm, dinner and Circle at the coven house. I could skip dinner. "I'm free until about eleven."

"What do you have at eleven?" he asked, sounding curious. "I mean, if that's not being nosy."

I started to fudge something, reflexively, then caught myself. "Every Tuesday my coven gathers for a ritual Circle at midnight. That's when we contact our ancestresses who have departed to the Beyond."

"Oh." He paused a moment, absorbing that. "Do you want to just do Wednesday, then? In case I get back late?"

"Just call me when you get in. If there's time, I'd love to see you then; if not, then Wednesday's fine."

"Sounds good!"

I stood holding the phone against my chest after we hung up, marveling at how normal this felt. I mean, how utterly bizarre that it *should* feel normal, if that made any sense.

Raymond had been shocked when I'd first revealed my nature to him, and angry at how I'd deceived him, but then he'd recovered, and now he just took it all in stride.

How cool.

Right?

I stuck my phone back in my jeans pocket and looked around the room once more. I had to do *something* with it; Jeremy's magical embellishments had all had traces of Gregorio's magic in them. I'd removed those, with the help of Niad, Sebastian, and Leonora, but what was left behind was just an unpleasant reminder of…too much.

I needed to make the space mine again.

Down the hall, I heard Rosemary babbling as Petrana gave her a bath. Then my daughter sent me a word: *Nice.*

I smiled and went to check on them. "Is it nice, having a bath?" I asked Rose.

Nice. Room.

I raised an eyebrow. "Nice room? You like Jeremy's old study?" I had made her a nursery next to my bedroom, of course, though she'd spent very little time in there as yet. But the study was indeed a pretty nice space, even though it looked over the street, and would be noisy for sleeping in.

I leaned against the sink as Petrana shampooed Rosemary's red hair. "When did you live on this plane, when you were Luna? Was it very long ago?"

Many. Long.

"And you probably lived in the Old Country, right?"

Old!

"So I guess a city like San Francisco is a novelty to you." I remembered how much she had enjoyed our trip to the Old Country as well, the big city of Balzt—which probably had changed quite a bit from her day. "Okay, kiddo, when you're big enough to sleep in your own bedroom, you can have the front room. If you still want it then."

She gave me a big toothless grin, and then tried to eat the bubbles of shampoo that dribbled down the side of her head.

———————————————————————

Raymond called at three on Tuesday, and we arranged to meet at the little dive bar in Noe Valley where we'd first met—where I'd watched his band play, and then invited myself home with him.

"Old times' sake?" he asked, when I suggested it.

"Something like that." I wasn't even sure myself, so I was just going with my gut here. "I like their beer."

"I had never seen a woman drink so much beer before that night."

"Oh, sure you had."

"No!"

We both laughed. "Okay, see you in a few," I told him.

He was already there when I walked in, at the table by the front window, and he'd ordered two drafts. "Mmmm," I said, grabbing a chair in one hand and my beer in the other, then draining half the glass before setting it down. "That hits the spot."

He just shook his head, smiling.

We chatted for a while—I asked him about his gigs; he said they were great, and told me a few road stories. Then he finished his beer and cleared his throat, looking serious.

I watched him, thinking about the contrast between this excellent, down-to-earth human man and the elegant, graceful, and also excellent warlock…who might or might not be headed out of my life…forever, or for a while, anyway.

How was it that both men were so very different, and yet both appealed to me so much?

(And both had such a hard time beginning important conversations?)

"How *are* you doing, Callie?" Raymond asked. His tone of voice made it clear that it was not a casual question.

So I thought for a minute before I answered him. "As good—and as bad—as you might expect. I think about my mom every day. I miss her—I think of things I want to tell her, and then remember she's not there to tell. I think about how she left us and wonder what I could have done differently to prevent that. I worry about my dad; he's keeping pretty much to himself, and that isn't good for him. But at the same time, I know that we all have to do our grieving in our own way. Every day gets a little bit easier. And I've got my best friend back, so that's amazing; and I'm sitting here having a comfortable beer with you, which is also pretty great." I smiled at him. "*And*, I can already see that things are changing, for the better, in all kinds of ways, both big and small. My coven is opening up a bit—all the old rules and customs are being loosened. We've told a few humans about magic, and the world hasn't ended."

"That's 'cause you told the right people," he said with a grin.

"True that." I grinned back at him, then frowned. "Actually, that's not quite accurate," I said.

"You told the wrong people?" He pretended to look offended.

"No, that the world hasn't ended. I mean, obviously it hasn't, but what I just said, about things changing—the world kind of *is* ending. The old world, I mean. The world where there were all kinds of secrets and divisions."

"Like between humans and witches."

"For example. But even within witchkind—between warlocks and witches; between covens and unaffiliated witches. The whole structure. I told you my dad is kind of in seclusion."

He nodded.

"Well, Dad was second-in-command in the Convocation of Elders, after Gregorio. But he hasn't even called a meeting, much less stepped up to formally become their new leader. I wonder if there will even *be* a Convocation going forward."

"What does that mean?"

I shrugged. "I don't really know yet. They always kinda acted like they were in charge of witchkind, but the covens never really took direction from them or anything."

"So, they were like the kings and queens of the Netherlands or something?" he asked.

I looked at him, startled. "Uh, actually, yeah, a lot like that. Figureheads, and everyone pretends they've got power, but they really don't." I laughed softly. "So they know not to push it, and everyone's happy. Except Gregorio *did* push it. And maybe it fell apart as a result."

"That doesn't sound like a bad thing."

I nodded. "I don't think so. And on the witch side, it's not just my coven loosening up. I'm hearing things—small things, but still—about other covens. Some of which have been relaxing traditions for a while now." I thought about Magenta's coven, how informal they had felt to me. How comfortable. "Leonora has surprised me several times in the last few weeks."

"Oh?"

"Yeah. The latest thing is, she invited Gracie to bring her girlfriend to the house, so more of the sisters can help her learn whatever magic she might have within her."

"Wow," Raymond said, looking thoughtful. "That's cool."

"Very."

"Do you…?"

"Hm?"

He shifted in his chair. "Do you think maybe…all humans can learn magic?"

I looked back at him, seeing the yearning in his eyes. "I honestly have no idea," I said. "Remember, we are all descended from common ancestors, so it's theoretically possible. Maybe it's like training muscles. Or maybe not—maybe it's like rolling your tongue or tasting soap when you eat cilantro; maybe there's a genetic component, and you either have it or you don't." I leaned back as the possibilities unfolded in my mind. "I've been at a bit of a loss wondering what I'll study next. This…this is interesting."

"It would be *so* cool to be able to grab a beer without getting up from the couch," he said.

I laughed as I finished my own beer, then glanced at his empty glass. "Want another?"

"Sure," he said, "but it's on me. Don't wave your finger and make it appear out of thin air in here, okay?"

"Don't worry," I said. "I do still understand how your human world works. But if I'm not mistaken, you bought the first round, so this round is on me."

"Fair."

I returned to the table after a minute with two more frosty glasses.

"This is my limit," he said. "I gotta drive home after this."

"This is fine for me too."

We drank a moment. Then he said, "I been thinking. About you losing your mom. About family; about how great my own mom is; heck, how great even my big sister is." He gave me a crooked grin. "How we just never know. You know? How easy it is to take stuff for granted."

"Right."

"How you and me made a baby together." He was keeping his eyes on his beer now. "An amazing baby, cutest baby I ever seen."

"She is pretty darn cute," I agreed.

"How family isn't something to just throw away," he almost mumbled.

I put a hand on his arm.

He looked up at me. "Callie, I want to be family with you—and our daughter." Before I could answer, he rushed on. "I don't know what that means exactly—I know you do things different; I'm not saying we should get married or whatever. I know you're older than me, and, well, you're gonna live a lot longer than me, and I can't do magic and all that. I know you got other arrangements, and duties, and stuff. But Rose is our daughter, and, and, that's important. That's huge. That's *everything*."

"Yes, it is," I said softly. "I want you in her life. I want you in *my* life. I don't know what that looks like either," I added, as relief spread across his face, "mostly because I don't know what anything in my life is going to look like going forward—not those 'other arrangements', not anything really. But I'm interested in finding out. With you."

He grinned and took my hand. "Okay, Babymama. It's a deal."

I rolled my eyes to the ceiling, beseeching whatever spirits lurked up there. "Oh Blessed Mother. 'Babymama'? What have I done?"

EPILOGUE

Following an enticing aroma, I headed downstairs and found Christine in my kitchen, her cheeks rosy from heat, a white apron tied around her waist. (Did I own an apron? Or had she brought it?) "You're just in time!" she said, bending down to open the oven door, then drawing out a big cast-iron pan with something fluffy and fragrant in it. "Dutch babies with fresh peaches. Go grab a seat in the dining room; I'll bring your plates."

"Where did you get fresh peaches in early May?" I asked, as I obeyed the order.

Christine grinned as she stepped into the dining room, a plate in each hand. She set one before me and one before Raymond. "Be right back with yours," she told Sebastian, and then to me: "Humans have to have some secrets, even in witch homes."

"Fair enough," I said, as the aroma of brunch wafted up. I moaned involuntarily.

"Don't wait! It'll collapse in a minute," Christine called from the kitchen. "Start eating!"

Raymond already had his fork in hand. I followed suit. "You don't have to tell me twice."

It was amazing. I barely looked up, because she was right—it settled on the plate, though was no less delicious for doing so. And the peaches... Wow.

After we'd cleaned our plates, I asked, "Was that an entire stick of butter on my portion, or just half a stick?"

Christine shook her head, smiling. "I will never tell."

Rosemary had watched the entire meal from Raymond's lap. They were so entirely cute together, it melted my heart. As she grew, her resemblance to her father grew as well—or, rather, her resemblance to her aunt. But I could see myself in her as well.

I still wondered every day about Luna Amadora, the other element inside my Rosemary. I was excited for my baby to grow up enough to tell me what she knew, what she remembered, from the person she had been before.

But for now, my weird baby was simply a joy.

I went to help with the cleanup and the preparation for this evening's much more elaborate meal, but Petrana had that all well in hand. "It was nice of you to let Christine make brunch," I told my golem.

"But of course," she said. "It was what she wanted." She washed another dish and set it in the drainer. "She does not seem to understand that I don't need to rest."

"She will eventually," I told her. "It took me a long time too, and I'm still not sure I've got it a hundred percent." I laughed, and added, "You're not making that any easier, acting more like a person all the time."

"My apologies," she said, with her little smile. "You will all just have to adapt, as I do."

I shook my head and went to join the others in the front of the house. As I walked past the second parlor, I caught sight of Raymond and Rosemary. He was holding her and looking at me with a suspiciously innocent expression.

"What did I just miss seeing?" I asked him.

He blinked at me. So did my daughter. "Nothing," Raymond said.

"Nothing?" I sent a silent message to Rosemary: *What is he not telling me?*

Fun! she sent back.

I narrowed my eyes at both of them. "Fun, she says. What is fun? I never authorized any fun. All fun needs to be approved in advance, with forms filed in triplicate with the head office, which is me." I was trying to glare sternly at him, but it wasn't working. They both just looked so…silly. "And if said fun involves any danger whatsoever to that child, it is automatically disallowed."

"Okay," Raymond said, also trying not to laugh. "Then I absolutely was not tossing this baby into the air and catching her at the last moment after pretending to drop her."

I opened my mouth to—I don't know what, scream probably—as Raymond's face fell.

"I'm sorry, Callie, god, I'm so sorry," he said. He hurried out and handed me Rosemary, then pulled us both into a hug. "Your face—god. So long as I live, I never want to see that look on your face again."

"It's all right," I said, slowly realizing that it was. Rosemary, for her part, was delighted to be so close to both of us. She reached out for both his hair and mine, seemingly unable to decide which braid she wanted to pull on first. Because now she was doing *that* again, apparently.

Christine called out from the front parlor: "Dude, that was hilarious but also just totally not funny."

"I really am sorry," he said to both of us.

"I forgive you, but just this once."

He nodded solemnly. "Thank you, Empress Callie. It will never happen again."

I snickered. "Well, if I have to have a nickname, I guess Empress is better than Babymama."

"Babymama?" Christine said, aghast. "Seriously, Raymond?"

He just laughed.

"Why Empress?" I asked him, as we joined the rest of the party in the front parlor. Flavius had arrived, as had Gracie and Rachel, as well as Logan; a number of my coven sisters had promised to drop by later, as had some of the younger witches from the community. Sundays were turning into a free-flowing open house around here, culminating in a large dinner, with far too many people to fit around my table.

I liked it. It was a bit like having a coven of my own, but without any rules or traditions. Or maybe we were making new traditions. But no rules.

(Well, except for the one I had just made: no tossing the baby up into the air and pretending to drop her. No matter that she was a magical being who could no doubt catch herself if she needed to.)

Rose was clearly enjoying the new routine; she absolutely loved having so many happy adults around who all wanted to hold her and play with her. Just now, she was reaching for Gracie, who took her gladly even as she kept practicing magic with Rachel.

Raymond sat on the arm of the couch next to me. "Why Empress?" he said, echoing my question. "I don't know—I was just thinking of Geneva's store, in Mendocino. The Empress and The Moon. Rosemary Luna is obviously the Moon, so you must be the Empress."

"Empress of what empire?" I asked, laughing as I looked at the motley crew around me. "The Realm of Strays?"

Christine, who had been watching Gracie with Rachel, glanced at Raymond, then at me. "Can I ask you something?" she said to me, quietly.

Raymond, picking up on the sibling-code, said, "Uh-oh, secrets time again, I'm in trouble."

His sister gave him a weary smile.

I got up and followed her out of the room. "What is it?"

She sighed and leaned against the wall. "He's putting a good face on it, but I think it's hard for him to see Rachel and, well, me getting some of the magic stuff, when it still just doesn't work at all for him."

"Hmm," I said. A burst of laughter followed us out into the hall. "Come with me," I said, turning to the stairs.

I brought her up to my lab on the third floor, and closed the door behind us. "I love this space," she said, walking to the back windows and looking down at the yard below.

"Me too."

She walked back to the middle of the floor and stood over the pentacle, careful not to let her feet touch any of the lines. *It won't harm you*, I told her, silently. *And you can't hurt it either.*

Her blue eyes widened as she looked at me. "It is still so strange that I can hear you," she said. "I wonder if I will ever get used to it."

"Try answering me," I said. "Silently, I mean."

"I did." She laughed softly. "Then I said it aloud when it was obvious you didn't get it. Are you making any progress on your research about it?"

"Not yet," I said, going to sit on my lab stool. "But I wouldn't expect to this soon. I'm still designing the experiments, figuring out what to test for, what to look at. Working with you guys is helping me narrow stuff down."

"It's truly weird," she said, rubbing her arms. "And it's very cool. I can see how useful it must be, why you guys would have worked to develop the skill."

"Yeah. It's hard to imagine life without it—or without any of my other magical abilities." I thought about Flavius, abruptly forced to live without half his senses, his strengths. Everything that made him who he was. He had insisted to me more than once that he was content to be human, but he still kept himself pretty reserved. I was glad at least that he came to the house most Sundays and seemed to find some enjoyment in our company.

Christine stepped out of the pentacle and walked over to sit in the guest chair. "Why do you guys even speak out loud if you can do this?"

I chuckled, thinking of the stories Jeremy had told me about the Old Country before I went there—that it was a place where nobody spoke aloud, that friends just kept mind-channels open to one another, like old-fashioned telephones left off the hook, connected. "Because that would be weird and creepy, for one thing. I don't know if you noticed, but it's really hard to convey tone or emotion in ætheric communication."

"I hadn't really noticed yet, but, yeah, now that I think about it."

I nodded. "So that's one reason. Another is that we—well, most of us, anyway—tend to live in at least some kind of proximity to humans. It's really hard to blend in with humans if you're sending silent messages back and forth." I smiled at her. "Even humans who have no idea what's going on tend to notice."

"Right," she said, with an answering smile. "But you didn't drag me all the way up here to just talk about this, did you?"

"Perceptive as ever," I said. "No, I dragged you up here to take some of your blood."

She raised an eyebrow. "Isn't it vampires that drink blood? I thought you were a witch."

"Ha. Ha." I waved at my lab bench. "When I talked about how working with you guys was helping my research, I didn't mean just in the abstract. If I can look at your blood and compare it to Raymond's, I might be able to pinpoint—or at least narrow down—the difference between you two."

"I could make another joke about that if you like," she said, rolling up her sleeve, "but I feel like I've been funny enough already for one day."

"You know it, sister," I said, gathering my blood-drawing equipment.

Later, when the house party was in full swing, with every downstairs room full of laughing, talking, nibbling, sipping, and in some cases singing people—witchkind and human alike—I left the baby with Petrana and headed upstairs to use my private bathroom, both to do the necessary but also to enjoy a moment of relative quiet.

I stepped into my bedroom, only to see the bathroom door closed. A moment later, it opened and Logan walked out.

"Oh sorry, Callie!" she said, smiling. "I hope that was okay—both downstairs bathrooms were full."

"Of course," I told her.

"I'll just get out of your way." She started for the door.

"No, wait here a moment—I'll be right out. I wanted to talk to you about something."

"Sure." She gave me a puzzled look on her way to the little table by my window.

When my business was done, I went out and sat on the bed.

"What's up?" she asked.

"Oh, just, well, something," I said. "Sorry—this is harder than I'd thought it was going to be."

Now she looked even more puzzled. "Callie, you can tell me anything."

"I know. It's not that." I leaned over and grabbed the strap of my purse, tucked under my nightstand, and pulled it up onto the bed. Then I hunted through it, coming out with her deck of tarot cards. "I've been meaning to give these back to you." I held them out to her.

Logan got up and took the box, turning it over in her hands as she gazed down at it. Then she opened it, slid out the deck, and handled the cards, moving them slowly through her hands. After a minute, she looked at me. "Thank you for keeping these for me," she said, very quietly. "And...for using them."

"Of course. They reminded me of you." I paused, then made myself say the rest of it. "And...they still remind me of Mom. She taught me a lot...with them. Using these cards."

Logan slipped them back into the box, folded it shut, and reached it out to me. "I think they're your cards now."

"What? No! They're yours." I crossed my arms over my chest.

She just smiled and kept holding the box out. "No, they're not. They've got far more of your energy on them than they do mine, now. And I've got plenty of other decks. These belong to you."

I blinked back tears, shaking my head, but finally relented and took them. "Thank you," I said, holding them to my breast.

"You are welcome. Always." Her smile grew sad. "I feel a bit of your mother on them as well, I think. Or possibly just your thoughts of your mother, but either way, she's here."

I nodded. I felt it too.

She sat down next to me on the bed and put a hand on my knee, still smiling at me. She looked so...happy. At peace. It warmed my heart. "How are your parents doing?" I asked her, after a minute. "I thought they might come tonight, but they begged off again."

"They're good," she said, but her smile fell a little. "It's a big adjustment for them, being back here after so long."

"I imagine. This world has changed greatly since they last lived in it."

"It's like they're not 'back' at all, but living somewhere new for the first time. I'm delighted to have them so close to me, but..." She shook her head. "I'm not sure they like this new San Francisco—this modern world at all. There's so much they don't understand about it."

"Maybe they would be more comfortable in the Old Country," I said.

Logan nodded enthusiastically and brightened. "I told them the same thing! I think they're seriously considering it. At least going there and visiting. And…" She paused, biting her lip, but her eyes shone with excitement.

"What is it?" I asked.

She grinned. "I, um, might go there with them. Just, you know, to get them settled and stuff. I've never been, of course."

"You'll love it. I thought it was great—well, Balzt was, anyway. Are they thinking of going there, or to Zchellenin where they were before?"

"Balzt, definitely. My mom particularly loved your stories about it."

There was something more, I could tell. And I was beginning to suspect what it might be… "Well," I said casually, "it's a big, confusing place; I hope you will seek out someone familiar with the lay of the land when you get there."

"You do always see right through me, don't you?" she asked, unable to contain her joy any longer.

"So, how *is* Jeremy doing?"

"Pretty good, I think." She reached into her pocket and pulled out a folded piece of paper. It was a handwritten letter, clearly well-read. She opened it up but didn't offer it. "He and Niad have rented a large apartment near the river in Balzt. He oh-so-carefully describes the floor plan, making it clear that they're not sharing a bedroom, but also that there will be a spare bedroom for me if I want to visit." Logan looked up at me, her eyes still shining. "Callie, I want to go."

"You should. Absolutely."

"Is that…okay with you?"

I gave her a long look. "I don't even know where to start with that."

Logan laughed. "I know, you're not the boss of me, and you don't know how you feel about Jeremy, and Raymond's here, and all that…"

"Yes, all that, but more even than any of that: my *life* is here. And it's a good life, a busy life, and incredibly satisfying. My house is full of people; my daughter is growing by leaps and bounds; I'm starting a fascinating new research project; I'm involved with the remaking of witchkind at every level of the city."

"You are." She nodded.

"Not to mention Jeremy invited *you*, not me," I added.

Her blush deepened. "I suppose you have a point."

I laughed, then turned more serious. "But you have to promise to come back. I didn't get you back from a year locked in the in-between space just to lose you to the Old Country. No matter how many tantalizing warlocks it may contain."

She looked at me a long moment, studying my face. Then she nodded. "I promise. I've never been there, but I think…I can already tell that I don't belong there, long-term."

"You don't know that," I argued. "But I hope it's true—selfishly, I admit."

"Why does travel have to be so hard for our kind?" she lamented, then added with a laugh, "Hey, that's what you should study next: what's in our blood that makes airplanes so difficult for us, and if there's anything we could do about it."

"That's not really my area…" I started, even as my mind grabbed the question and began chewing on it. I already had some of Christine's blood up in my lab, and some of Rachel's: humans with traces of magical aptitude. I could compare that with Raymond's, and then with mine…

"Earth to Callie," Logan said.

I looked up to see her grinning at me.

"I was just kidding," she added.

"I know, but…it's an interesting question, actually."

"Well, if anyone could figure it out, you could." We smiled at each other for a moment. Then she looked down at the box of cards in my hand, frowning slightly. Was she sorry she'd pressed them on me? Of course she was. "Can I ask you something?" she said.

"Yes, absolutely. You don't even have to ask." I held the box out to her.

She smiled and shook her head. "No, no—they're yours, I meant that."

"Then what is it?"

"I was just wondering…would you do a reading? For me?"

I stared at her. "You want *me* to read for *you*?"

"I do, Callie. I really do."

I swallowed, and gripped the box a little tighter. She wasn't teasing me, and she would never make me feel inadequate for being a relative novice with the cards. "Well. Hmm. Okay." I glanced over at my window, and the little round table under it. "Pull up a chair."

Once we were settled, I shuffled the cards, thinking about the many questions we had, thinking about the spreads I'd been taught. I had never fully gotten comfortable with the traditional Celtic Cross spread—it felt overly complex to me, as if it were trying to do too much at once.

Besides, this table was too small for that.

I closed my eyes, still shuffling awkwardly. Elnor brushed against my ankles; I hadn't even seen her come in. She sat on the floor by my feet, and as she did, the vision of what I wanted to do came to me: a melding of my logical, rational mind with the intuitiveness of the tarot.

"I'll do a one-two-three-four spread," I said to Logan, opening my eyes and smiling at her.

"One-two-three-four?" She looked puzzled. "I haven't heard of that one."

"I just made it up." I gave the cards one more shuffle, cut the deck in my hands and refolded the cards together, then held it to my heart. "Ready?"

Logan nodded. "Ready."

My bedroom door pushed open a few more inches, and Willson came in. He sniffed around and then came to sit by Logan, after exchanging nose-brushes with Elnor.

I laid the cards out quickly, trying not to react to what I saw. But it was hard not to.

Death

Nine of Swords　　Temperance

The Emperor　　Page of Pentacles　　King of Wands

The Devil　　The Hermit　　Five of Cups　　Queen of Wands

"Wow," I whispered, gazing down at the spread.

"None are reversed," Logan murmured, looking puzzled.

I gave an apologetic shrug. "I...keep them all right-side up," I admitted. "It was hard enough learning all the nuances of the upright meanings; I'll learn the reversed ones when I'm sure I've got these down." I looked at her. "Do you want me to do it over, the correct way?"

"This is the correct way," she said, definitively. "The way that you chose to do it: that's the way you should do it."

"Okay."

Logan gazed down at the cards, looking pensive. I so wanted to ask her what she thought—wanted the benefit of her insight, her years of working with the cards, with *these* cards—but she had asked me to do this, and I was going to do as my best friend wished.

At first glance, it looked like a very bleak spread—captivity and despair; the hopeless man in bed beneath the nine swords; spilled cups on a barren ground—but then I began to see a different story take shape.

Could I do it this different way? Could I tell the story that felt the most true?

But why not? I'd already invented the spread, just because it came to me in a moment and it felt right. Why not go with my feelings, not my thoughts, the rest of the way?

I leaned forward, studying the cards once more, rehearsing their meanings before I committed my ideas to voice. Then, at last, I felt ready.

Might as well start with the obvious. I pointed to Death, at the top of the stack. "The ending of something, and the beginning of something else—a new phase. But big: not just finishing a book you're reading, or Sunday dinner: a big life change."

Logan smiled at me. "I think that's clear."

"Yes." I pointed at The Devil next.

Logan glanced up at me in surprise; she'd obviously been expecting me to move down through the cards in the order I'd dealt them.

"I'm seeing a different pattern here," I told her, motioning at the spread as a whole. "Reading more left to right, rather than top to bottom, it actually looks...well, it tells a more coherent story. A more encouraging one, as well—not just for you, but for all of us. Our whole community."

"Oh?"

"Yeah," I said, beginning to find my stride. "Starting from chains and a wicked captor—" I pointed at The Devil. "—despair, hopelessness, and profound challenges—" I put my finger on the Nine of Swords. "—and an authoritarian father figure." I touched The Emperor. "From there, we move through wisdom and soul-searching—" I pointed to The Hermit. "—a whole lot of balance, cooperation, and working together—" I touched Temperance. "—and culminating in creative energy and hope for the future." I put my finger gently on The King and then The Queen of Wands.

"Interesting," Logan said.

"It's not perfect—not an entirely clear progression," I admitted. "The Five of Cups over here on the right speaks of loss, despair, and loneliness; and the Page of Pentacles to his left is a more positive messenger, of earthly achievements and physical health. But those too make a kind of sense, in their way; none of our paths have been straightforward. We bounce around, sometimes up and sometimes down; but the general progression looks to be a positive one. Leading to my old friend," I said, again pointing at The Queen of Wands.

"I do remember her from that reading we did for you," Logan said softly. "And her little black cat."

"But this is *your* reading, so all of this means something more specifically about you—not just the whole community, and certainly not just me."

Logan nodded. "But I like that the card that I think of as so closely associated with you appears in the final position in my reading." Then she shut her mouth and pantomimed zipping her lip.

I laughed. "I do too, and you don't have to silence yourself. Maybe, as friends, we can do the reading together."

"I don't want to stop you!" she said, laughing with me. "You're doing a great job."

"Thank you." Encouraged, I added, "I'm going to say that the Queen in the final position means that, however far you travel, and whatever adventures you have, you're always going to come back to me. Come back home."

She beamed at me. "I hope so. I like that interpretation."

"Me too." I looked again at the whole spread. "So, underneath that first interpretation—left to right, and generally improving—I'm also seeing a lot of power here. Ten cards, and fully half of them are major arcana. Three more are royalty."

"What does that say to you?" she asked, like a good teacher.

I thought about choosing my words carefully, but we were well beyond such sensitivities. "Well, you're not a witch who has historically been very powerful. And yet—there's a difference in you, since your ordeal."

She cocked her head, silently asking me to go on.

"Not just going to the in-between place, suffering there, and ultimately escaping. But what you and your mother learned to do there."

"What you taught us to do there," she said, gently.

I shrugged. "I figured out a thing based on what you told me Gregorio was doing to you, and I taught you how to do it yourselves. But you two took it much farther: you told me that you became comfortable with the procedure, found your way back to the other captive souls, and were teaching them how to do it." I watched her face. "The old Logan wouldn't have even tried. Wouldn't have dared. Wouldn't have believed she had the power."

"I wouldn't have had the power," she said. "I didn't."

"I don't know if you did or not, but you clearly do now," I said. "And I think this spread, this reading, is saying that—and implying that there is more to come."

She gazed down at the cards a long time. I could see her eyes moving across them as she thought about what she was seeing, and what I had said. At last, she looked up at me. "I like that the Page of Pentacles is effectively right in the middle of it all," she said.

"Oh?" I asked. "Why is that?"

With a shy smile, she said, "You called him royalty, but he isn't, exactly. He supports the royals."

I started to protest—was she trying to wiggle out of thinking of herself as important, as central? In her own dang reading? *Really?*— but she went on.

"He's a messenger—he's an in-between card. He is neither a numbered card nor a ruler. But he travels between all the characters—he goes everywhere. And his message is a good one: as you said, all about tangible things, but *big* tangible things: health, love, even money."

"And there he is, smack in the middle of your life."

"Just as I am." Her smile widened. "In the middle of everything, I have a bright new beginning. I can go anywhere, do anything."

I leaned back. "Yes, you can."

"So...I will."

We sat grinning at each other for another long moment. Then she said, "I'm starving. Do you think they left us any meatballs?"

I took her hand, and we stood, together—being careful not to trip over our cats. "Only one way to find out."

– ABOUT SHANNON PAGE –

Shannon Page was born on Halloween night and spent her early years on a back-to-the-land commune in northern California. A childhood without television gave her a great love of the written word. At seven, she wrote her first book, an illustrated adventure starring her cat Cleo. Sadly, that story is out of print, but her work has appeared in *Clarkesworld, Interzone, Fantasy, Black Static,* Tor.com, the Proceedings of the 2002 International Oral History Association Congress, and many anthologies, including theAustralian Shadows Award-winning *Grants Pass,* and *The Mammoth Book of Dieselpunk.*

Books include the four contemporary fantasies of The Nightcraft Quartet; hippie horror novel *Eel River;* story collection *Eastlick and Other Stories;* personal essay collection *I Was a Trophy Wife;* the Orcas Island-based cozy mystery series The Chameleon Chronicles and Tales from the Berry Farm, under the pen name Laura Gayle; and *Our Lady of the Islands,* co-written with the late Jay Lake. Our Lady received starred reviews from *Publishers Weekly* and *Library Journal,* was named one of *Publishers Weekly's* Best Books of 2014, and was a finalist for the Endeavour Award. Forthcoming books include a sequel to Our Lady;and plenty more Orcas mysteries. Edited books include the anthologies *Witches, Stitches & Bitches* and *Black-Eyed Peas on New Year's Day: An Anthology of Hope,* and the essay collection *The Usual Path to Publication.*

Shannon is a longtime yoga practitioner, has no tattoos (but she did recently get a television), and liveson lovely, remote Orcas Island, Washington, with her husband, author and illustrator Mark Ferrari. Visit her at www.shannonpage.net.